PIRATE HUNTER

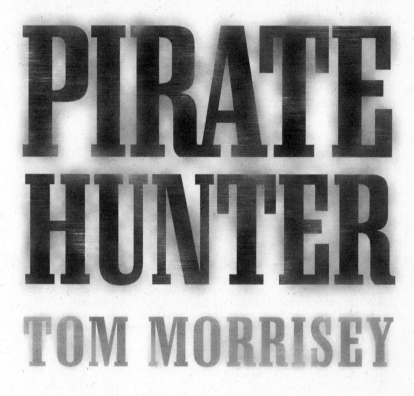

PIRATE HUNTER

TOM MORRISEY

BETHANY HOUSE
Minneapolis, Minnesota

Published by Bethany House Publishers
11400 Hampshire Avenue South
Bloomington, Minnesota 55438

Bethany House Publishers is a division of
Baker Publishing Group, Grand Rapids, Michigan.

Printed in the United States of America

Library of Congress Cataloging-in-Publication Data

Morrisey, Tom, 1952–
    Pirate hunter / Tom Morrisey.
      p. cm.
    ISBN 978-0-7642-0348-0 (pbk.)
    1. Pirates—Fiction. I. Title.

    PS3613.O776P57   2009
    813'.6—dc22

                            2009007608

Shortly after this manuscript was delivered to its publisher, I received word from friends in Key West that Captain Anthony Tarracino—"Captain Tony" in this book and to almost everyone who ever knew him—had passed away at the venerable age of 92, still looking two decades his own junior, and unrepentantly charming to the very end.

After consulting with friends and being assured that his widow, Mary, would be honored by the gesture, I decided to leave him alive within these pages. Death is, after all, a passage rather than an end.

Pirate Hunter is dedicated, then, to Captain Tony Tarracino and all the saints and all the sinners of the island of Key West. As a recent saint and a lifelong sinner myself, I've always felt a special bond with you.

—TM

And I saw a new heaven and a new earth:
for the first heaven and the first earth were passed away;
and there was no more sea.

Revelation 21:1

ONE

"I favor the red ribbons because they look like blood."

The pirate worked as he spoke, plaiting thin lengths of crimson silk into the raven hair of a wig on its tabletop stand. His own hair was almost exactly the same color of black, but closely cropped, the short growth even, suggesting that he had shaved his head a fortnight or two back. His beard, on the other hand, was thick and long, the ends of it bleached to a lighter brown by salt air and sun. Every strand had been combed and lightly dampened with sperm-whale oil, the scent of it warm and very nearly spicy in the small, close cabin of the sloop.

The pirate stepped back a bit to look at his work, leaning naturally to keep his footing as they canted over onto a fresh heel. Above their heads, the ship groaned and creaked with the turn, the mate's commands coming through the wooden bulkheads as a series of curt, muffled shouts.

The pirate gazed down his nose at the barefoot and bare-chested fifteen-year-old on the other side of the table. The younger man's skin was a deep chocolate brown, almost as dark as his jet-black hair, a fact that made his eyes appear larger than they were, giving him the appearance of an innocent.

"Why do you think that is, boy?"

The young man startled and stood a little straighter. "Sir?"

"The ribbons, boy." The man's voice was a calm baritone. "Why would I favor ribbons that resemble blood?"

The younger man kept his eyes fixed on those of the pirate but canted his head slightly down and to his right, a mannerism he had when he knew the answer to something but was thinking it through, just to be certain. Lips still closed, he took a quick dart of breath through his nose.

"Because a fierce man, streaming blood but on the attack, would present a most frightening aspect, Captain. Because a person so startled would hesitate in his own defense, and a moment of hesitation is an opportunity in which to attack. At very least that is how I see it, sir."

The pirate stopped his work and touched an index finger to his lower lip. "Tell me, boy—have you been speaking with my crew, discussing my manners, my ways?"

His companion shook his head. "No, sir. The crew doesn't talk about you. The crew doesn't talk about anything but women and riches and rum."

The captain laughed. "And which of those three interests you?"

"The riches, Captain."

The pirate laughed again and started another ribbon into the wig. He turned it to look at his work. The younger man watched and then cleared his throat.

"Might I ask you something, Captain?"

The captain lifted a single eyebrow—his right. "You cannot learn if you do not ask."

"Yes, sir. Thank you, sir. . . . When you took the slaver? When you took the crew . . . ?"

"Yes?"

"You sold all the rest of the . . . cargo. Yet you did not sell me. Why?"

"Because you speak the King's English, lad. Speak it, read it, write it as well as any Yorkshireman. Because you are familiar with Scripture. Because you seem to have an extremely able head on you."

"Those things—the learning and the Scripture—they were the doings of the Scotsman who raised me. He and his wife. Before he came to Africa to start his chandlery, Mr. Bascombe was a vicar. He taught me the Scripture, and history and philosophy."

The pirate smiled. He had white, even teeth. "Then, when you say your prayers, you must thank God for Vicar Bascombe."

He tied off another lock of the wig.

"But, Captain, does a slave not fetch a higher price if he speaks English?"

The captain looked up from his work. "I sold those men and women to save them, boy. They'd made it all the way across to the Indies; they were strangers in a strange land. If I'd put them ashore on some island, thirst and starvation and the Arawaks would have killed most of them off by now. And those who lived would be hanged for escape when the colonists found them. By making them chattel, I gave them food and a roof and the hope of still being alive by this time next year. Slavery may be the devil's own commerce, but death is irreversible. So I sold them to save them, lad. That and put a few farthings in our pockets. But you?" The captain picked up another ribbon. "What you've got between your ears is all you need to survive, boy. I kept you apart because you showed that promise. Why? You had no kin among the others, did you?"

The teenager shook his head. "They were people of the bush. I was raised in town."

The pirate shrugged. "Then what I did was best for all concerned."

13

The teenager handed the pirate another ribbon. "May I ask you another question, Captain?"

"Has your learning come to an end?"

The younger man shook his head.

"Then the same principle still applies. Ask away."

"Well, Captain, you seem to be a man of principle."

"Principle?" The pirate laughed. "There are those who might argue that point, but we shall grant it for the moment. And as you precede your question with it, I take it you are going to ask about behavior that appears . . . unprincipled. You want to know why I—why my crew and I—take ships. Is that it?"

The younger man's eyes widened. "Why . . . yes, sir. That is it precisely."

"Open that chest." The pirate pointed with a hand that was uncallused, its nails neatly trimmed and filed. "Bring me the case that you find on the very top."

The young man peered into the open chest. "A tube, like a chart case?"

"The very one. Bring it to me."

The young man did as he was told, and the pirate unwound the leather lace that secured the cap, then extracted a rolled sheet of parchment. When he unrolled it, it was clearly a government document, written in the thin, iron-gall cursive favored by government clerks. The foot of it was stamped with a wax seal and tape, and signed with an ornate scrawl.

"This"—the pirate tapped on the parchment with a manicured finger—"is a royal letter of marque, signed by His Majesty's lord governor of the colony of Tortola. The king has lands in this new world which are presently . . . uhm, occupied by nations other than his own. As such, they steal from the royal coffers, so we overhaul ships flying the flags of those nations and take back what is rightfully our own."

The young man worked his lips.

"Say it, lad. What is on your mind?"

"Well, sir, if they take from the king, should we not return what we . . . retrieve? To the king?"

The pirate nodded. "We do, lad. When one gives a thing to the king's lord governor, it is the same as giving it to the king himself. And the workman is worthy of his wage; I believe that is in your vicar's book. So, in his graciousness, the governor—on His Majesty's behalf—allows our crew to keep part of what we take: the greater part. The . . . well, the *considerably* greater part. Very nearly all of it, if truth be told."

"So!" The young man brightened. "You are not a pirate at all. You are a privateer."

"That all depends—" the pirate laughed as he replaced the document in its case and handed it back to his young compatriot— "on whether you are on the giving or the receiving end of the transaction.

"I daresay the captain of that slaver we took you from is calling me a pirate. In point of fact, I would venture that he is calling me considerably more than that. But he is an enemy of His Majesty—and I rather imagine an enemy of yours as well."

As the boy returned the case to its chest, a knock sounded above them at the cabin's hatch.

"Come." When the pirate spoke in commands, his voice went lower, from a baritone to a bass.

The oak hatch swung open, sending sunlight streaming down into the tiny cabin. A barefoot, bearded man descended the ladder on the forward wall; he was wearing a faded Royal Navy officer's waistcoat over canvas breeches. When he turned, his tanned and naked chest showed in the gap of the coat, which was a full size too small for him. He gave a nod by way of a salute.

"Begging your pardon, Captain, but we've closed half the distance on the merchantman."

"Near enough to make out her ensign?"

The mate nodded. "It's the old flag, sir. White cross on a blue field."

"Servants of King Louis. Splendid. We'll have to air her out if we take her, but I'll wager she has brandy. How many guns, Ben?"

"Ports for ten each side. Plus a swivel gun or two: that'd make twenty-two. Looks like deckhands in her rigging, not marines, but she could be carrying some."

The pirate looked at the young man. "Twenty-two guns to our twelve four-pounders and the chance of two dozen muskets, to boot. What do you think, boy? Try to take her, or let her run?"

The teenager straightened. "Take her."

The pirate returned to his plaiting. "You'd risk my men's lives for a prize when we don't even know what she's carrying?" He looked up again.

"No, sir. But I'd risk *her* men's lives."

The pirate tied off the tip of a lock with a silver bead. "How so?"

The younger man motioned toward the silver brush and a tortoiseshell comb on the tabletop. "May I?"

The captain nodded once, slowly, his eyes on the boy.

"Say your brush here is the merchantman. Even if she has guns we can't see atop her aft castle, she'll still be blind in the quarters. She can shoot broadside and possibly straight aft, but she cannot shoot at an angle astern—not without repositioning a gun, and that takes time. So we sail straight into that unprotected quarter." He moved the brush. "Then we turn broadside and fire chain shot: take down her rigging and maybe even her masts. That puts her adrift; she can no longer maneuver to return fire. We can stand off and fire solid shot at her until she surrenders."

"Well." The captain looked at his mate. "It seems that young . . . What's your name, lad?"

"Theodore, sir. Theodore—"

The captain shushed him. "Your Christian name alone will suffice on this ship, unless you're married, which I doubt very much that you are."

He divided his beard in two and began plaiting the left side with the scarlet ribbons. "So, Ben, it seems that young Ted has a knack for the scheming of things. What think you of his plan?"

The mate hoisted his breeches a bit. "It leaves us with a crippled prize, Captain. We can't put the half of what she's carrying in our hold; the rest would go to waste."

The pirate glanced up at Ted. "He's right, you know."

The young man scowled. "Then we take her gold and silver and burn her."

Both pirates laughed, and the teenager's face reddened.

"I like the cut of your jib, Bold Ted," the pirate said. "But that's an inbound merchantman. She carries very little gold or silver; only what her frightened passengers might have stuffed away in the corners of their trunks. Her cargo is probably cloth and tools and furniture, gunpowder and shot and some cannon, I wager, in her bilge as ballast. And perhaps—if Providence smiles upon us—some brandywine, seeing as she's French."

"Cloth and tools? What good are those?"

The pirate finished plaiting the other side of his beard.

"Those goods are needed by merchants here in the Indies, Bold Ted. They order them from the Old World, and pay when they arrive on the dock. Now, those merchants—or one of their cousins—will still get those goods, but they will buy them from us for a few shillings on the guinea. We can do that and still profit, because we paid naught for their manufacture, nor for the cost of crossing all of that." The captain waved a hand in the general direction of the great rolling Atlantic.

The boy's eyebrows rose. "You mean you buy and sell like common shopkeepers?"

The captain shrugged. "Not 'buy,' perhaps. But sell? Yes. That we do. Help me on with this wig, lad."

The captain sat on a three-legged stool, and Ted, waiting a moment while the deck assumed a new angle beneath him, lifted the wig from its stand and settled it on the pirate's close-cropped head, placing it with the care of a pontiff consecrating a king.

"Excellent," the pirate said, admiring the result in a looking glass. He topped it off with a scarlet-plumed tricorner hat, slipped a brace of dueling pistols into his golden sash, and turned to Ted. "When a shop owner or a chandler or even a military garrison buys from us, lad, they save money, and they save a great deal of it. It is far cheaper to buy from the brethren of the coast than it is to do business with the trading companies. That tends to make them like us very much. It tends to make them rather lax about demanding protection on the high seas.

"And as for burning that ship, we'll do that only if she fights us. She is manned by a crew that was either pressed into service or signed on out of desperation for what amounts to ten pence a week, maybe less after they've drawn goods and provisions. They have no interest in protecting a rich man's fortune, not unless they feel they are in danger of losing their lives as well. That is the key to the whole thing."

The pirate held a finger to his lip again, as if thinking. He opened a chest next to his bunk and took out a rolled piece of muslin. He unfolded it, revealing a handsome flintlock pistol with a well-engraved, heavy brass bolster on its grip. Working with the speed of a man long accustomed to such actions, he swiftly loaded, tamped, primed, and cocked the foot-long gun. Then he handed it to the young man.

"There you are, Bold Ted. That is a Spanish-made half-inch from the shop of Geromino Menandez, one of the finest pistol-smiths in old Madrid. Tuck that in your belt. If we have to board in force, fire the shot to help clear the deck, and then use the gun as a club until the prize is ours."

Ted looked at the pistol in his hands. It was the finest thing he had ever seen.

"Captain," he said, "I have no way to pay you for this."

The captain cocked an eye toward the ceiling. "Now that you mention it, nor did I when I acquired it. Now slip it in your belt, Ted, and mind the trigger. That ball can take your leg off."

Ted put the pistol in its place. He seemed to grow an inch taller in the process.

The captain held a hand out, toward the ladder. "Shall we take the air?"

The three of them climbed to the open hatch and the deck—the teenager first, then the mate, and finally the captain, who had topped his finery off with a brocaded velvet waistcoat. The crew, on the other hand, had opted for practicality, pulling on tarred breeches and jackets and leather jerkins—clothing designed to turn a light sword's blade. All around them the Caribbean Sea shone a deep and rolling blue under a sky dotted with only a few small clouds.

Their quarry, a three-masted ship, was under what seemed its own small constellation of cumulus—a full set of snow-white sails straining concave before the wind. But it was plain to see that she was losing her race to the pirates' faster Jamaica-built sloop. Already they were close enough to make out the men in her rigging, shielding their eyes as they watched the closing pursuer.

"Colors," the pirate said evenly. Behind him, a man ran up a black flag. On it was a winged skull wearing a white crown. In its lower left was an hourglass; in its lower right, a pair of crossed bones.

The captain accepted a spyglass and took a look at his quarry. He lowered the glass, still gazing at the distant ship. "Raise ports. Run them out."

On both sides of the sloop, hinged gunports were lifted. Gun crews hove together on thick, greased ropes and rolled deck cannon out so their muzzles cleared the sides of the ship.

"Vapors," the pirate commanded.

Musicians—a fiddler, a piper, and a horn player—began playing a screeching, cacophonous melody, a veritable hornpipe from hell. All along the deck of the pirate ship, men shouted, barked, bellowed, and screamed as they jumped into the air, stomped on the deck, and rang cutlasses together.

The captain pointed to one of his crew. Raising his voice to be heard over the din, he shouted, "One across her bow . . . at your leisure, Jack."

Standing well to the side, a gunner waited until the sloop was rising on a swell and then lowered his improvised match—a piece of burning hemp—to his cannon's touchhole. Sparks shot up, thunder erupted, and the cannon leapt back on its carriage. A thick cloud of smoke wafted by—foul, sulfurous, blue-gray in color. When it had cleared, the pirates could see a geyser of white shoot up from the blue sea on the far side of their quarry's bow. Moments later, the merchantman's acre of sail collapsed as she came sharply about and spilled the wind. Her gunports remained shuttered. A man with a cutlass ran back to her ensign and hacked at it. The crossed flag fluttered and fell into the sea.

The pirate crew roared their approval.

The captain smiled down at Ted. "And that is how it is done, lad. We'll still keep our guns on her, and we will sink her in a minute if anyone decides to be brave or foolish. But I doubt anyone will, and we've a fine prize with no unsightly gaps for our carpenter to patch."

He turned to the mate. "Ben, would you be so good as to assemble a prize crew?"

The mate saluted—the first time anyone had executed a proper shipboard salute all morning—and chose men from the volunteers clustered around him.

The captain clapped the teenager on the shoulder. "You are a good lad and a bright one, Bold Ted. But I daresay that this Vicar Bascombe of yours took his knowledge of tactics from the histories of Caesar, and perhaps from naval accounts; we will have to do our best to clear your head of all that battle nonsense. Ships of the line fight to the death, and if hard-pressed, so shall we. But for men in an enterprise such as this, our stock in trade is the option of surrender, and surrender is always what's best for all parties. If one of our men is maimed in a fight, we must pay him a pension and buy him a plot of land, and that expense reduces considerably the prize share for all concerned. Not to mention that the prize is worth more if taken whole.

"And those lads over there"—he nodded at the merchantman—"are highly relieved now that things are proceeding in a civilized manner. Most of them will volunteer to crew our prize and receive shares for their cooperation. As for the ones that don't, they will be locked in the hold and set ashore at the nearest landfall."

Ted shook his head, his close-cropped black hair glistening in the bright Caribbean sun, as the sloop closed in on the drifting merchantman. "It's not how I thought it worked at all."

The pirate laughed and lifted a hailing trumpet.

"I am Captain Henry Thatch, a servant of King George." Behind him, the first mate coughed. "And you are my prize." The captain squinted at the mate, then continued, his deep voice amplified nearly threefold by the brass horn. "We give you all quarter so long as you submit; on that you have my word. Drop us a net and stand by to assist as we board."

He handed the horn to a crewman and smiled once again at Ted as the crew swarmed around them. Grappling hooks dangled from the tan hands of several. Most had exchanged their cutlasses and muskets for smaller arms—dirks and clubs and cocked flintlock pistols slung in pairs on cords about their necks.

"Consider this the beginning of your finer education, lad. There are things in this world and the next—things worth knowing of which you have probably never so much as dreamed. But you have a good head on your shoulders, and I shall do my best to enlighten you."

The pirate looked down and cocked his head.

"Let us begin," he told the teen, "with the brighter points of history. What would you say was the seminal accomplishment of the year of our Lord sixteen hundred and twenty-three?"

TWO

I blinked at the question and became acutely aware of the background noise of the office—the air-conditioning hissing out its temperate consolation, the distant warble of a fax machine making a connection.

"Of 1623?" I asked, buying time.

Across the battered steel desk from me, Phil Rackham rested his chin in his hand, cradling a couple days' worth of stubble in his thumb and fist. He nodded, crow's-feet becoming more pronounced in his tanned face as he did so. Most of him, from the thinning, sun-bleached hair to his callused hands, looked a little bit weather-beaten, but his sea green Columbia bonefishing shirt appeared brand-new, fresh off the rack. At its neck, a gold doubloon, framed in silver, rested in a thicket of equally sun-bleached chest hair.

It made what I was wearing—a sport coat, necktie, and Dockers—seem hopelessly out of place, the very picture of job-interview desperation.

I glanced out the window beyond him. No answers there—just tourists posing with the life-size bronze statue of Hemingway in front of the old post office building, Papa holding a fishing rod outfitted with a big, heavy saltwater reel.

Rackham's office, like those around it, was glass from waist height up, cubicles built into the high-ceilinged space of an old marine warehouse. The building had probably already been ancient back when it was Hemingway himself—and not just his statue—standing on the streets of Key West. In the office to my left, a pretty young woman was talking to a middle-aged couple: probably investors, because as they spoke, the girl took a gold chain out of a purple velvet bag—it reminded me of something that would come with a gift bottle of Canadian whiskey—and put it around the older woman's neck. It worked; the woman beamed.

Off to my right, two white-jacketed preservationists were discussing a black object that looked to be an iron musket-ball mold. The way they were handling it, it appeared to be very light. I assumed that it was a resin replica molded from a concretion.

Concretion takes place as living matter and underwater grit become plastered around a sunken object over the years. If the object is a ferrous metal and relatively small, it will often rust away to nothing, leaving a void within the concretion that can be detected by X-ray. Drill into it carefully, introduce resin until all the encapsulated seawater has been displaced, allow the resin to harden, break the concretion mold, and you can have a near-perfect, if flyweight, copy of the metal original. I had made hundreds of such molds when I'd interned at the North Carolina Maritime Museum.

Rackham cleared his throat, and I snapped back to the present.

"Well," I said slowly, "there's the loss of the Spanish Tierra Firme Fleet off the Dry Tortugas, west of here—the *Santa Margarita*, the *Rosario*, *Nuesto Señora de Atocha*, and the rest. But that's 1622, not 1623."

"And if I'd asked about 1622, that would be an excellent answer," Rackham told me. "Spain had a weak economy made weaker still by her insistence on basing it upon the mineral wealth of the New World. When her treasure fleet was lost with five years of accumulated wealth to the 1622 hurricane, it threw the Spanish economy into deep recession—some would say a full-blown depression. That, plus the actions of the buccaneers—the first pirates in these waters—loosened Spain's hold enough for the English and the French and the Dutch to gain a foothold."

He smiled, lifting one corner of his lips only. The left corner.

"But the year in question, Mr. . . . ." He glanced at my résumé. "Mr. Rhode—"

"Greg," I said.

"We'll see," Rackham told me, still looking down at my cobbled-together list of academic honors and accomplishments. He glanced up. "The year in question is 1623."

In the next office, the middle-aged couple was nodding at whatever the pretty girl was saying. The woman hefted the heavy gold-chain necklace and grinned.

I glanced out the window again. The tourists had walked on, leaving Papa posturing ebulliently at no one.

I looked Rackham in the eyes.

"I don't have a clue," I told him.

He smiled—both corners of his mouth this time.

"That's an even better answer. I like people who aren't afraid to admit they don't know things. You give most people a master's in marine archaeology and they think they have to have an answer for everything, but the truth of the matter is, if we had all the answers, we wouldn't be full-time treasure hunters—we'd be full-time treasure *finders*."

He made a note on the margin of my CV. "We work on salary plus share around here, Greg. An eighth of a share for you to start, up to a quarter-share after you've been here three months. Sassy in Administration will give you the details, but the upshot is that the salary will keep you in pizza and beer and a used trailer or a studio walk-up on Truman, if you haggle over the price of your rent. The share, if we strike the right find, can make you rich. But you can't count on the share: not the time of it, nor its size. You up for that?"

I wondered if he could hear my heart.

"I sure am."

We shook on it.

"Okay." Rackham made another note on my résumé and handed it back to me. "Give that to Sassy. She'll give you a draw against your first month so you can put rent plus deposit on a place to live and enjoy your first week here in Key Weird. Come by Monday at eight and we'll get you set up. Fair enough?"

"Yes, sir. Thank you."

I stayed in my seat.

"Is there something else?" Rackham asked me.

"Well." I straightened up. "Yes, sir. There is: 1623—what happened that was so significant?"

Rackham repeated his one-ended smile.

"We have a pretty fair library down the street here, Greg. What say, Monday morning at eight, you stop back in here and you tell *me*?"

THREE

"You lost the sport coat." Phil Rackham's Monday morning attire was strikingly similar to what he'd worn on Friday, only now the Columbia bonefishing shirt was a pale pink. It reminded me of a '63 Thunderbird that my uncle had once owned. "Good. May want to invest in some mothballs; Key West isn't really your sport coat sort of place."

"I noticed."

Rackham laughed. "So what's up?"

"Well . . ." I took a breath. "Blaise Pascal was born in 1623."

"Aha. The 'God-shaped hole in the human heart.'"

"Actually, there's some dispute as to whether he ever really said that."

Rackham leaned back in a gray desk chair that looked decidedly Navy-surplus. "You study Pascal?"

"No, but I know how to use Google. And I doubt Pascal's birth is the event you were looking for, anyhow."

"It wasn't. What else have you got?"

I looked over his shoulder, out his window. A group of Japanese tourists were playing pass-the-camera in front of the statue of Papa Hemingway.

"The first North American temperance law was enacted in

Virginia in 1623," I told him. "But from what I saw on Duval Street Saturday night, I wouldn't say that had any lasting ramifications."

"Yep." Rackham nodded. "Duval Street pretty much any night will testify to that. Anything else?"

I took a breath. "The First Folio of Shakespeare was published."

"Aha. Very good. And that is significant—why?"

I took another breath. "One of the plays printed in it was *The Tempest*."

"Ah, yes. *The Tempest*." Rackham closed his eyes and lifted his head, as if he were peering though his eyelids at the ceiling.

" 'Full fathom five thy father lies,' " he began to recite, " 'Of his bones are coral made; those are the pearls that were his eyes; nothing of him that doth fade but doth suffer a sea-change . . .' "

Rackham opened his eyes.

" '. . . Into something rich,' " he said, dropping his voice half an octave, " 'and strange.' "

I didn't say anything; what *could* I say? But Rackham was looking straight at me, as if expecting a remark of some kind. I glanced through the glass walls at the adjoining offices. The pretty young woman, Miss Drape-'Em-with-Gold, was drinking coffee. She lifted a hand in greeting. I waved back. The other office was unoccupied.

"*The Tempest*," Rackham explained. "Second scene of Act One. So what's so important about that play, Greg?"

I looked at Rackham. "It's about a shipwreck. It's believed by some scholars to be based on a historical event, the stranding of the . . ." I paused for a moment, trying to remember the name.

"The *Sea Venture*, a ship bearing colonists from England to Jamestown," Rackham said, stepping in. "In 1609 the ship was taking on water catastrophically in a hurricane, and her commanding officer deliberately steered her onto the Bermuda reef in order to keep from sinking. Not a soul was lost; the survivors were able to live on fish and feral hogs that had been turned loose by the Spanish decades before. That's why the hog penny has been a Bermudian coin for centuries now. When a new ship was built so they could continue on to Virginia nine months later, two of the company stayed behind to claim Bermuda as a Crown Colony. The rest finished the trip to Virginia."

"Um . . . right." It took me a second or two to get that out.

"Of course," Rackham said, standing, "there are others who make equally compelling claims that the play was based on the loss of another ship entirely, the *Edward Bonaventure*, and that Shakespeare used Henry Mays's account of her loss as his source."

Rackham's eyes had a way of making you feel like a bug pinned to a piece of cardboard. I shifted my gaze to the statue of Hemingway across the street. There was a seagull by his feet, pecking determinedly at something.

Rackham was still looking at me.

"Okay," I finally said.

"So." Rackham sat on the edge of his desk. "Why's that so important? Why is a shipwreck such a great big, world-changing deal?"

I looked around Rackham's office. He had a small sixteenth-century swivel cannon, the kind that would mount on a ship's rail, propped up in one corner. A couple of nineteenth-century deadheads were in another. On the one wall that actually was a wall—except for the window with the view of the Hemingway statue, that is—there were pictures of Rackham with Jacques Cousteau, Rackham with Bob Ballard, Rackham with Mel Fisher. A gilt frame held the first page of the admiralty court decision that had given him title to the *San Pedro*. There was a foot-long gold bar in a display case on his desk, rolled maps of the Gulf and the

Keys were sticking out of an amphora in another corner, and from the ceiling dangled a detailed scale model of a Benthos open-frame submersible ROV.

I held my hands out to either side, "Because . . . of all this."

Rackham gave me half a smile and stood. *Meeting concluding.* Picking up on the signal, I got to my feet as well.

"Who," he asked, "led the first expedition to salvage the *Atocha* and the *Margarita*?"

I thought for a moment. "Gaspar de Vargas."

Rackham nodded. Then he put an arm around my shoulders.

"You know that," he told me as he opened his office door. "And I know that. And so do pretty much all of the people here."

We stepped out into the hall.

"But I'll tell you something, Greg. Most of the people in the world do not know that. What's more, if you told them, they wouldn't care. Yet everybody knows who Shakespeare was. That's why the *First Folio* was so important. Not because it contained *The Tempest*, but because it passed on to us the works of a man with profound insight into the workings of the human soul."

We stepped into an old freight elevator and went down one floor. When the door opened, it did so onto a broad floor filled with tarp-covered plastic tanks with wires leading out of them: reverse electrolysis vessels, to stop the corrosion in large ferrous metal artifacts and leach the salt out of them. Maybe Rackham sensed my stiffness, because he took his arm off my shoulders. We walked side by side down a raised wooden walkway between the tanks.

"Shipwrecks are a very big deal within this organization, Greg," Rackham told me. "But not so to the world outside. We're a curiosity, an adventurous insight to most people, but—except maybe to the folks who invest with us—we are not the end-all, be-all of life. There are hundreds of other things ahead of us on that list. You'll want to remember that. When this job gets to you—and it will—a little perspective might be just what you need to make it through to the end of the day."

We stopped in front of a door with a frosted glass window in it.

"The *Peabody* is going out in two weeks' time, and I'd like you aboard when she departs. It's a new phase, the fourth, on a wreck we've been working for the past year—the *Rosarita*. Have you heard of it?"

Heard of it? It was part of the reason I'd applied for the job. It took me a moment to stammer, "Uh—I have. Sixteenth-century treasure ship, isn't it?"

Rackham nodded, his hand on the door. "It is, although thus far we've also found a couple of flintlock pistol barrels and actions."

I found myself cocking my head. "Flintlocks are what—eighteenth century at the earliest? What do you think you have? Two wrecks on the same site?"

Phil shrugged. "Either that or a period wreck contaminated by later objects: some sailor dropping his seabag over the side. Either way, it wouldn't hurt to have along a marine archaeologist who hasn't been influenced by our previous surveys. But until then, we have a backlog of small preservation items that I'd like to put a serious dent on processing. Mind pitching in on that?"

Out working a site in two weeks; I'd never dreamed it could be that soon.

"Sure." I hoped I didn't look as dazzled as I felt. "My pleasure."

"I think that just might be so."

That part didn't make sense to me. At least not for another ten or fifteen seconds. Then Rackham opened the door.

"Sheila McIntyre, meet Greg Rhode. He's going to be giving you a hand here for the next week or two."

"My knight in shining armor."

The voice, a little bit sultry and a little bit amused, came from behind a steel rack at the far side of the room. Sheila McIntyre stepped out from behind it.

And took my breath away.

FOUR

She was as handsome a woman as Ted had ever seen; comely and fine, draped in a dress crafted from silk as white as a morning cloud, and rich blood-red velvet. In the spyglass she appeared to be in the center of a rainbow-rimmed drop of water, but even in that imperfect image, occluded by the partial shade of her parasol, her face had the perfect beauty and symmetry of a chestnut-haired china doll. She stood near the edge of the wharf as if it were her dais, and those about her kept a deferential distance.

Ted tugged at the spyglass, trying to eke a bit more magnification from it.

"Did Vicar Bascombe not teach you that it is impolite to stare?" Henry Thatch asked.

"I don't think," Ted whispered, his eye still to the telescope, "that Mr. Bascombe ever saw anyone like *her*. She's an angel."

He handed the telescope to the pirate, who took a long, leisurely look and nodded. "That she is."

Their ship, the *Regent*, lay at anchor, her sails tightly furled. Behind them, in the broad shelter of Road Town Harbour, the French merchantman sat similarly at rest, a Union Jack now flapping listlessly at her stern, even though the *Regent*'s days of privateering had long since passed. Both ships had set longboats in the water, the pirate crew and the prize crew pulling smoothly for the docks.

"Captain!" Ted's eyes were still glued to the wharf. "She's waving!"

The pirate said nothing, but lifted his hand and waved back. The ship's musicians were toying with an Irish reel, considerably more melodic than the din they'd raised for the taking of the merchantman. Off to the side, several of the crew were at the rail, awaiting the return of the longboat, one of them dancing to the music as the others laughed and clapped time. And behind them, the mate and the ship's carpenter were rigging a boatswain's chair.

The *Regent*'s longboat reached the dock.

"Captain!" Ted's voice was very nearly a whisper. "That lady is getting into our launch."

"That she is." Thatch kept the spyglass to his eye.

"She's coming out here?"

"She is."

Ted watched as the crewmen carefully helped the woman into their boat. He looked up at the pirate. "Why?"

Thatch collapsed the spyglass and slipped it back into its leather case. "The merchantman carried sufficient specie for me to make a portion to the crew. Enough to enjoy an evening ashore, that is."

Ted nodded and fingered his share, three silver coins, through the plain leather pouch at his waist.

The pirate looked down. "But for the majority of the Frenchman's cargo, I am going to have to negotiate with the merchants of Road Town. That, or if their coffers are too shallow, take a skeleton crew and sail on at first light to Saint Thomas, see what the trade will bear there. So I shan't be leaving the *Regent* this night, and the lady will be spending the evening aboard."

Ted's jaw dropped. "You mean she's a . . ."

Thatch quirked an eyebrow. "A what?"

"No." Ted shook his head, stared down at the deck. "No. She is a lady—far too fine to be anything such as that."

Behind him, the mate started laughing. The captain began to laugh as well.

Ted's eyes screwed up in anger. "What?"

The pirate continued to chuckle and wiped the corner of one eye. He turned to the mate. "Tell you what, Ben. You keep mum on this and so shall I. Mistress Anne would not be amused to hear what she'd been mistaken for."

The pirate doffed his hat and bowed toward the longboat. It was near enough now for Ted to see the lady smiling in return.

Ted blinked. "But if she's not a . . ." He looked from the captain to the mate and back again. "Who is she?"

The captain smiled.

"That, Bold Ted"—he nodded toward the woman in the longboat—"is my wife."

Mistress Anne would not, as it turned out, be the only feminine occupant of the longboat. A young woman boarded after her, a girl in her teens, wearing a calico dress and a plain white bonnet. And because the bonnet was a poke bonnet, not covering the young woman's face, Ted did not require the spyglass to see that her face and arms were the color of mahogany. He turned to Hatch and glowered.

The pirate lifted his chin a bit. "What earns me that look, Bold Ted?"

"That." The teen pointed at the longboat.

"You object to the launch?"

Ted shot him a glance from the corners of his eyes. "Don't

toy with me, sir. You told me to my face that you cannot abide slavery."

Hatch shrugged. "Nor do I."

The younger man pointed at the launch again. "Then how do you explain her?"

The pirate stared at the longboat as if trying to puzzle out a distant inscription. Then he laughed, a loud bark of a laugh that only deepened his young companion's scowl.

"You mean Sally?" The pirate turned to his mate. "He means Sally." And the mate laughed as well.

"Sir?" Ted gripped the rail so tightly that his fingertips paled. "Do you mock me? She is clearly your servant."

"My servant?" With that, the pirate made an effort to contain another round of laughter, but failed, holding one hand out as he fought to regain composure.

"Oh, dear." Hatch wiped his eyes. "I'm sorry, Ted. Yes, Mistress Anne and I have servants—a whole family of them from Cornwall, in fact. But they are neither slave nor indentured; I hired them. And as for Sally, well, suffice it to say that, were I you, I would forego guessing any other woman's occupation for the rest of the day."

"She's not your . . . ?"

"She's not my anything. She is Mistress Anne's young friend. The two of them sew and read together."

Ted looked at the longboat again. "They read?"

Hatch nodded: once, quickly. "Bible, mostly. Or the odd broadsheet that makes it here from London in one piece. But as for Sally's profession, I would not get on her bad side were I you, or you shall have a very dry stay ashore."

"Dry?" Ted scowled again. "How so?"

"Her father," the pirate said. "He owns the best public house in Road Town."

The longboat drew next to the sloop as the boatswain's chair was lowered, the captain's wife sitting daintily on the broad plank seat. Her young companion had a white length of silk draped scarf-length about her neck, and she removed it and bent to Mistress Anne's ankles.

It took Ted a moment. Then he figured it out; Sally was binding the captain's wife's petticoats closely about her legs, preserving her modesty as the crew winched her aboard. It reminded him of something Bascombe, the Scotsman, had told him about—how the warders at Wapping Stairs in London had bound the skirts of condemned women on the gallows.

It was a distressing image, and by the time he had chased it from his mind, the crew had winched Mistress Anne aboard and the captain had taken a knee to free her from her bondage. The young man turned once again to the rail; the longboat was pulling away.

"Captain?"

The pirate was holding his wife's hand in his own, bending toward her as she spoke. He turned.

"Yes, Ted?"

"The young lady, sir." Ted glanced at the receding longboat. "She is not coming aboard?"

"Sally? No. I daresay she's due at the inn. She only came along to help with this." The pirate held up the length of white silk.

Ted turned to the rail again. In the longboat, Sally was gazing back at him, and he raised a hand in greeting.

She waved back, and she looked at him, and for a very long moment the only thing he saw was her eyes.

FIVE

I've never been much for those love ballads, where the singer is going on and on about the color of his true love's eyes. And poetry? The sort of stuff that does the same thing, only without a guitar and a melody to take the edge off? A jock in one of my lit classes at Duke probably said it best when, after the graduate assistant—one of those pale women dressed in earth tones—had finished an overly dramatic reading of a love poem by Burns, or maybe Wordsworth, one of the two, he stage-whispered, "Whoa. I think I just threw up a little in my mouth."

But Sheila McIntyre's eyes put that whole body of music and literature in an entirely new perspective. They were, to begin with, two entirely different colors—one deepwater blue and the other walnut brown, a combination that I was pretty sure I had seen before only in *National Geographic* portraits of timber wolves. Yet there was nothing canine about those eyes at all. Framed by her boyishly short cap of soft blond hair, they made her look almost pixie-like, a quality accentuated by that fact that even in her Crocs flip-flops, she stood all of five-foot-four. Add in a Pepsodent-white smile, and Sheila McIntyre had a face that could light up any room.

Even a barroom. Even the Green Parrot Bar.

A word about the Green Parrot. Key West has bars the way most towns in the South have churches. Not just a bar on every corner; on some streets, bars appear with the regularity of the black keys on a piano.

And we're talking some passing strange establishments here. There's Captain Tony's Saloon, where patrons of decades past have left undergarments stapled to the ceiling beams, and the tree growing up through the center of the building is rumored to have once doubled as a gallows. There's the Garden of Eden, a rooftop establishment that is—and I swear I am not making this up—clothing-optional. There's Sloppy Joe's, where cruise-ship tourists come looking for the ghost of Ernest Hemingway, even though during the time that Papa lived in Key West, the building occupied by today's Sloppy Joe's was a hardware store or something like that. And there's Hog's Breath Saloon, which sells liquor, but probably makes most of its profit off the sale of T-shirts with its enigmatic slogan: *Hog's breath is better than no breath at all.*

All together, Key West—particularly after the Sunset Celebration has concluded on a Friday night in Mallory Square—is the sort of place that, were Carrie Nation still around, would give the old girl a triple coronary in about two seconds flat.

Yet at the far end of all of this licentiousness, in a little city where hedonism seemed destined to thrive in a subtropical climate, the Green Parrot is the sort of place that most tourists take one peek into before moving on.

How to describe the Green Parrot? Well, to start with, the sign out front reads, *Sorry, We're Open.* Another one, over the bar, admonishes, *No Sniveling.* Above the bar itself is what appears to be an artistically draped parachute, and if you select anything but blues on the jukebox, people complain. There is both a dart board and a pool table—things conspicuous by their absence in many Key West bars, because darts and pool cues and billiard balls make handy weapons. And the place is open-air; if you sit in the wrong place and it rains, you'll get wet. But the thing that makes the Green Parrot closest to the hearts of Key Westers are its prices—lower than the tourist bars on Duval Street—and its happy hour, which is generous.

Even in this environment, even illuminated by a neon sign advertising the availability of Landshark Lager, Sheila McIntyre had this very nearly saintly presence. She did not say a lot, but when she did, it was in the most beautiful accent imaginable.

She was . . . Well, let's put it this way. On my first day at work, when Phil had walked me down to the preservation lab, Sheila had been radiant—and she was wearing latex gloves and an ancient black rubber apron that reached well below her knees. Furthermore, the room was cooled by a window air-conditioner that did not quite have the BTUs for the job, and most people would have looked wilted, but Sheila McIntyre simply glowed.

"Ever grade pearls?" That was the first thing she had asked me, and those three words—plus the knight-in-shining-armor comment—were enough to speak volumes on her background.

"You're Australian."

She nodded. "I do believe I am."

"And your folks . . . named you *Sheila*?"

She grinned. "My dad's always had this wicked sense of humor."

Then her face had straightened. "So . . . ever grade pearls?"

She appeared unsurprised when I told her I had not. Actually I was surprised that she had asked. Pearls—pearls liberated from their parent oyster, at least—are not the sort of thing one generally expects to find on a centuries-old shipwreck. Without the protection of an oyster's mantle, pearls generally erode down to gritty spheres and eventually dissolve into sand when lost under water.

But on a wreck from the previous season, a galleon known as the *Santa Maria*—no relative to the Christopher Columbus ship—a pewter chest had been recovered, and when it was opened, it was found to contain more than a thousand pearls of various size: most of them the size one would use for embroidery, though some large enough to be set in earrings or necklaces.

These, Sheila told me, had been irrigated with filtered fresh water for the last six months. Now they were about to be shipped to a gemologist for appraisal, but first they had to be graded by size and color.

It was not the sort of work that one would need a master's degree to perform. A six-year-old could have done it. All I had to do was use a pair of nylon tweezers to group them by size—there was a plastic gauge with various-size holes in it to assist in this task—and then re-sort the sized pearls by color: white, light gray, medium gray, dark gray, and black. Once that was done, I was to cut appropriate-size pieces out of a length of soft foam rod, slit the rod with an X-Acto knife, put one pearl within each piece, and then pack everything for shipping in a set of aluminum Halliburton cases.

It was grunt work of the most basic kind. I did it all week, and I didn't care. For one, I was going to be out working a site soon, a relatively unexplored site, and I would happily have scrubbed the floors for that opportunity. And for another, I got to watch the constantly attractive comings and the goings of Sheila McIntyre, and even had lunch with her a couple of times. When she asked me if I wanted to go to the Friday night happy hour at the Green Parrot, I was beside myself.

But I should have guessed we wouldn't be alone.

It turned out that something like half of Phil Rackham's operation went to the Green Parrot on Friday nights. There were five at our table: Sheila; the young investor-relations woman who had the office next to Phil—her name turned out to be Robin—a couple of divers who introduced themselves as Panhead Mikey and Malibu; and me.

Robin had changed out of her preppy polo shirt and khakis into something a little more Key West: hair back in a ponytail, faded denim short shorts, pink flip-flops, and a baby blue T-shirt that read, *I Taught Your Boyfriend That Thing You Like*.

Panhead Mikey was wearing board shorts and a Henley tee from Orlando Harley-Davidson. Malibu had on a black wife-beater with a skull and crossbones, the better to show off his ink. And he had apparently added to it recently, because he kept pressing a piece of damp gauze to a fresh, crisply outlined, slightly pouty mermaid on his forearm.

"Must you do that at the table?" Sheila asked him.

"Just got it," Malibu said. "Me and Mikey stopped in at Paradise Ink on the way here."

"You couldn't have gotten it later, so you could do that at home?" I asked.

Malibu glanced at Panhead Mikey, and they both laughed.

"What?"

"Dude, everybody knows you can't get a tat when you're drunk," Malibu said, spacing the words out, as if instructing an imbecile. "It'll bleed like a stuck pig."

"And I suppose," Sheila asked, "staying sober is not an option?"

Malibu and Mikey cracked up again.

"Babe," Malibu said. "It's like . . . Friday night."

As if that explained everything.

The bar was beginning to fill up. The band scheduled for

that evening was Pet Boys, out of Lauderdale, and they enjoyed a pretty vigorous following at the Parrot. The Green Parrot was a rarity in that way as well; a Key West bar where you could sit all night and never hear "Margaritaville" played once—not unless Jimmy Buffet was in town and he dropped by to play it himself.

It had given me pause when we joined Robin and Panhead Mikey and Malibu at their table. True, to do anything else just would have seemed weird, particularly as I didn't know anybody in Key West but Rackham's people and my landlord. But in the underwater treasure-hunting world, divers tend to be the cowboys: wild and unbroken, the kind of roughnecks that repulse many women—okay, *most* women—but attract enough that you have to consider them a threat. Sheila and I had only recently met, and we were still more acquaintances than friends, but it would have shattered me if she were anything more than cordial to either of them.

My one hope was economic. Malibu and Panhead Mikey were first-year divers, and Rackham paid first-year divers minimum wage plus one percent of anything they found. But since *Peabody* was at the dock getting her engines and transmissions serviced, they weren't finding anything but the business ends of mops at the moment. True, they lived and took their meals—even while in port—on the converted minesweeper that served as Rackham's principal salvage vessel, and Rackham deducted only a token amount from their wages for these amenities. But minimum wage is minimum wage, and while the Green Parrot's drinks are a bargain by Key West standards, they can drain a limited coffer fairly quickly. So I had a glimmer of a hope that the two of them would run out of gas before they could flirt Sheila McIntyre right out of whatever limited connection we'd made thus far.

The strange thing was, except for the exchange about the tattoo, the two divers acted as if they didn't even know Sheila was there. Their attentions were directed toward Robin—couldn't have been any more strongly directed toward her if each had launched independently into the courtship dance of the blue-footed booby.

From where I was sitting, Robin seemed to be biding her time. It was pretty clear that the woman's intention was to share a table with the scuba twins, but nothing more. Sure, she was laughing at their jokes and chatting with them . . . just a bit. But my guess was, if she was looking at all, she was looking for someone beside them. Maybe somebody with table manners. And a real job. And it seemed odd to me that they were so focused on her; Robin was pretty enough, but Sheila was in a class by herself.

The folks one section over started getting noisy with root-beer barrels: the Green Parrot's version of a boilermaker, made with root-beer schnapps. Lots of table thumping and cheering. Behind the din of the growing crowd, Muddy Waters's "Mule Kicking in My Stall" was wailing on the jukebox, the slide guitar just barely audible above the fifty or sixty conversations all going at once, and night was coming on through the open sides of the bar. Robin got up to visit the ladies' room, and in that female show of restroom camaraderie that I have never quite understood, Sheila went with her.

I watched them go. Or maybe I should say that I watched Sheila go. We'd worked late, getting the last of the pearls packed and locked away in the safe, to wait for the morning's armored-car pickup, and we were both still wearing what we'd had on at the lab: in her case, khaki shorts, a sleeveless chambray shirt, and a pair of navy Crocs flips. Didn't matter; I watched until she got swallowed up by the crowd.

"Yo." Malibu nudged Panhead Mikey and pointed his

longneck at me. "I think Rhode Scholar here is having a Schmack attack."

"Schmack" was the way Sheila McIntyre's name got condensed into a nickname by some of the guys in Rackham's operation. I'm pretty sure she liked it about as much as I enjoyed being called "Rhode Scholar."

Yet if a Schmack attack meant that as far as I was concerned there were only two kinds of people in the Green Parrot that night—Sheila McIntyre and everyone else—then Malibu was right. And knowing that, and knowing that he knew, made my face feel hot.

"Rhode Scholar," Mikey said. "You're, like, blushing, man."

Both divers looked at each other and cracked up. More than the situation would warrant, if you asked me.

Malibu took a breath and fought to regain composure. He leaned on the table, looked at me more closely. "You don't know, do you?"

He turned to Panhead Mikey. "He doesn't know!"

Both convulsed in fresh laughter. Now my face got hotter, but I was no longer blushing.

"What?" I asked.

"Dude," Malibu gasped, trying to stop laughing, "Schmack is, like, you know . . . a rainbow warrior."

"A what?"

"Oh, for crying out loud. She bats from the wrong side of the plate, dude."

I got a little dizzy there. "You mean she's . . ." I shook my head. "Nah—no way."

"Oh, way." Malibu was enjoying this way too much. "Definitely way."

"He's right," Panhead Mikey chimed in. "We've, like, you know, researched it, bro. It's a bummer, a real shame. But it's true."

I had no ammunition to counter their claim. After all, what did I know about Sheila McIntyre, other than that she came from a cattle station outside Brisbane, was cuter than the proverbial button, and had a seemingly encyclopedic knowledge of sixteenth-century New World goldsmithing?

Besides, even if I had the wherewithal to counter the scuba twins' claim, Sheila was on her way back to the table. Looking beautiful.

And unobtainable.

6

SIX

Well, what can I say? After all, I didn't make the trip from Durham to Key West to meet Sheila McIntyre. I went there to get a job with Phil Rackham, and a job with Phil is what I got.

And it wasn't as if Sheila had rejected *me*. From what Malibu and Panhead Mikey had told me, she had pretty much rejected my entire gender, a vast crowd of humanity, of which I was merely a part. So I certainly couldn't take it personally.

Seven years of university-fostered political correctness had left me ambivalent on the subject. I mean, why gay guys prefer other guys has always just left me baffled; half the time I'm pretty near nauseated by the smell of *myself* after a long, hot day. Just the thought of snuggling up to another man is enough to give me a gag-reflex sort of moment.

Now, girls preferring girls: that's always made at least a little more sense to me. After all, *I* like girls.

So I guess I'm judgmental, but not so bigoted that I worry about hate-crime charges.

And, as my undergrad roommate had once told me, "We gotta support the gay dudes, Greg. Myself, I encourage them. After all, if they weren't interested in each other, we'd be having to compete with *them* for all the babes on Saturday night. And face it, bro, most of those guys look, dress, and clean up way better than us."

I can't say I totally endorsed my old roommate's views on gender preference. But I wasn't repulsed by the news about Sheila, either.

Confused, sure, but not repulsed.

And in a way it was liberating. I mean, rather than sitting in the conservation lab every day, looking at this way-beyond-cute girl and suffering that simmering mental anguish, *Should I ask her out? Will she say yes? If she says yes, how do I keep from messing this up? And what if somebody else comes along for her?* Rather than Rolaids-ing my way through that train wreck of certain misery, I could just enjoy her company. I could take her as she was. We could talk without deception. There was nothing to read into our conversations.

We could be friends.

Who'd have thought it?

We began doing the small things friends do—looking after each other, doing favors. She called around and found a shop that carried the battery I needed for my underwater camera. I helped her recover the system in her aging notebook computer when it glitched after a software upgrade. She brought in a little black and silver espresso machine and set it up in the lab so she could make us lattes in the morning before we put on our aprons and set about preserving the past. She claimed that in the same way *café con leche* helped locals fight the heat in Puerto Rico, lattes would help us soldier on through a Key West summer despite the lab's ailing air-conditioner. Some mornings I would stop in at La Dichosa on White Street to pick up a small loaf of warm Cuban bread and a little tub of honey butter for our at-work breakfast.

There in the conservation lab she and I became comfortably domestic. No courtship, no gamesmanship, no where-were-you-this-weekend jealousy and suspicions. In short, none of the relationship baggage. We just enjoyed each other's company. It was nice.

Around about the middle of my second week in the lab—my last before the *Peabody* left to go on-site—I was walking down the hallway with our baked goods when I heard music coming out of the lab: banjo, guitar, bass, fiddle, and a click. It was something traditional but rollicking, and I paused when I got to the doorway, listening. Sheila looked up from where she was making notes on one of the tables.

" 'Cluck, Old . . .' " I started. Then I shook my head. "No . . . It's not that; it's 'Devil in the Strawstack.' "

Sheila's iPod was stuck in the slot of one of those Bose portable speaker systems. She peered over the top of her glasses and checked the screen from several feet away.

"Right you are." She smiled. "You know this album?"

I shook my head. "No, but I recognize the tune."

Sheila brightened noticeably. "You enjoy bluegrass?"

"Sure." I set the butter down and pulled out a Swiss Army knife to slice the bread. "I grew up in Black Mountain, North Carolina. Music like this is pretty much what I was weaned on. Just haven't heard much lately. Everybody at Duke was into hip-hop and metal."

Sheila wrinkled her nose, opened a bag next to her, and took out a bread knife and paper napkins. She set my Swiss Army knife aside and offered me the bread knife. I laughed and began carving our breakfast into thick, warm slices.

"Who is it?" I nodded toward the stereo.

"Ron Block." She said it brightly, glad to be talking about it. "And it is, in fact, the *Devil in the Strawstack* album."

"Ron Block . . ." I looked up, trying to place the name.

"Banjo and guitar—Alison Krauss and Union Station," Sheila offered. She accepted the first slice and buttered it.

"Sure." I nodded, listening to the intricate picking. "Makes sense. Talented picker. Wow . . . wish I could play like that."

That really got her attention. "You're a musician?"

Okay—what are you doing? My throat tightened. *Why go there?*

"No," I finally managed to say. "I mean, I used to be. High school and when I was an undergrad. But no. Not in years."

"What did you play?"

"Guitar, banjo . . . mandolin. You learn to play one of 'em, you pretty much learn to play them all."

Stop it. Just shut up. Now.

"Get . . . *out!*" Sheila clapped her hands like I'd just offered her ice cream. "Oh! Do bring them in. I'd love to hear you."

I looked around, glanced into the electrolysis tanks, trying to avoid her eyes. "Naw. Don't have them down here. Not even sure where they are now, to tell the truth."

She cocked her head.

"I got . . . uh, busy in grad school," I stumbled through the fabrication. "Field projects, thesis . . . took up all my time."

And what do you call that, Greg? A half-truth? A half-truth is still half untrue.

"Well, that's a shame," Sheila said. Then, mercifully, she dropped it.

I guess I shouldn't have been surprised when I got to the lab the next morning and mandolin, fiddle, bass, and banjo were pouring out of the lab. A real toe-tapper. Only this time there were vocals. I paused in the open doorway to listen.

> *I'm not holding onto Jesus; He's holding onto me.*
> *He died and rose again to set me free.*

I am resting in the Spirit, not afraid of what will be.
I'm not holding onto Jesus; He's holding onto me.

This was Key West in late June. The morning was hot already, and the air-conditioning situation had not improved one iota. But it didn't matter.

I felt cold.

Take it easy, man. Lots of spiritual lyrics in all that old traditional music. Comes with the territory. "Down to the River to Pray" and all that. It doesn't mean a thing.

A finger poked me in the small of my back, and I about jumped out of my skin.

"Hey, and good morning to you!" Sheila was standing there with a carafe of water for the espresso machine. She nodded at the stereo. "More Ron Block—*Faraway Land.* Got it off iTunes last night. You like?"

"Nice," I said weakly.

Sheila smiled and closed her eyes. "I never knew there was music like this until I got to this country. I love it." She opened her eyes. "But you're right; most everybody here wants to listen to rock. I'm so glad you're the exception."

She rubbed my forearm softly as she said this. I should have been thrilled, but mostly I just wondered if it felt clammy.

The morning's work was silver coins. Silver and gold may go hand in hand in most people's minds, but when you put them under water, they are two very different animals. Gold is nearly impervious to salt water. As long as sand and such doesn't get the chance to erode it, if you take a piece of gold out of the ocean, it will look as good as it did the day it went in the drink, even three or four hundred years later.

Silver is another matter entirely. As soon as you put silver in salt water, electrochemistry takes over and it starts to oxidize and bond with other metals. It tarnishes until it looks like nothing but a black stone. Coral will grow on it. So will barnacles. And if things don't stick to it, it sticks to them.

Drop the average person on a wreck site strewn with silver—even lots of it, even millions of dollars' worth of it—and he or she will probably swim right past it, because it doesn't look like anything at all. Silver on a wreck site looks mostly like clumps of old black rock.

The coins I was working on were already about sixty percent of the way through the preservation process, which is to say that the gunk and tarnish had been cleaned off their rims with a weak acid solution. Now, using an ultrasonic cleaner and a soft brass dental pick, it was my job to separate a column of coins—they'd bonded after sitting atop one another in a long-since-dissolved wooden box—into individual eight-*reale* coins, the legendary "pieces of eight."

I tried to concentrate on my task, but the music was still playing in the background, Sheila humming along with it. As I listened, I realized it was not an album of bluegrass music with some old-time spirituals mixed in here and there. It was an entire album of original spiritual music, most of which was bluegrass.

Great.

I got clammy again, but I tolerated it. Then a new song came on—slow, rising and falling guitar and fiddle, with a bit of mandolin, the music coming like slow raindrops. And much as I tried to block it, I was hearing the words:

> *Life is odd; do you know why?*
> *You never live until you die.*
> *Chasing life, it runs away.*
> *Living in tomorrow kills today.*

I swallowed. With difficulty—my throat was closing up on me. And I was having a hard time seeing what I was working on;

my eyes were blurring up. I set the dental pick down, afraid I'd scratch a specimen. The song swelled into a refrain:

> God is love and we're the branches on the tree.
> Depending on the love to live a life we cannot lead.
> If only God is good, then good we cannot be.
> In our weakness He is strong.
> It's another life we're living on.

Game over. My diaphragm began quivering on its own. Not bothering to take off the magnifier I was wearing, I staggered out of the lab and half-ran to the men's room, nearly kicking in a stall door to get my head over the bowl.

Nothing came up. To get control over my breathing, I placed a hand on either of the metal stall walls and closed my eyes. Finally, after a good three minutes had passed, I felt composed enough to shuffle to the sink, take off the magnifier, and throw some cold water on my face.

Suck it up. You've left that; it's behind you. It's gone. Now get ahold of yourself.

When I came back into the lab, Sheila was peering through a desk magnifier—one of those stanchioned magnifying glasses with a fluorescent ring light—and cleaning what appeared to be the frizzen from a flintlock pistol. She looked up and set her tools aside.

"Greg? You all right, mate?"

I sat. "Just a little woozy."

"Woozy?" She crossed the lab and put the back of her hand against my forehead. "You don't feel feverish."

She bent and looked into my eyes. Hers were brown and blue and alive and amazing, and her breath smelled like peppermint. "Are you faint?"

I waved her off. "It was just a . . . a moment. That's all. I'll be fine."

She stepped behind me and began kneading my shoulders, my neck. It felt good.

"You've a boat to catch in two days' time," Sheila told me. "We can't have you ill. Perhaps you should go home."

The neck rub was feeling too good. I wriggled free. "I'll be all right. Really."

Sheila moved to my side and crossed her arms. "You need a bed."

I shook my head. "I'd rather be here. Here with you."

Her face softened. "Well, all right then. If you're certain."

"I am." I managed a smile. "But would you mind if we turned off the music?"

Saturday night, late, was embarkation for the *Peabody*. The memo Phil sent around had been very clear. He wanted everyone aboard by midnight, the gangplank would be pulled at half past, and the ship would be ready and under way an hour later in order to put us on-site by sunrise.

Because the *Peabody* could potentially return from any outing loaded with precious metals and antiquities, using the public marina was out of the question, and Phil had leased a secure berth alongside one of the big concrete wharves at the old Navy sub base. The wharves were empty concrete, wider than a road, and the submarine docks that had once projected from them were long gone. That made loading the ship easy—you could just drive a truck right alongside the docked old minesweeper, and that's why I'd asked to use one of the Rackham Treasure Hunters' pickups.

I'd been on enough research vessels to know not to overpack for the trip. I'd brought along two pairs of board shorts, three T-shirts, a ball cap, and a set of foul weather gear. That plus the polo shirt and khakis I was wearing would, I knew, see me through the next week easily, as long as I regularly rinsed things out and dried them.

My equipment was another matter. Phil had asked me to bring my rebreather along, and while the rebreather itself—a Dive Rite O_2ptima FX—was compact enough to fit in an airline carry-on bag, by the time I'd finished adding a week's worth of scrubber cartridges, two sets of oxygen and diluent tanks, and all my tools and spares, it came to more than a hundred pounds of stuff, all packed into one large cardboard box and a waterproof case that was a meter square.

And that didn't count my regular gear bag—wetsuit, masks, fins, buoyancy compensator, regulator, and lights. Normally I would have hauled along either the scuba gear or the rebreather, but Phil had made it clear he wanted me to bring both.

I also had my electronics gear—notebook computer for writing reports, a digital camera with watertight housing and underwater strobes, portable hard drives for storing digital images, and extra cards for the camera. It was a pile of stuff, any way you looked at it. I said I'd be happy—well, maybe not happy, but willing—to drive my gear to the ship, return the truck to Rackham's offices, and then walk back. But Sheila had insisted on driving me.

Sheila was in rare form, chatty and happy, probably because, seeing as she'd volunteered to be my chauffeur, I'd dipped into my dwindling savings so I could spring for dinner at Kelly's Caribbean. Sitting outside, under the stars and the party lights on Kelly's brick patio, it had felt almost as if we were on a date. I'd just wished it could have been so.

"I am *so* wishing I could be diving with you, instead of being stuck in the lab this week," she told me as she drove.

"Didn't you dive Phase Three on the *Rosarita* last month?"

"Sure." Sheila waited for a pedicab to clear the intersection ahead of us. On either side, the sidewalks were full of revelers trudging to the next party stop on Duval. "But that was last month. I want to be in the water *now*."

"Water's getting warmer; it's hurricane season."

She shot me a sidelong glance. "It's just barely July."

"And besides, all we're going to be doing this week is establishing the site and doing initial surveys."

"Oh, yeah." Sheila waved to Captain Tony, well into his nineties and on his way home from holding court at Captain Tony's Saloon, as he did every Saturday night when he was in town. Tony waved back because, in his nineties or not, Tony *always* waves at pretty girls. "It wouldn't be fabulous at all to be there right at the beginning, surveying a new section of the wreck."

"We'll just be moving sand."

"And uncovering who-knows-what."

A bunch of guys with military-short haircuts straggled across the street in front of us, and Sheila slowed to let them cross.

"Okay." I finally said. "You're right. I've got the dream job here; you're getting the shaft."

She grinned and punched me in the shoulder. I grabbed my sleeve and feigned pain. Okay, I *half*-feigned pain.

She turned in to the old sub-pens area and rolled down the window. Evening warmth and a distant scent of frangipani wafted in. The guard leaned forward for a glance, said "Hey, guys," and waved us through.

Portable halogen lamps on tripods, powered by a muttering Honda generator, bathed the *Peabody* in light from the wharf. The cook and a couple of the deckhands were unloading canned goods from a van while the divemaster supervised dockhands wheeling large green cylinders aboard: oxygen for mixing nitrox. People were tending to lines and doing some last-minute tweaking to the communications array forward of the navigation mast. *Peabody* looked like a vessel being readied for war.

Refusing Sheila's help—which, truth be told, I could have used—I muscled the rebreather case out of the bed of the pickup. Sheila found me a handcart, and I set my gear bag on top of it and ran it down the gangplank onto the ship, where the divemaster showed me to the gear locker. The scrubber cartridges weren't heavy, but the boxes they were in were cumbersome, requiring another trip.

When I got back onto the wharf, another truck had arrived to off-load frozen food, and Sheila had moved our truck down to make room. She was standing next to it, my clothes and shaving kit in a small canvas duffel at her feet.

"Hey, sailor," she teased. "Got everything?"

I nodded at the bag. "Just this and I'm ready to go."

"So I'll see you in ten days?"

"Give or take."

We were out of the wash of the floodlights, but darkness did nothing to diminish how pretty she was.

Shake hands or hug? I didn't want to screw this up.

Sheila solved the dilemma for me. She opened her arms.

I gave her a squeeze, said "See you soon," and let go.

She didn't. All she did was lean back a little.

"Greg," she said softly. "It's okay. You can kiss me, if you want."

If I want?

I wanted. I gave her a peck on the cheek.

She gave me a half smile. "That, sir," she said, "is not a kiss."

It wasn't? I looked at her and I was wrong. She was not pretty; she was drop-dead beautiful. And she wanted me to kiss her? Worlds were in collision.

Let them collide.

I kissed her.

I kissed her again, on the lips this time. Tenuous, we barely touched. And when I opened my eyes, Sheila's were right there looking back at me, and she was smiling, rubbing my arms gently.

Sheila smiled.

"Sheil," I finally said, my voice thick. "I'm . . . confused."

"You are?" She dropped her hands to my waist.

"Well, I thought you were . . ."

"What?" Then her eyes opened wide. "Oh my . . ." She began laughing—laughed so hard, tears began rolling down her cheeks. "You've . . ." she managed between gasps. "You've been talking to Malibu and . . . Mikey, haven't you?"

I nodded and she laughed even harder.

"Well, no wonder you've been the perfect gentleman." Sheila wiped her eyes with the back of her hand. "Oh my."

I just stood there, one of her arms still around me, looking stunned.

Sheila composed herself. "When I first got to Florida, I flew in to Orlando and spent a week with a mate from university; she's working as a concierge at Disney?"

I nodded.

"And she got me a pass for the parks, and you know how they have those kiosks selling the souvenir pins? Well . . . I'm so dense. I found one shaped like Mickey—head and ears—only it was done up as a rainbow with all these multicolored rhinestones, and I've always loved rainbows so I bought it. Then I got back to my mate's apartment and she about drops her jaw; explains to me it's the pin Disney has done up for this Gay Days event that's held at the parks every year."

She glanced skyward at the memory and shook her head. "I couldn't very well take it back, could I? I mean, what does one say? 'Sorry, I didn't realize the implications'? So I threw it in my bag, and then I got down here, and Phil had me go out for that turn on the *Peabody* last month."

I nodded again.

"Well, as soon as they hear I'm coming aboard, Tweedle-Dee and Tweedle-Dive go into full-out prowl mode." Sheila held her hand, fingers outstretched, perpendicular to her forehead: the universal divers' signal for "shark."

"And I figure that's going to be less than pleasant, shooing the two of them away for a whole fortnight," she continued. "But then I remembered that pin. So I stuck it on my sun hat, went to a rummage shop and found a T-shirt from last year's Key West Gay Pride parade, and stopped by the library to check out *Three Lives* by Gertrude Stein . . . which, this being Key West, they had three copies of. So, I came onboard with all that lot, and . . ." She chuckled at the memory. "Bob's your uncle: Malibu and Mikey couldn't have given me wider berth if I'd tested positive for typhus."

"So," I said, feeling like the world's slowest student, "you're not . . . ?"

In answer, she started laughing again.

"Okay," I said when she'd finished. "I get it. You're not."

Behind us, on the water of the harbor, there was a splash: a jack or a barracuda chasing a baitfish to the surface. Off in the scrub near the gate, a mangrove cuckoo called sleepily.

An hour before, I'd been looking forward to shipping out on the *Peabody*. Now I didn't want to be anywhere but where I was. I took her hands, she took mine, and together we just stood there, eyes locked.

Sheila gave both my hands a squeeze, and then she showed me the dive watch on her wrist.

"Almost midnight, boyo. You'd best board."

"I know." I didn't move.

Sheila smiled. "I'll be here, waiting, when you get back."

"Promise?"

In answer, she kissed me on the cheek. "I'll be waiting," she whispered in my ear.

Fish or cut bait; I knew that if I didn't leave right then, I never would. I picked up my duffel and walked—more unsteadily than I would have liked—to the gangplank. With one last wave to Sheila, I stepped down onto the deck.

SEVEN

From the deck of the *Regent*, Ted looked for a second time at the Road Town waterfront. Since the pirate schooner had first arrived there with him aboard, he had traveled with Hatch to St. Thomas and back, selling the remainder of the merchantman's goods. And in all that time he had not set a foot ashore.

The schooner had been Ted's entire world for three weeks now. And for a month or more before that, he had been chained in the dark and putrid hold of the aging Dutch *fluyt* that had carried him away from the fort at Shama, three days' forced march from his home.

It seemed an eternity distant now, and that was just as well. Days and nights had come and gone unnoticed while he was confined in spaces so close that a man could not even get on all fours. The hell of Vicar Bascombe may have been filled with lakes of fire, but to Ted it was dank and putrid darkness, plunging on a strange hostile sea, and waking on the rough, hard wood, your hips and shoulders rubbed raw, to find the man chained beside you cold and dead.

Hatch had forbidden him to go ashore when they'd run the slaver into port and sold the rest of the captives aboard in Jamaica; the captain had said that he didn't want any trouble over holding anything back. And Ted had complied, trusting him intuitively.

Nor had Ted left the vessel in St. Thomas. The captain's lady had stayed aboard while they were there, and Ted had wanted to stay near her, to do duty to his captain and afford Mistress Anne his protection while the *Regent* was moored in the harbor. Not that she needed such; the pirate sloop was always under an armed watch. But it had satisfied Ted to do it.

Even when the deals had been struck and he and the rest of the skeleton crew had taken the schooner in tow with the longboat, bringing it next to the docks for unloading, he had gone from the ship to the boat and back to the ship again, never taking so much as a single step ashore.

Now, standing at the rail, looking out again at the shops lining Road Town Harbour, and down at the waiting longboat, he found himself hesitant to move. The *Regent* was the only safe haven he had known in better than three months. In no small measure it had become his very home.

"I'll wager I know what you're waiting for," boomed Henry Thatch's deep voice behind him.

Ted turned. "Sir?"

"Your share," the pirate said. He drew a leather bag from the belt at his waist. "It was as I'd thought; we did well in Saint Thomas. Open your hand, lad."

Ted did as he was told, and the pirate put three heavy coins in his palm—gold sovereigns.

"Three quid?" Ted's eyes opened wide. "But, sir, you already paid me. And I did nothing, neither in the taking nor the crewing of the prize."

The pirate laughed. "You did nothing because nothing was required. But I'm certain that, had we been required to take that merchantman by force, you'd have done your part. Besides, just the presence of an additional man on deck may be enough to cow an opponent. Our strength is in our numbers, boy. And what you got before was just a division of the coins onboard. That share is yours, fair and square."

"Then thank you, sir." Ted checked his pocket for holes and then slid the three gold coins deep within it.

The pirate smiled and glanced down at the longboat. "Well, over you go, then."

And that was that. Checking to make certain his pistol was secure in his belt, Ted swung his legs over and clambered down the knotted rope to the longboat. Moments later, Mistress Anne was hoisted over in a cloud of yellow chiffon, and the captain clambered down the rope as well, the two of them getting the lady safely settled on a seat in the bow. The captain bent to undo her bound petticoats, and Ted averted his eyes. Then three more crew came down to help man oars and they were off.

Only the lightest of chops was blowing in the harbor, and the blue sky was punctuated only by the smallest, lamb-white, fair-weather clouds. The sun was shining down on his head and neck, and the oar felt good in his hands, the boat leaping in time to the cadence of its rowers. In the stern, the captain held the tiller, and he shot a knowing smile from time to time to the lady in the bow. Behind the captain, the *Regent* shrank smaller and smaller in the dying light of the day, her sails tightly furled, a little wooden toy upon a periwinkle sea.

"Ship oars," the captain said softly, and following the others' example, Ted lifted his oar blade-first into the air. Then he laid it lengthwise within the boat while the captain hove on the tiller and someone behind Ted attended to the lines: bow, stern, and spring. Ted and the other crew swarmed to the dock and stood by to help Mistress Anne from above as the captain assisted from

TOM MORRISEY

the boat, watching carefully lest his wife slip on the wet, mossy wood of the steps.

Soon all were safely on the dock, with Ted on dry land for the first time in . . . he could not count the time. Too many days and nights had slipped by, and he had not seen the half of them.

The largest congregation of buildings lay to his left, and that was the direction the rest of the party took. By and by, Ted fell in behind the captain.

As he walked, Ted fingered the coins in his pocket. He cleared his throat. "Begging your pardon, sir."

The captain glanced back. "What is it, Ted?"

"I was just wondering, sir. Your share of the prize. How do you keep it safe?"

"Safe?"

"Yes, sir. From those who would take it. From thieves, sir."

The pirate's laugh boomed and echoed from the shop buildings, and people far down the street turned to look. Thatch motioned for Ted to come up next to him.

"That is actually an excellent question, Bold Ted. Very soon these islands will be gentrified and piracy will be no more. So, in anticipation of that day, I have been buying land and investing in businesses upon the shore. My share from this taking is going into a sugar mill that my friend Elder Hobbins is building on Jost Van Dyke. Treasures can be stolen and ships can be taken, but I calculate it would take a better man than I to carry off an entire sugar mill."

Ted nodded at the soundness of the logic, and they walked in silence for several steps. Then he dug into his pocket and fetched the three gold coins.

"Sir," he said, "would you be so kind as to do likewise with my share?"

The pirate glanced down. "You propose to be my partner?"

Ted nodded.

"Why, then, I would be honored." The pirate accepted the sovereigns, hefted them a moment and handed one back. "A gentleman needs a suit of clothes, Bold Ted. You might wish to attend to that. And perhaps there is a lady in Road Town that you will wish to entertain?"

Ted grinned despite himself and accepted the bright sovereign.

An hour later, Ted was walking down Front Street with a parcel beneath his arm. The vest, woolen breeches, blouse, and silk stockings had all seemed practical to him, as had the single-buckle shoes, even though he was not accustomed to anything on his feet.

The tricorner hat, on the other hand, had taken a bit of persuasion on the shopkeeper's part. But finally, when the rotund, aproned man had pointed out that, "No gentleman takes his lady out for the air on a Sunday afternoon without something fine upon his head," well, at that Ted had relented. And now he was carrying it all with care lest he crush the hat, because he had one more thing to attend to before he could don any of it.

He walked down the street, past chandlers and shipping companies, passing yet another tailor and an assortment of coopers and carpenters, until he came to a two-story clapboard building with a swinging signboard out front that advertised, in both lettering and image, *The Rose and Crown*.

He entered into a small lobby. To his left was a bar and dining parlor. To his right was a doorway, attended by a man who was missing many of his parts: his left eye and ear, his right hand from the wrist down, and his right leg from the knee down, the last replaced with what looked like a peg fashioned from a piece of stairway banister.

"Something you're after, young man?"

"Yes, sir." Ted straightened up. "Have you any baths here?"

"We have baths for those who have sixpence."

Ted felt the collection of coins in his pocket. "That is rather dear, is it not?"

The man pointed through the open doorway with a stump. "Last I checked, the water in Road Town Harbour cost nothing. Bit tepid, though, if you ask me. Salty too."

Ted dug into his pocket again and came out with three copper coins.

"You're in luck," the man told him, dropping the sixpence into a wooden box. "We've just hauled and boiled for the day, so the water's fresh as a daisy. You'll be first one in. Down the hall and make the turn, lad, last door upon your left. Lift the latch and you're good as scrubbed."

Ted followed the directions and came to a door with a simple lift latch. Inside was a room with a three-legged stool, a low bench with a bar of lye soap and a boar's-hair brush upon it, and a large copper tub, which unlike the simple basin he'd used at Vicar Bascombe's, had a tall back to it. Steam was rising from the water within, and he tested it with his finger and then jumped back quickly.

Ted set his pistol on the stool and put his parcel atop it, then slowly removed his shirt and dropped it on the bench. He tested the water a second time and kept his thumb in a good second before jerking it back. It felt as if it would be appropriate for cooking a chicken or scalding the hair off a hog.

His breeches went atop his shirt, the worn leather belt coiled atop them. Brush in one hand, soap in the other, he swung a leg over the side of the tub and slid his foot slowly into it. A full minute passed before it was resting on the bottom of the tub, and even then he was prepared to jump back out at any moment. But he stepped in with the other foot, holding it high like a wading bird before slowly lowering it in.

Once both feet were in the tub, Ted stood there for a long moment with the steam wafting up around him. He began to settle in, then quickly stood again. Going very slowly, he began to ease himself down a second time.

He had just settled to midthigh when a knock came at the door.

"Sir?" A woman's voice called as the latch swung up and the door began to open. "Coming in, sir; is that quite all right?"

In answer, Ted sat all the way down and gritted his teeth to stifle the scream.

The woman stepped into the room and peeked around the open door.

It was Sally.

"Well, good afternoon." She smiled as she said it. "Looks as if you found everything. Is the water to your liking, sir?"

Ted, incapable of speech, simply nodded.

"That's good." Sally turned and began setting stacks of folded laundry on a set of wooden shelves. "Very good. Take your time, and when you're all through, there are sheets aplenty here—for drying or to wrap yourself while you cool, whatever you may prefer."

"Much obliged," Ted said weakly.

Sally turned. "You are sounding feeble, sir. Are you quite all right?"

Ted nodded.

"Some people still advise against bathing," Sally observed. "They say it opens the pores excessively and allows bad humors to enter. But I myself have never believed such a thing. Do you?"

Ted shook his head.

"Quite sensible." Sally looked at the neatly folded parcel. "I see you have fresh things to put on. Would you like me to launder your other clothes? I could have them dried and ready by this time tomorrow."

Ted nodded.

"Very good, sir." Sally gathered up the salt-stained blouse and pantaloons. "Enjoy your bath, then, sir. A man stays at sea long enough, he needs to rinse the spindrift and the sea wind from his skin. You are a seafaring man, are you not, sir?"

"The captain told me," Ted said by way of reply, "that you worked in your father's public house."

"But I do, sir. It is next door, part of this inn." Sally cocked her head. "And what captain is it who speaks of my affairs?"

"Captain Thatch. Captain Henry Thatch."

Sally brightened. "Anne Thatch's husband?"

"Yes, miss." Ted nodded. "Mistress Anne. That is she. The very one."

The copper bathing tub issued a loud metallic *tick* as it cooled a degree or two.

"Of course!" Sally touched a finger to her lips, a gesture at one time both coy and demure. "You were there, on the deck of the *Regent*, this Tuesday, after she reached, sir, were you not?"

"I was."

Sally smiled, displaying fine white teeth. "Well, I beg your pardon, sir. I did not know you immediately with your clothes off."

She laughed as Ted sank lower in the tub. "Not to worry, sir. You are quite modest. I see more bare chests on the stevedores unloading at the wharfs every weekday. Well, I will give you your privacy." She pronounced it *priv-us-see*. "Take as long as you like."

She reached for the door latch.

"Miss?" Ted's voice had come back to a surprising strength.

Sally turned.

"I was wondering, miss," Ted asked, "if you would take your supper with me this evening?"

"Supper?" Sally shook her head. "I am working at supper this evening—and every evening."

"I see." Ted looked down at the soapy bathwater.

"But if you take your supper here at the inn," Sally added, "you shall surely see me. I will be serving."

"Well, then." Ted smiled. "I shall look forward to that."

Sally stepped halfway through the door and turned. "As shall I."

Still smiling, Ted sank to his neck in the hot water and scrubbed absently at his arms with the soapy, thick boar's-hair brush.

"Well, what have we here? A banker or a publican or a lord of the manor? Some such man of great means, I daresay."

Ted grinned and turned a full circle at Henry Thatch's table, doffing his crisp new tricorner hat to Mistress Anne.

"Join us, Bold Ted." Thatch pushed a stool back from the table with his booted foot.

The pirate was dressed considerably less flamboyantly than he had been when they'd taken the merchantman. Yet, while most of the revelers in The Rose and Crown made do with plain muslin shirts and leather vests, the pirate was still in a coat. His shirt had a freshly starched ruffle at his throat and a plume in his hat—modest, but a plume nonetheless.

Mistress Anne's gown was a deep and regal blue, trimmed with lace so white it seemed to glow in the candlelight of the wood-paneled room. Night was falling on the harbor front outside the windows, yet the lady's face gave off its own soft glow, as if morning were just the briefest of moments away.

"Sit, Ted," the pirate said a second time, and the young man came back into the moment and sat.

A good number of the *Regent*'s crew were scattered about the large, dark room, some seated at rough tables and some leaning against the wooden columns of the room. Laughter and rum were both running unabated, while off in a corner a man slightly too drunk to be doing so was trying to coax a hornpipe from a dusty accordion. Yet despite the rough-and-ready look of the place, the only smells were those of tobacco and rum and the distant scent of roasting meat.

"We are about to sup, and as your commanding officer I order you to do justice to all that finery and join us," Thatch said with a smile.

"Commanding officer? We are neither aboard ship nor in the heat of battle," Ted pointed out.

"Then, in that case, Mistress Anne and I humbly beg you to be our guest."

Ted doffed his hat again. "And if Mistress Anne asks it, I most gratefully accept."

Anne covered her mouth with her hand and laughed.

Dinner was mutton with potatoes and carrots and Bermuda onions, which Ted assumed was excellent. Although he ate it and washed it down with ale—the weakest libation available other than tea, which cost dearly—he did not remember a bit of it, because their server was none other than Sally, who teased Mistress Anne for being accompanied by "Not one, but *two* fine and handsome gentlemen."

The plate and mug seemed to empty themselves before him. In no time Thatch was asking him if he'd care for a brandy and a pipe after dinner, and Ted was answering, "Thank you, sir, but my head is a bit light just now from the ale. Would you and the lady excuse me for a moment?"

Thatch nodded as Ted stood and moved to the side of the room where Sally had been returning regularly to fill mugs from a pair of large tapped barrels. Sure enough, she came back a moment later.

"Hello." She smiled slyly as she filled the first of two clay mugs.

"Good evening, miss. I was wondering if I might call on you."

She began to fill the second mug. "For what, sir? More ale?"

"No. Not that. I meant . . ." Ted glanced up and to the side, as if the words he was searching for were out there somewhere.

Sally laughed.

"I know what you mean, sir." She let the foam settle just a bit and topped the mug off. "And that is a question you would have to direct to my father."

Ted's eyes opened a bit wider. "But of course. I would be most pleased. Can you tell me where . . . ?"

"Certainly." Sally lifted the mugs and smiled again. "He is standing directly behind you, sir."

Sally left with her mugs. Ted turned and looked up at the largest man he had ever seen in his life, an ebony tree of a man, standing with his arms crossed, his biceps bulging under rolled sleeves. The man leaned his shaved head forward and asked, "What is your business here, boy?"

"Sir?"

"Call me 'landlord,' if you are a patron here, or 'Mr. Emmons' if you are not." He squinted at Ted. "Looks of you, I'd say you'd best call me 'Mr. Emmons.' Now, one more time—what business have you here?"

"My, uh . . ." Ted gulped. "I am here having dinner with my captain, sir . . . landlord . . . Mr. Emmons."

"You are having dinner at my taps?"

Ted looked at the big barrels as if they had suddenly materialized there next to him.

"No, sir, I . . ." Ted took a breath. "I was asking your daughter, Mr. Emmons, if I may have the privilege of calling upon her."

The landlord's eyebrows inched lower. "That privilege is not hers to grant, boy."

"A distinction of which I am recently informed. Mr. Emmons . . ." Ted removed his hat. "I beg your pardon, sir. I am unschooled in such matters, having never asked to call upon a lady before."

"I see." The landlord straightened up. "You say that you are here with your captain. Do you mean your captain, or your master?"

"My captain, Mr. Emmons." Ted moved his hat so the landlord could clearly see his shod feet. "I am not chattel."

"Your shoes appear quite new," the landlord observed. "And who is your captain?"

"Captain Thatch, sir. Captain Henry Thatch."

"So, then." The landlord wiped his hands on his apron and recrossed his arms. "You are a pirate."

"No, sir. I am not." Ted looked back at the broad, towering landlord. "Captain Henry is a privateer."

Emmons glowered back, obviously unimpressed by the distinction. He tapped his booted foot.

"Well," he finally said, "better a pirate than a soldier. The garrison here has proven the truth of that."

The landlord glanced around the room until he spotted Thatch and Mistress Anne. Then he glanced down at Ted. "Come with me, boy."

The two of them crossed the floor, Ted feeling like a calf following a bull. They stopped at Thatch's table.

"Oscar!" Thatch got to his feet and shook the big man's ham of a hand. "You have given me this evening the finest meal I have had this season. Quite wonderful. Lady Anne agrees."

"It does my heart good to hear that," the landlord said, his face visibly softening. Then an edge came back into his eyes. "Is this your boy, captain?"

"Bold Ted?" Thatch glanced at him. "He is no one's boy, Oscar. In fact, he travels armed. Show him, Ted."

Ted moved his vest back to reveal the flintlock pistol in his belt.

"He is either free, then, or risking the gallows," Oscar muttered. He looked Thatch in the eye. "Has he a freedman's papers?"

A roar erupted from the back of the public house as one sailor bested another at arm wrestling. Glancing back in that direction, Thatch smiled. "They are being drawn up as we speak."

"Well, then." Oscar looked down at Ted. "You may bring those papers with you when you come on Sunday."

"Here, sir?" Ted waved at arm at the room.

"No, not here." Oscar grimaced. "No proper public house opens its taps on the Lord's Day. You may bring those papers with you when you come to church."

"Church, sir?" Ted's eyes widened.

"Yes. Church. You attend church, do you not?"

More cheers erupted as the arm wrestlers made it two out of three.

"I was raised by a vicar, sir," Ted said. He did not add that Vicar Bascombe, while he had taught Ted to read from the Bible, and prayed—oftentimes overlong—before meals, had not once, to Ted's knowledge, entered a house of worship since arriving in Africa.

"Well, then." Oscar shook the captain's hand, but did not shake Ted's. "Sunday it is. If you wish to see my daughter, you shall see her in the Lord's house. And don't forget those papers."

"Papers?" Ted pulled out his stool and sat. "Is such a thing even possible, Captain?"

"I do not lie, Ted." The pirate told him. "Not to my friends, at very least. And there are people in these islands who will trouble a black man greatly unless he can prove himself free. So I stopped in to see a magistrate this afternoon. A cask of the merchantman's brandy convinced him that articles of emancipation are entirely in order for you."

"But the slaver who was transporting me," Ted said, "did he not have papers making me *his* property?"

"He did." Thatch nodded. "And as I recall, our cook used those to light his stove ashore the very next day. Do not be troubled, Bold Ted. The magistrate is a friend of mine, and even if that Dutchman manages to row the dinghy we set him in all the way here, nothing he says will stand against an Englishman's word in His Majesty's court. Steer clear of Sint Maarten and the other Dutch colonies, and rest assured you shall be safe as houses.

"And besides," the captain said, holding up the two gold crowns that Ted had handed him earlier, "you are my business partner."

The prospect of proof of Ted's emancipation, combined with the hope of calling upon the lovely Sally, wore away at Ted's resolve. Eventually he consented to join the captain in a cup of rum. And then another. And then one more.

By the time they rose to depart, the younger man had a definite weave to his step.

"Why don't you come home with us this night?" Thatch asked. "We've an extra bed."

"No, no. None of that." Ted wagged his finger. "I've a fine snug hammock, wait . . . waiting for me on the *Regent*. A shen . . . a shent . . . a *gentleman* and his lady need their, uh, their privacy." He said it the way Sally had said it: *priv-us-see*.

"Quite thoughtful," Thatch said. Mistress Anne stifled a giggle, and Thatch glanced at her, one eyebrow raised. "Well, let us walk you to the wharf, see you safely onto the boat, then."

They made their way onto the hard-packed dirt street. The Southern Cross was hovering above the horizon, the Milky Way a luminous fog across the sky, and the warm night air was fragrant with tropical flowers. They walked onto the dock—Thatch steering Ted with his hand away from the edge—where a small crowd of men was waiting for the longboats that would return them to their ships.

Ted peered at the men, particularly at a taller man who was standing in their midst. He slipped away from Thatch's grasp.

"Excuse me?" Ted pronounced the words carefully, trying to keep the slur from his speech. "I beg your pardon, sir—is it Captain Dickson?"

"Who is that?" At the mention of his name, the tall man turned.

"It is me, sir," Ted said. He tried to sound as cheerful as he could. "Ted, sir. From the chandlery. Back in Axim Town, on the Gold Coast. I helped your men load your wagon when you came to us to supply your refit, earlier this season."

The man peered down at him. "Of course. Bascombe's boy, is it not?"

"I was a member of Mr. Bascombe's household. Yes, sir."

"What'd he do? Sell you off?"

Ted blinked. "Mr. Bascombe? Oh no, sir. He has no dealings with slavers."

"No dealings with slavers?" Dickson uttered a sharp bark of a laugh. "Who do you think he came to Africa to sell his wares to?"

Ted looked around. All of the tall man's companions were grinning at him.

"Well, he trades with folk such as you, sir."

Another bark of laughter. "And what did you imagine I carried?"

The rest of the men were chuckling at him now.

"I saw you unload in Axim, sir. You carried cotton. You carried molasses."

"Eastbound I most certainly did." The tall captain nodded. "But westbound . . . tell me something, boy. Did you not ever wonder what we did with all the lumber Bascombe sold us?"

Ted was momentarily without words. One of his most vivid memories of being loaded onto the slaver in Shama was that the wood of the narrow, close pallets in the slaver's hold was all new, freshly milled and still smelling of its sap. And it made sense. A slaver would sell its pallets with the rest of the cargo—rip everything out to make room in the hold so it could carry a paying cargo both ways.

"I myself have offered fifty quid to Bascombe for this boy here," the slaver captain told his cronies. "Nine will get you ten, some Portuguese or Dutchman gave that penny-pinching old Scotsman a farthing more. I'll wager he was saving this one up for a rainy day."

He looked up at Thatch, who had said nothing to this point. "Will you sell him to me, Henry? Sell him and I'll see what Emmons wants for that young wench of his in the pub. Put them together, I'll wager we could raise enough black stock to work a goodly farm."

Without even thinking about it, Ted pushed back his vest and drew the finely worked Menandez pistol from his belt.

"Here, what are you about with that, boy?" Dickson said.

In answer, Ted cocked the pistol.

Put his finger on the trigger.

Aimed at Dickson's heart.

But before he could loose a shot, two strong hands had clamped him about the waist, lifted him clear of his footing, and tossed him like a bundle of cordwood.

Next thing he knew, he was in the humid night air.

Then he was under water, all sights and all sounds nipped off suddenly by the dark and mottled surface of Road Town Harbour.

EIGHT

Blue seawater closed over my head and a thousand tiny crystalline bubbles rose past me to the surface. Behind me, on the rebreather, there was a muted pop and hiss as the oxygen and diluent valves opened and then closed. In the lower right-hand corner of my mask, a light-emitting diode blinked red three times, paused, and repeated the sequence two times more. That meant all three oxygen sensors were reading the same: an oxygen partial pressure of point-seven and no glitches. I pivoted head down and began to kick rhythmically for the sea floor some forty-five feet below. The valves popped and hissed again as I descended.

It was good to be in the water again, and the conditions—sixty feet of visibility and little perceptible current—couldn't have been more different than the low-viz, surge-swept diving I'd done the previous winter in the chilly waters of Beaufort Inlet. Already I could tell that the thin three-millimeter wetsuit would be more than adequate for even a three-hour rebreather dive, and knowing that relaxed me. Adding a touch of air to my buoyancy compensator, I came to a hover a yard above the sandy bottom and let the warm sea hold me there, motionless.

Looting of ongoing search sites is always a hazard in the treasure-hunting business. Every small plane overflying a working salvage vessel could hold some ambitious cowboy with a GPS unit. And even though *Rosarita* had been formally arrested—that's what they call it—under Phil Rackham's name in an admiralty court, chasing stolen artifacts is a time-consuming and rarely fruitful process. So the company had kept a small cabin cruiser on-site as a watch boat while *Peabody* was in for refit, and as all three of the smaller boat's crew were divers, they had occupied themselves by laying out the search grids for the next phase of exploration. Hundreds of rebar stakes had been hammered into the bottom, with more than a mile of nylon line strung between them, dividing the search area up into discrete ten-meter squares.

Except for a five-minute foray by Malibu and Panhead Mikey to set the *Peabody*'s anchor, I was the first diver in the water, and my mission on this first dive of the trip was remarkably simple. I was double-checking the previous divers' work, verifying the compass heading of each run, and then measuring each line with a stadia reel, making certain the squares were indeed squares and that the grids were positioned precisely in the locations specified on the site map. Once I'd verified the first grid, I was supposed to send a marker buoy to the surface, and the actual work would begin. Being on a rebreather, I had a bailout bottle and a scuba regulator with me to handle any problems under water, so I didn't need a dive buddy and we could concentrate the working divers on search and recovery.

I got to the first stake, distinguished by a knot of fluorescent orange tape. A quick wrap of a Velcro fastener secured the stadia reel's tag end to the stake, and I swam it down the boundary line, unreeling as I went.

Stopping halfway—well away from the magnetic influence of the steel rebar stakes—I made sure the bubble level on my compassboard was centered, shot a heading, then turned around and shot the reciprocal heading. Both matched the specs cribbed onto my slate, and I crossed them off with a pencil. And when I got to the next stake, the taut tape read ten meters right down to the millimeter. This was going to be easy.

I made the quarter turn of measuring tape around the stake and set out down the second leg of the square. But when I got halfway along and stopped to shoot a compass heading, I noticed something glittering in the surface-filtered sunlight, not two meters into the square. Something green.

Curious, I set down the stadia reel and my compassboard and swam over to it. The green part looked glassy. An exposed bit of beer bottle tossed overboard by some passing fishing charter? I took a closer look, and gulped.

It wasn't a piece of beer bottle. It was a gem—large, green, exquisitely pearl-cut, flawless.

For better than a minute I just hovered there, staring at it, not touching a thing. Was it really what it appeared to be? And if it was, how had the mapping crew overlooked it?

Then the mouthpiece of my rebreather began vibrating and the LED in front of my dive mask flashed yellow. Carbon dioxide warning—I was forgetting to breathe.

Inhaling and exhaling deeply and regularly, I flushed the sensors with fresh gas, making the warning go away. Then I became a marine archaeologist again and went into action.

First step, complete the heading readings on the line I'd been double-checking: done. Second step, use the compassboard to determine a point exactly perpendicular to the artifact: five meters, three centimeters from Stake 2. Third step, measure from that point to the artifact so it could be mapped on the grid: two meters exactly—what were the chances of that?

Fourth step . . . *What is the fourth step?* Of course—document provenience. Unclipping the small camera housing from my harness, wishing I'd brought the larger flash, I laid my dive watch next to the bright green jewel for scale and took two digital photos, checking the screen on the camera's back to make sure they came out.

Now I could touch it. Gingerly, I pinched the faceted stone between thumb and forefinger and lifted.

Resistance.

It was attached to something.

Clipping the camera back onto my harness, I began to fan the sand away from the jewel. A small tan cloud erupted. Ten seconds later I saw yellow metal.

Gold?

I fanned more sand away, and for the second time in five minutes my buzzing mouthpiece reminded me to breathe again.

It was a gold cross, larger than my open hand. Green pendent gems—emeralds?—easily five carats apiece, hung from the ends of the crosspiece and the base, and in the center was what appeared to be a blood-red ruby easily ten carats in size. I remembered to unclip the camera and take another picture. Then I picked the cross up. It was heavy—a good three pounds.

Three pounds of South American gold, three emeralds and a ruby . . . What would something like that be worth, just in the value of the materials? Tens . . . no, *hundreds* of thousands. And the artifact value, because this had to be sixteenth-century Spanish: this had to be priceless.

Somehow, putting something that fine into the net goody bag at my waist just seemed wrong. I kept it in my hand, clipped my compassboard and stadia reel off to the line I'd been measuring, and started up for the *Peabody*.

Hans, the Dutch divemaster, had made it clear before I'd gone in that, regardless of what anyone's dive computer said, each dive from his boat had to conclude with a five-minute safety stop at ten feet, rebreather or no rebreather. So I got to the weighted trapeze-like bar that was hung at ten feet, grabbed hold, and watched the seconds count down on my dive computer, occasionally stealing a fresh glance at the cross.

It was exquisite, finely worked, and my heart started thumping again. What I had in my hand could potentially not only pay for the time the *Peabody* would spend on this dive site but could pay for every trip Phil Rackham would make for the rest of the year.

Jubilant, I went up, barely remembering to close the mouthpiece on the rebreather before dropping it out of my mouth.

"Something wrong?" Hans asked. He was bent over the swim ladder.

Saying nothing, I held up the bright gold cross.

Hans's eyes opened wide. "Stay there!"

He disappeared for a moment, then came back with a Nikon SLR and began snapping shots.

"Hold it higher," he said as he shot. "Turn it so the light hits it. There!"

Then he turned and shouted, "Jack! Come back here! Come see what Greg has found!"

"Jack" was Jack Egan, captain of the *Peabody* and second only to Phil in the organization's hierarchy. He and Hans put a hand under each of my arms and helped me up the last two steps of the ladder as a crowd began to gather on the swim deck. Everyone was beaming—even Panhead Mikey and Malibu, which pleasantly surprised me. I would have thought they'd be jealous.

"Good work, Greg!" Jack told me. "Can I see it?"

I handed it to him, and he picked up a hose and began misting the excess sand and mud from it. The entire crew was gathered around us, and I was still standing there soaking wet in my fins and wetsuit, the hose of the rebreather draped around my neck. I felt like Amundsen at the Pole, like Armstrong setting foot on the moon.

Jack turned the cross over and looked at the back.

"There's an inscription," he said. He moved the cross close to his eyes and then held it at arm's length. He patted his shirt pocket with his free hand. "Left my reading glasses in the wheelhouse. Can you make it out, Greg?"

I squinted at the tiny letters. Then I made them out.

"Made," I muttered, "in China."

Jack glanced at the divemaster. "What do we get for those in the gift shop back on Whitehead, Hans? Fifty bucks? Sixty?"

He clapped me on the shoulder. "That's a valuable find, buddy."

The entire crew erupted in laughter and walked off, leaving me red-faced on the swim deck.

NINE

Yes. I felt pretty stupid.

Salting a dig is the oldest practical joke in the archaeologist's book. Once, when I was doing a conventional dig next to the Cooper River—a shipwreck landlocked and then buried when the river changed its course two centuries earlier—we'd had a cocky and loudmouthed graduate assistant who had made it his responsibility to step in and take the trowel whenever an undergrad found so much as a pottery shard. So one of my classmates had salted his feature with a replica of a first-century Greek drachma.

It was a museum-quality replica, so it looked exactly like the real thing, but it still had a dot of epoxy on its obverse, where it was attached to the card it had been hanging on in the museum shop. But my friend had pressed the coin into the clay with that bit down, and the graduate assistant had swallowed it, hook, line, rod and reel.

He was certain he had evidence of not only pre-Columbian, but pre-Viking contact. And when—after he had spent the better part of an hour easing the "coin" out of the substrate—someone had pointed out the bit of glue on its back, he changed his tune and decided that perhaps it had belonged to a sailor of a later time who carried a family heirloom on a necklace and attached it in that fashion. It wasn't until we showed him another example of the coin, still attached to the card, when he realized he'd been had. Red-faced, he stormed off the site.

That had been a fairly extreme example. Still, one of the first things you learn when you study field methods is that people tend to think they have found the things that they are looking for. So old Sears Craftsman Arkansas sharpening stones are mistaken for period lithic artifacts, and modern black-powder bullets are misidentified as Civil War-era Minié balls.

But I had handled hundreds of Spanish New World artifacts, and while I may not have had the experience of a professional curator, I nonetheless knew enough to tell the difference between a sixteenth-century precious metal artifact and a twenty-first-century pot-metal knockoff. Even under water.

But I hadn't. And the reason I hadn't was because I'd let my enthusiasm get ahead of my education.

So I opened the rebreather mouthpiece, bit down on it, checked my partial pressure presets, resettled my mask on my face, and jumped back into the Gulf of Mexico.

And this time I didn't care if I stumbled across the Ark of the Covenant or a jeweled scepter sticking out of the sand. I was going to measure baselines and check headings. If I found anything, anything at all, I was just going to tag it, note it, and move on.

In five minutes I had finished the first square and sent up the surface marker. Right after that I had company: Mikey and Malibu and two other divers on hookah rigs—surface-supplied air.

For the next two hours I worked methodically, checking, measuring, verifying, getting accustomed to the sound of four regulators growling in the near distance. Only one stake was off, and that one by just two centimeters. I reset it and remeasured all four grid squares it was associated with.

I was just finishing that up when Malibu—I could tell it was Malibu because he was wearing just the Farmer John bottoms to his wetsuit, and I recognized his tats—swam up and handed me a slate.

Found wood, the penciled scrawl on it read.

Another gag—that was my first thought. But then I thought about all the money Phil Burnham was no doubt spending to keep a salvage ship on this site. *Esprit de corps* was one thing, but there was no way anyone could justify nonstop gags on an operation such as this.

Still . . . *wood*? I thought of RMS *Rhone* in the British Virgin Islands. It had been decked with teak, the most impervious to seawater of all the woods, and yet, after a century and a half under water, only a bare yard or two of her decking remained. From teredo worms to barnacles to sheer solvent strength, the ocean had its ways of consuming wood, one way or another. The only times it did not was when the water was extremely cold—so cold that the normal biological and chemical processes slowed way, way down, or when the wood was encapsulated or buried.

As Malibu and I finned our way back, a tan cloud began to materialize before us, and the likelihood of truly finding a wooden object became substantially higher. Like sites on land, marine archeological sites, and particularly those in stretches of ocean with clay or sand bottoms, become covered with what's known as *overburden*: bottom material that engulfs and covers a site's features. On dry land that's where shovels come in. But here the divers had been using an air lift.

Air lifts work on a very basic hydrostatic principle: release a bubble at depth and it will expand as it rises. Release that bubble near the mouth of a tube or hose, and as long as the tail end of that hose is substantially higher than the mouth, the bubble will eventually enlarge to the point that it makes a moving seal in the tube as it rises.

The result is a sort of underwater vacuum cleaner. You can use it to suck material off the bottom and release it in the shallow water above you. The sandstorm that follows closes viz down to two or three feet, but two or three feet of viz is all that's really necessary for most site exploration. And in the right hands, an air lift can be guided in such a way that it removes lighter material, such as sand, but leaves the heavier—tools, coins, large gold crosses—right where they are.

I'd read in my notes that the hurricanes of the previous season had already shifted much of the overburden, leaving the *Rosarita* a fairly shallow, covered site. Sure enough, the grid square had only been lowered by a foot and a half at most, to begin exposing the various amorphous lumps and random linear features of a scattered shipwreck. And near the center of the grid square were what appeared to be long pieces of gingerbread broken at the ends and lying parallel to one another; hull or decking, it was hard to say which.

I examined it and ascertained that all edges had been exposed by the air lift. Taking out the camera, I photographed it, then I measured it and—borrowing a slate from Panhead Mikey, because mine was full of notes—drew a sketch of it lying *in situ*, because I knew that details you could see to sketch oftentimes did not show up in photographs.

I fanned the edges of the remnant with my hand; it appeared to be mostly more sand underneath.

Mikey crooked a finger: *question*. He pointed to the wood and pantomimed levitating it with his hands. I shook my head, held both hands out, level with each other, then folded them together:

too delicate. Motioning for his slate again, I wrote: *Can u cover it back up w/ sand?* He nodded, and I scrubbed that side of the slate clean with sand and wrote, *Do that then, & leave this square for now—work on next one*. He gave me the OK signal, and I started up for the *Peabody*.

TEN

Jack Egan studied a photocopy of my on-slate sketch and paged through the digital images on the laptop screen. He turned to me. "Decking?"

"Possibly. That or an upper hull segment from a ship with a pretty fair amount of tumblehome."

With most people I would have explained that last term. *Tumblehome* is an inward curve of the upper part of a vessel's hull; the thing that gives sixteenth-century naval vessels such a pronounced rubber-ducky appearance. Shipmakers have used it over the centuries, particularly on warships, as it allows the heavy cannon on upper decks—which tend to have a more pronounced influence on how the vessel rolls—to be placed nearer to a ship's centerline.

But I figured Jack had been in the business long enough that he was more than familiar with most of the vocabulary of marine architecture. It looked as if I was right. He didn't ask me to explain; he simply nodded.

He tapped my sketch. "Any ideas on how to get it up in one piece?"

I drew four lines on the copy. "Strapping like this would bring it up level. Thing is, strapping tends to load the edges, make it want to bend or break, and we don't know how solid this is. So I'd recommend passing the strapping through something stout enough to give it some support. Thick-walled PVC tubing, like what you'd use for a wastewater pipe, would work. Put tubing on top as well, strap it in place, and that would make a pretty good cradle for transporting it."

"How much tubing?"

"Four six-foot lengths of four-inch ID, and four eight-foot lengths should do it. Zip-strips where they intersect for stability."

Jack thumbed something into his BlackBerry. He looked up at me. "What about after we have it up?"

"That's the tricky part." I began to tick points on my fingers. "One, the wood fibers on the outside can dry away to dust while the inside is still saturated. Two, there's sulfur in old wood and oxygen in the air, plus oxygen released by any iron bolts or nails holding it together. These will begin to create sulfuric acid practically as soon as it hits the air. To reduce both of those things, you want to get it into a controlled environment—fifty to fifty-five percent relative humidity—just as soon as you can. Keep misting the outside with mineral-free fresh water so the piece desaturates and loses contaminants at a steady rate, inside and out. And then once you've leached the salt out of it, you need to replace the water in the wood cells with PEG—polyethylene glycol. It's a long, drawn-out process—we're talking years, not months. But you have to start it just as soon as you can. Pretty much once it's up, it should be in a conservator's hands."

Jack studied the drawing again and then set it aside atop a flatbed scanner. "Doesn't sound like anything we can start onboard."

I shook my head. "If it was smaller, maybe we could jerry-rig something. Tent it with plastic sheeting belowdecks. Piece this size, we can't even *get* it belowdecks. It has to go back to a lab right away."

"Okay." Jack thumbed new data into his BlackBerry. "It's reburied. Let's leave it that way for now. Good job, Greg."

When I'm making rebreather dives, I only make one a day. Technically, this first day on the *Peabody*, I'd violated that policy, but I wasn't counting the dive on which I'd "found" the cross—I'd barely been under water five minutes before I'd started up on that one.

At any rate, I'd finished my diving for the day with my cursory survey of the wood remnant, so after a quick lunch of burgers and fries, I did the after-dive service on the O$_2$ptima and then settled down to attend to the day's paperwork.

Actually it was paperwork in name only; all the stuff I had to record would fit in the Microsoft Excel templates I was carrying in my computer. I had to verify every grid I'd double-checked, document the one stake I'd moved, and then do the after-dive report on the planking.

It kept me at the little steel desk in the wheelhouse most of the afternoon. Our divers were all out of the water, and I'd just gone belowdecks to stow the computer, when I heard the motor of a smaller vessel drawing near. It cut its engines as it pulled alongside. Curious, I went back topside.

It was the cabin cruiser that had been site-sitting when we'd shown up that morning, and the mate and a deckhand were already catching the bow and stern lines, so I stepped amidships to take care of the spring. There was a young woman bent over picking it up, and when she turned my way to toss it, I nearly missed the catch.

It was Sheila.

ELEVEN

It wasn't just Sheila. It was Sheila and Phil Rackham and a cheerful blond woman who introduced herself as Betty—Phil's wife. And apparently the cook had been clued in that the boss was on his way out to the site, because a large propane grill had been set up next to the winch on the broad, open work deck, and a small herd of New York strip steaks was sizzling and smoking fragrantly on it.

I tied off the spring line robotically—take a bight, flip it, loop the davit and wrap—still pleasantly stunned that Sheila was out on the site. She held out a hand, and I helped her up onto the *Peabody*.

"Hey, you." I gave her a hug.

"Hey, yourself." Sheila glanced around, made sure no one was looking our way, and gave me a kiss that landed half on my lips and half on my cheek.

Holding her out at arm's length, I was aware that I was grinning like an idiot. Not that I really cared who saw it. "To what do we owe the honor?"

"You." Sheila pointed to a bundle of PVC pipe on the smaller boat's deck. "Phil wants us to get that planking ready to be lifted tomorrow morning. We can bring it up at the end of the day and run it back to the lab when the sun's not beating down on it."

"No joke?" I looked a second time at the bundle of pipe, as if I thought it might go away. "He's that interested in getting it to the lab?"

Sheila smirked. "He's that interested in getting it off his work site. Phil's like that kid in the story, furiously shoveling out the stables, sure he's going to find a pony under there somewhere. In his mind, there's every chance of a pile of gold bars and a sackful of scepters under that big hunk of wood."

I must have looked a little deflated, because Sheila quickly added, "Oh, he wants to preserve the planking too. That's why he brought me along—to stabilize it for the run back to Key West. Minding the material with historical value is brilliant PR for the operation. It gives us something substantial to show the people who think we're just ocean looters, and it keeps the state archaeologist off Phil's back. Plus we get something new to go into the museum."

I nodded. Rackham's Key West Treasures—the tourist museum that made up most of the bottom floor of his old warehouse—was an important part of his operation. Between admissions and souvenir sales, it probably contributed as much to the bottom line as the net from the salvage operations.

Sheila smiled brightly. "Good first day, then?"

I nodded.

"They salt the site for you?"

A little of the wind went out of me. "How'd you know?"

"They salt the site for everybody, the first dive. For Malibu and Mikey, I heard it was seventy pounds of lead, spray-painted to look like a huge gold bar. By the time they got it to the surface, half the paint had rubbed off and they *still* thought they were rich."

I gave her a glance. "How about you?"

"Oh, for me they had a tiara, complete with rhinestones." She rolled her eyes. "I left it where it was, and on the next dive I stuck a little price tag on it: twenty-five ninety-nine."

My already stratospheric estimate of Sheila McIntyre ratcheted up a notch or two.

She leaned forward, gave me a peck on the cheek, and whispered, "The divers are already in queue for the steaks, mate. We'd best get in line or we'll starve."

Blatant suck-up to the boss or not, the steaks were amazing; big, thick, done to just slightly on the rare side of medium, and accompanied by loaded baked potatoes and plenty of grilled fresh vegetables: green peppers and sweet onions and wax beans and broccoli. Malibu and Panhead Mikey registered the opinion that it was the sort of meal that required a case or two of beer to be complete. They may as well have been asking for snow in the tropics; what with the heavy machinery onboard and the near-constant diving operations, Jack Egan's ship ran strictly dry.

As for me, sweet tea and Sheila McIntyre were more than enough to make the meal complete. We carried our plates and flatware to the bow and sat side by side on the ship's big bollard so we could enjoy the steaks and the sunset and each other's company in private.

How shall I describe it? There I was with this amazing woman, who actually seemed to like me, and we were on a treasure-hunter's ship, on the site of an historic shipwreck. We were exploring it, and we were part of it, this project. We were central to it. And here, at the end of this astounding day, this amazing woman and I were sharing a sunset. It was very nearly perfect.

"You know," I began tentatively, "this could be—"

"Shhh . . ." Softly, gently, Sheila put her hand on mine. She did not so much shush me as she invited me to join her in silence.

"Look." Sheila nodded, almost a bow of sorts, at the setting sun, settled now in a melting orange omega on the steel-colored sea. "There."

We watched the sun sink down, shimmering and liquid, until it seemed to be nothing more than a red-orange waxen oblong floating at some infinitesimal height above the distant horizon. Sheila squeezed my hand.

"Look," she whispered. "Here it comes."

Silence. The molten oval of orange light contracted until it was a single, glowing, miniscule dot.

"Keep watching." Sheila's fingers tightened on mine.

The dot disappeared. For a fraction of a very brief moment nothing happened; the world holding its breath. Then, as if a candle had been kindled just beyond the edge of the sea, the tiniest jet of emerald flame appeared and then expired.

The green flash. Arguably one of the rarest meteorological phenomena in the world. I'd heard of it from just about every sailor and diver I knew. But I'd never seen it. Not until then.

And with that, the moment was no longer very nearly perfect. It *was* perfect.

What happened next, I lay at the feet of Phil Rackham's environmental policy. You see, on many workboats, dinner gets served on paper plates; at the end of the meal, you just trash-can whatever you've been eating with. But the *Peabody* had been outfitted with a high-capacity freshwater generator, not only to provide a means of washing artifacts but to provide a means of washing dishes as well. Even the coffee got served in ceramic mugs, which meant that after every meal you walked your plates and your flatware and your cups or glasses down to the galley, rinsed them off, and set them in the dishwasher rack.

So rather than staying in seclusion on the bow and watching the stars come out, Sheila and I were good campers and bussed our own dishes. And as we were leaving the galley, Sheila put her finger to her lips and asked, "What's that?"

I listened.

"Banjo," I told her. "Being played badly. Very badly."

"Splendid." She took my hand, and we followed the sound up to the work deck, where the cook was squaring away the grill and most of the crew was gathered around, sitting on canvas chairs or flat on the deck while Malibu coaxed a semi-melodic noise out of a banjo—a Kay Bluegrass model, from the looks of it.

" 'Lo, all," Sheila said. "What's up?"

"Hey." Panhead Mikey jabbed a thumb at his buddy. "Malibu here won this thing off some dude playing poker on a shrimp boat before we shipped out last night."

"Yeah." Malibu dragged a thumb across the strings, and the banjo complained in response. "New band at the Parrot last night. The guitarist doesn't know squat about Texas hold'em. If we'd had more time, I woulda got his Stratocaster too. But all I had time to work him for was this crummy piece of junk." He strummed it again.

"Dude," Mikey said, "you, like, really stink at that."

"You're doing okay," I told Malibu. "You've got the fretting. You just need to pick it instead of strumming."

Malibu stopped strumming. "Say what?"

Shut up now.

"It's a banjo," I heard myself saying. "You pick it."

"Hear that?" Malibu glanced around. "Rhode Scholar jams." He held the banjo out. "Show us."

You see? You see what you've done?

"No, really." I waved it away. "You're doing fine."

"Take it, Greg," Mikey chimed in. " 'Bu's, like, totally abusing our ears."

Malibu stood and put the instrument in my hands. "Wail on, Santana."

I looked around. The entire crew was there, even Phil and Betty. And when I turned to Sheila, she smiled and raised her eyebrows a bit.

Okay. Done like dinner. I took the banjo, put the strap over my shoulder, sat, and gave the instrument a light strum; the two highest strings were just a little flat, so I tightened them.

"That Chinese melody," Mikey said.

"How's that?" Malibu asked.

"Tu-Ning." It got the light laugh it deserved.

Then the strings sounded fine and I started to play: just the easy stuff, because I hadn't had a banjo in my hands in better than two years.

I did a couple of picking exercises first, listening to the banjo, which had a fairly good sound: brass tone ring, mahogany resonator. I did the answering phrase from "Dueling Banjos," which got a chuckle from Phil and Jack. Then I started into "I Am a Man of Constant Sorrow."

Panhead Mikey picked up on it almost immediately. "Hey— from whatcha-ma-call-it: that George Clooney flick."

I nodded and kept playing, slowly and simply at first, as if I were just finding my way in and learning the tune. Then I picked up tempo, adding undertones and complexity. I looked up and Sheila was beaming, so I went into even more intricate picking, the sound coming out as if it were two banjos playing rather than one. And when I finished, the whole boat applauded.

"Where," Jack Egan asked, "did you learn to play like that?"

But before I could answer, Malibu groused, "So he can play one song. Probably all he knows."

It was an odd way of asking for an encore. Didn't matter. It worked.

"You're right," I told Malibu. "Only one I know."

Then I launched into "Pike County Breakdown." It's a bluegrass classic, in every picker's repertoire, the sort of thing that players dust off for festivals and contests: a lilting melody backed by a syncopated counter-pick, interspersed with an aggressive hammering twang that was just plain old showing off.

Toes were tapping all around the deck. "Yeah, play it," the engineer said, the encouragement rising out of the background like an "amen!" in church.

Jack's question floated back into my head: *Where did you learn to play like that?*

Where? This song?

As I played, the salvage crew around me dimmed and I was back on the front porch in Black Mountain, the Blue Ridge Mountains standing like torn-paper shadows against the early evening sky, the yellow bug light burning in the porch fixture while my father and I sat with our banjos on the steps.

It is late summer, firefly season, their second-long green-yellow glows punctuating the growing darkness in the yard, cicadas buzzing high above in the trees. I am twelve years old, and my father has the week-old beard and the bleached, short-but-shaggy hair that was his album-cover look back in the nineties. He is sitting where the porch light will fall full on his picking hand, so I can watch him and mirror his technique.

When I get it, he nods three times, beaming, and we take off on it together, him riffing on the already intricate foundation I'm playing, a rollicking train ride of music. And in that memory I look up as the melody carries us along, and there is my mother, sitting on the porch swing, reading glasses perched on her too-young-for-them face, knitting needles poised over an unfinished sweater, honey-blond hair back in a ponytail, and the look in her face is a mixture of love and pride, that mixture that only a mother can conjure.

Then I was back on the *Peabody*, playing the banjo on muscle memory alone, the fretting and the picking progressing as if it were someone else performing, not me. My throat was tightening, my eyes welling, and although I kept it together long enough to see the piece through to the end, it could not end soon enough for me.

I stood as the resonator rang with the final note, handed the instrument back to Malibu, and rushed off as the crew applauded, the sound of their clapping becoming patchy and sporadic as I fled for the darkness of the bow.

My father never discouraged tears, which is probably why I have grown to hate them. So as I stood there, hands on the rail, the distant stars blurring, I heard footsteps behind me. I kept my back to the boat, not wanting to say anything.

"That's a rare gift you have there."

I tensed. I'd expected Sheila, but it was a male voice: Phil Rackham's.

"Can you give me a moment?" I stayed looking out at the blank, black sea.

"A moment, yes. But I'm afraid I can't give you much longer than that."

I wiped at my eyes with my wrists.

"This isn't like being ashore, Greg." Phil laid a hand on my shoulder, and I tensed, but he left it there. "There's no way to give somebody space on a working boat. When something is eating at you, it affects the rest of the crew. Morale suffers. Work suffers. Safety suffers. And from the looks of things, I'd say you came aboard with some baggage. Is that right?"

I nodded, not turning.

"Who taught you to play that way, Greg?"

I swallowed. "My father." I had to push the words out. The distant stars were blurring again.

"Is that it?" Phil's hand tightened on my shoulder, his voice gentle, softer. "Did you lose your dad?"

"No!" I turned, more quickly than I'd intended, Phil's hand dropping from my shoulder. "That's not it."

Phil was nothing more than a shadow outlined by the dim lights coming from the wheelhouse, the white navigation light atop the stubby mast, indicating a vessel at anchor. He cocked his head.

"The problem"—I hated the bitter roughness in my voice, was grateful for the darkness all around me—"is that I *didn't* lose him."

TWELVE

"I cannot say that I fault your convictions." Henry Thatch spoke to Ted's turned back. "But you must remember that however excellent your English might be, you come from a colony that owes its allegiance to Lisbon rather than London. For you to shoot an Englishman, in a Crown Colony, on King George's own dock? It simply wouldn't do, Bold Ted. Don't you know what they do to men who settle matters in that fashion? They hang them, boy. They carry them across the Atlantic in chains and then they take them to Wapping Old Stairs, and they hang them on the gibbet, and they leave their bodies there on the rope until the tide has baptized them thrice."

"They would have to catch me first."

Thatch rubbed his forehead. Between the two men, atop the binnacle, lay a linen-wrapped parcel—a new set of clothes—topped by a fresh tricorner hat, spotless and perfect in the late morning light. And Bill, the mate, had personally attended to the Menandez flintlock pistol, removing the stock, pulling the ball, rinsing the barrel and mechanism several times with boiling water, then coating the entire thing with whale oil. The only thing the mate had not done—at the captain's request—was reload the pistol.

"Lad." The captain kept his voice low so only the young man

could hear him. "There is a behavior ashore and there is a behavior at sea, and what is fitting in one place is not fitting in the other."

Ted turned. "Do you think . . . do you dream that I do not know that, Captain?"

Thatch blinked. The young man before him seemed to have gained a foot in stature.

Ted lifted a belaying pin from its place at the base of the rigging, set it back again. He gazed at the islands across the channel to the south, and when he turned back to Thatch, his face was strangely calm.

"They took us from the pens at the fort and loaded us into the hold of the slaver at night," he told the pirate. "And I did not see the sun again until you took the ship. Weeks, months . . . I do not know how long we were all chained down there."

When they brought us into the hold, it was crowded with shelves about four feet deep, five shelves high for the length of the vessel, and so close together we were forced to walk sideways to make our way through. But these were not shelves; they were pallets, the places where we would be carried for the voyage across the ocean.

If you were to carry a horse, or an ox, or a hog across the sea, you would put it in a pen with ample room for it to stand and lie, and you would provide it with bedding and fodder every day. But they did not give us those things. We were placed headfirst onto that hard, cramped planking, placed like spoons, one against the other, the next man's nakedness pressed against your back, your nakedness pressed against the man before you, your shoulders hunched so they did not chafe against the planking of the next level up, and yet they chafed nonetheless. The space was not sufficiently long for a person to lie at length, and we were forced to contort ourselves with our knees drawn up into the thighs of our neighbors. Our wrists were bound, and our ankles were shackled, both to keep our bodies full upon the planks and to prevent any hope of overpowering our captors.

We were kept this way the entire time until you took us. When the man before you emptied his bowels, he did so onto you. When your bladder was so full that you had to release it, you did it onto him. Throughout the first few days I would hear people saying *"samahani"*—*I am sorry*—when they could no longer hold their wastes. But after a week no one said it any longer, because they were all too ill to speak. Every couple of days crewmen would come down into the hold with their shirts tied across their noses and mouths, and they would sluice us with buckets of seawater. But we never dried, and the salt rose carbuncles thick upon our skin.

The very first night we were at sea, the sailors came down into the hold and each selected a woman, always the younger ones, and dragged them up onto the deck. And one that they took was the wife of the man chained behind me, because I heard her scream *"mumeo"*—*husband*—and I heard him shout back, his breath hot upon my neck, *"mkewangu, mkewangu"*—*my wife, my wife*.

That first hour of the first night, not even the deck above our heads could muffle the screams of the women as the crew raped them. The second hour, from time to time I would hear a woman call out *"siyo!"*—*no!* Or *"tafadhali"*—*please*.

Every day a child would be sent around with a ladle and a bucket of fresh water, and we would each be given a drink—one ladle only. And every two days there would be two children, and the second child would give us each a piece of ship biscuit, or hardtack, to eat. Our mouths blistered and cracked from the lack of water, and I had to choke to get the hardtack down, but I did it, because if I did not, I would perish.

At first, this both mystified and outraged me, because if we were taken to be sold as goods, why would the slavers not wish to keep us healthy? But then I understood that it was for our captors' convenience. The less we drank, and the less we ate, the less waste we produced, and the less the crew had to swab from the decks once they had sluiced us.

Starving us and parching us also weakened us, and that was to our captors' advantage as well. And who knows? Perhaps it was a way of proving to the planters here in the colonies that they were getting good stock, because no weakling could survive a voyage under such conditions. A man who could live through that would be strong, capable of being worked the whole day long for years on end.

After two, perhaps three days upon the sea, some of the women began to beg the sailors to choose them for their lust. The sailors washed the women that they took on deck. They fed them salt pork and rum. And while they were being raped, the women were out of the stink and the filth and the horror of the hold. I do not blame them at all; they begged to be taken up, because to be left in the hold was akin to asking to die.

One night when the sailors brought their lanterns down into the hold to select their women, I heard a familiar voice—the woman who had been calling for her husband. Only now she did not call out to him. She was beckoning to one of the sailors, calling him "*nyonda, nyondangu*"—*lover, my sweetheart*. And then she added in Dutch, her words slow, newly learned, "*wees zo goed, neem me*"—*please, take me*.

Her husband wept all through the night, and from that time on his woman did not return to the hold, and her man accepted neither food nor water. This was before I had learned to count the visits of the children with the water in order to gauge the passage of days. But I would imagine that the man behind me survived a week in that fashion, perhaps more. Then, one day when the sailors sluiced us with the seawater, the man behind me did not flinch, and the sailors realized that he was dead.

Ted stared down at the *Regent*'s teak deck, stared at it as if he were trying to read his story from the grains and the whorls of the dark, smooth, holystoned wood.

He looked up. "May God forgive me, Captain, I was glad when he died. Glad because I would no longer have to stomach his moaning and his sobbing and his suffering. And glad because they took him away and, for the first time in longer than I could remember, I could move a bit. I could turn off my right side and lie mostly upon my back."

Ted cast his eyes down once more. "May God forgive me," he said again.

Thatch cleared his throat. "I am certain, Bold Ted, that He already has."

A shrill and thin call, a distant *klee*, sounded from the blue sky above them, and both men looked up, following the high flight of a kestrel until they lost it in the glare of the sun.

"I let that captain and his crew escape," Thatch said, his face still turned to the sun. "I put them in a longboat with some water and provisions, and I gave them a compass and a heading to the nearest land."

The captain took off his hat and he looked at it, smoothing some imagined imperfection with his thumb.

"If ever I see that man again, I will bind him in his own shackles for you, Ted. I will bind him in his own shackles and give you free rein to shoot him on the spot, or put him over the side: the quick death or the struggle, whichever you prefer."

The kestrel called again, but he was full in the sun now, impossible to see.

"I thank you for that, Captain," Ted finally said. "But I would rather that you teach me your craft."

"You want me to teach you the trade?"

The younger man nodded somberly.

The pirate lowered his hat to his side, tapped his leg with it. "I am hardened to this work, and that is the fact of it. It is the thing I have come to do with my life—to take a man's goods, a man's ship, at the muzzle of our cannon and our guns. But it is no life for a bright man such as you, son. Be a planter. You will live longer."

Ted dipped his head and peered up at his captain. "You expect *me* to be a planter?"

Thatch laughed. "Keep a shop, then. Or an inn with Oscar and Sally. Those are honorable trades. You are welcome to crew with me as long as you please; no one remembers who *crewed* the ship that robbed him. But I would not want to see you the captain of a pirate ship."

No kestrel called, and the men of the ship were not speaking—only singing a chantey as they hoisted a sail.

"There is honor in being a privateer," Ted observed.

"Only to those who owe allegiance to the king beneath, whose aegis the letter of marque has been written. If I so much as step ashore on a Dutch island, or French, or Spanish, men would break their legs in the race to fetch a rope. I would be disappointed in myself were I to teach you to follow this path."

Ted cleared his throat as if about to say something long practiced. "Then I hope that you will teach me to sail, Captain, and perhaps I can have my own ship after you have relinquished yours. Tell yourself that you are training me to be a merchantman. Perhaps I will. Perhaps I will go far off the main, miles away from where you take the *Regent* now."

Thatch smoothed the brim of his hat again. "How far, Ted?"

"All the way to the Gold Coast. To Africa. To Ghana."

Thatch squared his hat upon his head, then shook his head. "You cannot stop the slavers by yourself, lad."

"I cannot." Ted took his own hat from atop the bundle and put it on. "But I can find my way back to Mr. Bascombe."

"The vicar? And what will you say to him when you do?"

"Say?" Ted looked east. "I shan't say a word. I mean to kill the man—nothing more."

THIRTEEN

Phil Rackham joined me at the rail, the two of us looking out at black ocean and a starry sky.

"Do you know what a worship leader is?" I asked.

Phil shook his head. "Sounds like something to do with a church."

"It is. It's the person in charge of the music. Only it's not traditional—pipe organs and stuff. Worship leaders usually take things into more mainstream styles of music, and some worship leaders are actually recording artists in their own right. Ever heard of Michael W. Smith?"

"Think so."

"He's a worship leader. Actually he was pastor first, then became worship leader. Well, sort of a worship leader. At New River Fellowship Church in . . . um, Franklin, Tennessee, I think. Anyhow, that's what my dad is, or what he was. Worship leader at a big church in Asheville. But his thing was traditional music—bluegrass. Much smaller world than CCM: contemporary Christian music. But he's a big name in it. Ted Rhodes. He added the *s* at the end because people said it sounded better. Fake name, fake man."

"You don't like your father because he added a letter to his name?"

I patted the rail. "He can do what he wants with his name; that doesn't matter to me."

Beneath us, water lapped against the hull.

"So, Greg," Phil said, his voice low, "what's Ted Rhodes's story?"

"It's a long one."

Phil glanced at his watch, tritium numeral markers glowing greenly in the dark. "I have all night."

"Well," I began, "it started with my dad's second record deal. His first album was more of a homegrown sort of deal. A friend of ours in Black Mountain had done his garage over as a studio, and we did the sessions between Thanksgiving and Christmas one winter. This guy was in our church, and my father and he were volunteers in the fire department together. My father was once a paramedic. Anyhow, I was sixteen that year, and my dad had been teaching me, letting me play slide guitar on a couple tracks of that first album.

I remember there was a Christmas tree set up in the studio, with lights around the window to the recording booth, and it was just nice, you know? I remember thinking that, it being the season, somebody's Christmas lights were sure to short out and scorch the house, and my dad and his buddy would get called out to go attend to it, but it never happened. We got to record all night.

My mom was there, and she'd bring along a thermos of hot chocolate and a big plate of cookies for between sets, and like I said, it was nice. Fun.

That first album wasn't any big thing. We had a distributor, but most of the sales were regional: people who'd heard of him. Still, it got us invited to a lot of festivals, and one of them was Wolf Trap, up by D.C., and a producer heard him there, and he must have recognized the . . . I don't know, the synergy between bluegrass and Christian worship music, because he signed Dad on the spot. That was with Rounder—major independent record label. And *that* album was very much a big deal.

They were smart, how they did it. My dad wrote the whole album, and most of the songs were solos, but he wrote two duets, and somebody had the pull to get Vince Gill to join him on one, and Bonnie Raitt to join him on the other, and that guaranteed airplay, and the album just flat took off. It made the country Top 100 list its first month out, and what can I say? It changed our lives.

There was good and bad in that. Good in that he was happy and was able to get my mom this piano she'd been wanting, and they set up a college fund for me, and we all took a cruise together. But then he got more and more requests for personal appearances. Not just concerts, but radio and TV as well: *Focus on the Family*, *The 700 Club*. It was a big deal.

That all built up a lot of anticipation for his next album. So Rounder put this event together in Nashville. It was Easter weekend, and they wanted to have a meet-and-greet with a bunch of music critics, and then that Saturday they were going to make him a member of the *Grand Ole Opry*.

A photo shoot was going to be part of it all, and he and his publicist had this idea. My dad had this old Harley, a 1980 Shovelhead he bought used back in college, and they thought it would add some color if he could bring it along for the photo shoot that Rounder had planned. Only my dad wasn't the kind who would trailer the motorcycle up for the shoot. If the bike was going to Nashville, he was going to ride it there. So he shipped his instruments and his stage clothes up and then, early on Good Friday morning, he got on the Harley and took off.

Black Mountain to Nashville's normally not that bad of a ride— you can take I-40 practically the whole way. It's about five hours, and that includes stops for gas. Only that morning there was a tractor-trailer rig that had jackknifed just outside Asheville, and traffic was backed up for miles, so Dad decided to take another way. He figured he could take 19 down to US-441, cut across the middle of the Great Smoky Mountains National Park, and then pick up I-40 again.

Problem was, lots of people had the same idea, which meant 441 was backed up as well. So instead he went to the next road down: US-129, west end of the park.

There's a stretch of US-129 that's sort of a legend among bikers. They call it "Tail of the Dragon." It averages a turn every two hundred feet for eleven miles. And it wasn't as if he was pressing it or anything, not on that old touring bike. But he was coming around a blind turn when some guy in a U-Haul van coming the other way lost it, right in front of him. He slid into my dad's lane and there wasn't anyplace to go. The Harley wasn't moving that fast, maybe twenty-five miles an hour. But it was enough.

Phil patted his left breast pocket and then pursed his lips— the deeply ingrained habit of a lifelong smoker who'd quit. He looked down as he was doing it, then looked back at me. "But he didn't, um . . ."

"Die?" I shook my head. "No. Like I said, he's still alive. But he broke a few things: his leg, some ribs."

"Ribs?" Phil grimaced. "Even one busted rib'll hurt."

"Oh, I know." I nodded slowly. "And that was what started it all. You know that old saying, 'There's no such thing as bad publicity'? Well, the old man proved it true that weekend. The cast wasn't even dry on his leg and Rounder had the news up on the wire services. *Entertainment Tonight* even picked it up, and they'd never so much as mentioned his name before. The record started getting more airplay than ever, and the *Opry* let Rounder know that as soon as he was ready to play, they'd have a place for

Ted Rhodes on their lineup. All he had to do was pick a Saturday, let 'em know, and he'd be on.

"And I guess my dad figured he'd better collect on that promise while it was still fresh in everyone's mind. But he was in so much pain that he couldn't even sleep, let alone practice. Then our doctor upped his pain medications—just enough that he could function, but not so much that he'd be out of it."

I fell silent for a moment. In the darkness, we heard something—a turtle or a dolphin or a shark—break the surface and then submerge again.

Phil cleared his throat. "You want another moment?"

"No." I shook my head. "I don't need a moment. I've had years.

"What the doctor prescribed got my dad to Nashville," I continued. "My mother and I drove up with him, and we had to stop several times. Even with the meds his leg throbbed—it was in a walking cast by that point—and his ribs bothered him with every breath."

We stayed overnight in Nashville. He took an extra dose of his meds so he could sleep. The next morning my mother was begging him to forget about the *Opry* and just go back home. But he said it would be crazy to put up with all that discomfort for nothing, so we dropped him off at the Opry House and went out front.

They had him on in the second half of the show, and it was as if he'd never crashed the bike. I mean, he still had the cast on his leg, and the hosts even cracked a few jokes about that, but his voice? His performance? Never better.

My mother and I just figured that he reached down deep inside and found something we never knew was there. That, or maybe God had stepped in. But then later we learned the truth. It wasn't courage, and it wasn't God. It was chemical.

He got backstage and I guess he kind of freaked. He got the stage manager to call a doctor for him, and from what we put together later on, he just flat-out lied to the guy; told him that he'd forgot his meds at home and couldn't reach our regular doctor and that he didn't have an answering service—none of which were true. And like I said, he used to be a paramedic and so he knew about drugs and what to ask for. So this new doctor prescribed what he wanted, and they sent a runner to a drugstore to pick it up.

It was different from what he was already on, and he was lucky the two drugs together didn't kill him. Or maybe not lucky. Like I said, he knew his barbiturates. And the drugs didn't kill him, didn't hurt him, didn't even impair him that much. They just got him high. Not high enough that he couldn't function, or that anyone could tell he was messed up, but high enough that he felt like he could take on the world, that he could walk out on that stage and cut loose with the performance of his life.

I'm not going to say that it happened that night, but it happened. Percocet, Oxycodone, you name it. He was hooked on pain relievers. Even after his ribs had healed and he was back to walking without a limp, he claimed he was still in pain and got doctors to prescribe for him—doctors, because it turned out he had at least three, all of them prescribing for him, and none knew about the others. He was also using several different pharmacies, different chains, so no red flags ever went up.

He even had us buffaloed—my mom and me. I mean, as far as we could tell, he was a hero. He was in this pain, or so he told us, yet he was still writing songs and getting into the studio, and he was doing a steady concert schedule, in addition to his services at church.

Then one night, the summer after I graduated from high school, he came back from church. We heard the garage door go up; heard him cut the engine on the pickup. But ten minutes passed, and he didn't come in. So I went out to check on him, and he was passed out cold. I couldn't wake him up. Then my mom tried, and she couldn't wake him. He barely had a pulse and it was slow—really slow.

We called 9-1-1, and he was rushed to the ER at Mission Hospital, Asheville. And once they did a tox screen, they figured out that he'd overdosed. Actually he'd gone beyond overdosing. He'd built up so much of a tolerance to pain meds that his heart should have stopped cold within minutes after he took the amount he was doing. But in some perverse way his addiction saved him—kept him alert long enough to get him home, and alive long enough for the hospital to get amphetamines into him and save his life.

You can probably fill in the next parts yourself. First he insisted he'd made a mistake and taken a dose twice, but the docs said the amount of drugs in his system couldn't have been a mistake, so he finally confessed. We had this confrontation—my mom, the lead pastor, his agent, some people from the fire department, and a couple of the guys who backed him when he was on the road. He agreed to go into rehab, and we agreed to hush it up and concoct some story about him needing follow-up treatment after the accident—which of course was a lie.

Well, three months later, he was back home, clean and sober. They even let him play his banjo that last month in rehab. The fire department pulled his ticket as an EMT; you don't give an addict easy access to morphine. But other than that, everything seemed to be back to normal.

"Greg." Phil's voice was muted; he was looking down at the deck as he spoke. "People . . . they mess up. You were lucky you got your dad back. People need a second chance."

Tears began to cloud my eyes again. "He had his second

chance." I was fighting to keep the tremor out of my words. "He
had it. . . ."

I looked out to sea. Something large and alit and very far
away—a container ship probably—was at the horizon, at the place
where dark sea met the star-strewn sky.

"Do you know who you meet while you're in rehab?" I asked
the question as I was still facing out toward the sea. Then I turned
back to Phil. "You meet other addicts. People who can tell you how
to get drugs without using a pharmacy.

Dad didn't go straight back on; he stayed clean for . . . I don't
know, two months, maybe three. When he did go back on, it wasn't
as if he was on the street corner buying powder from gangsters.
He'd met somebody who had contacts in England, and the UK, it
turns out, treats late-stage cancer patients with diamorphine, which
is just another name for pharmaceutical heroine. So he never did
street drugs, but he became a junkie just the same.

And he was a lot more careful this time. He got high at home,
late at night, when he was supposedly out practicing in his studio.
He'd get high, stay up late, sleep in, and we didn't think much of it
because he was a musician, and he hung out with other musicians,
and musicians stay up late and sleep in all the time.

Except sometime after he first got home from rehab, my mom
got pregnant. And although I'd stayed home the first term, they
both insisted I go and start at Chapel Hill after Christmas.

So I wasn't there when, in her sixth month of pregnancy, my
mom woke up, spotting heavily. Dad was out in the studio, wrecked,
and when she came to find him, I guess he was able to get it together
enough that she never suspected he was messed up.

That didn't mean he could drive, though. But he tried anyway,
and made it a whole three miles from the house before driving off

the road. All the way off into the ditch, and the ditch was steep, so the truck rolled.

And then I was tearing up again. I hated it. Hated the fact that I was on the verge of blubbering in front of this man I barely knew, a guy who wore Spanish gold on a chain around his neck. I hoped the darkness hid some of what I knew had to be showing on my face. I took a deep breath and tried to recover.

"The baby," I finally got out, "she . . . died in the crash. My mom? She stayed alive for a week after. I was able to get home from school, see her before she passed. She wasn't conscious, though. Never knew I was there.

"As for my dad, he came out of it with a bump on the head and a scratch on his hand. He was back in rehab so quick he missed the funeral. My college had been set up with a fund they'd put together a couple years before, so after I buried my mom, I just went back to school and stayed there. I got a job and an apartment over the summers, applied for grad school at Duke after graduation. I found every reason I could to stay at school and . . . and I made it pretty obvious that he didn't need to come see me.

"People I know back home claim the accident changed his life. He went straight, started working with a support group, and from what I hear, he gives most of what he's making from his music to missions work. People think he's come full circle, but from where I stand, full circle would mean more than clean and sober. Full circle would mean having my mom back. Her alive, my baby sister alive. Full circle would mean . . . It would mean things would be different.

"But that's not going to happen. And every time I hear his sort of music, or anytime I play a mandolin, a banjo . . . ?"

I stopped talking. If I went any further, I'd be risking another meltdown. And besides, Phil knew what I meant; I could see him nodding in the starlight.

He patted his breast pocket a second time, then shoved his hands deep in the pockets of his jeans. He was silent for several long seconds before clearing his throat.

"Not that it's any of my business," he said, "but when did you last see your dad?"

FOURTEEN

"I last saw Mr. Bascombe the morning I was taken," Ted said. His back to the sun, Ted raised the backstaff and aligned it so its shadow vane cast a shadow on the instrument's horizon vane. "It was the dry season—our well was low, and he'd dispatched me with a donkey, a cart, and two barrels to fetch water from a falls outside of town. I remember he'd told me to wear my oldest clothes lest I muddy my better things. I wore patched breeches with rope for a belt, and a shirt that was nearly a rag, and once I'd left the town I'd stripped off the shirt. The dry season is hot."

"Try not to disturb that shadow while you make your horizon sighting," Thatch said, watching the younger man work the instrument. "Fetching water. That sounds innocent enough."

"Yes." Ted moved the sight vane, aligning it with the horizon vane. "But two men had come to the house the evening before, and there'd been shouting. Mr. Bascombe had the chandlery, just across the road from our house, but he'd also kept a warehouse ten minutes' ride down the road, and he rented space to other merchants as they needed it. The warehouse had burned two weeks before, and one merchant had lost some goods that had just come in and were being stored while he made room in his shop. He was holding Mr. Bascombe liable for the loss, but we had just purchased a great deal of lumber and fittings and we didn't have the money. I couldn't hear the entire exchange; I was in the next room. But I remember Mr. Bascombe saying that he would be outfitting a ship in a fortnight and he would have the money then. But the men were insisting that they could not wait."

"Sounds as if your vicar was in a fix," Thatch said. He glanced at the backstaff. "There, you have it. What is your reading?"

Ted told him, they consulted the ship's chronometer, and then he checked a page in the pirate's leather-bound journal.

"We are at seventeen minutes and forty-eight seconds of north latitude," the young man finally declared.

"Capital." Thatch smiled. "Deduct the semidiameter of the sun and that puts us at seventeen degrees and forty seconds, which is perfectly correct."

He continued watching as Ted wrapped the navigational instrument in muslin and put it away in its protective oaken box.

"So," the pirate said, "it is your belief that Vicar Bascombe sold you and arranged for your capture to settle his debts?"

Ted closed the latch on the box and secured it with a small polished horn of whale ivory.

"He rescued you as an infant after your village was destroyed, took you into his home, nourished you, clothed you, educated you, raised you beneath his roof for nigh on a decade and a half, taught you to speak like a Scotsman, and then decided one day he would sell you as livestock? As common, removable property?"

Ted stood with the box in his hands, swaying naturally with the movement of the sloop.

"Ted," the pirate said. "Bold Ted. What credence, what fact could possibly lie behind such fancy?"

Ted canted his head slightly down and to his right. He worked his bare right foot on the dark gray of the teak deck. He looked up, his brow knitted.

"Mr. Bascombe," he said, "came to Africa to sell goods to slavers. He left Scotland with the fullest intention of increasing his own comfort through the pain and the terror and the misery and even the death of others. Of hundreds, of thousands, of tens of thousands of others. He not only tolerated the trade, he encouraged it. He helped it to grow through his support—his material support."

"Yet he raised you as his son."

Ted hefted the box, looked down at it. "Mr. Bascombe is a businessman. For fifteen years I watched him at his work. He knows how to better his investment. And he knows how to reap his reward."

Thatch shrugged and started across the deck, the younger man falling in beside him.

"What manner of man," the pirate asked without looking Ted's way, "would stoop to such a level?"

He opened the hatch to his cabin, stepped down and stood on the upper rungs of the ladder. Ted handed him the backstaff in its case.

"What manner of man," Ted asked him, "would turn to piracy? Yet turn we surely have."

Thatch balanced on the ladder rung, the instrument in his hands. Ted looked around. Beyond the perimeter of the small ship, far past the sweating men heaving upon their ropes, the ocean was spread in a perfect blue, white-flecked circle.

"Somewhere out there," he said, "is a French merchant, fat and heavy for the harvest. Let us find and take him."

Thatch fixed the young man in the eyes.

Ted grinned. "This is why God gave us the sea."

FIFTEEN

Sheila McIntyre's smile looked genuine. Even in the sunlight on the deck of the *Peabody*. Her short blond hair, tossed lightly by the sea wind, seemed to complement the amiability.

It threw me. I was at a loss for words.

"Looked for you at breakfast," she said. She put a little yellow oxygen analyzer up to the valve on the metal manifold joining a pair of scuba tanks, cracked the valve to bleed a little gas out, and watched the black numerals flicker and morph on its gray display. She glanced my way again. "You just get up?"

"Didn't feel like breakfast." I watched as she logged her mix on the daily slate and shifted while the *Peabody* rocked beneath me.

Sheila handed me the analyzer. I switched it off, waved it back and forth to let regular air into the sensor orifice, and switched it on again. The little display dimmed, darkened, then showed the numerals 20.9—the percentage, rounded off to the nearest tenth, of oxygen present in ambient air.

"Yeah," Sheila said. She slid a stainless-steel backplate onto long bolts extending from the metal bands holding the two scuba tanks together. "Dinner last night was fair extreme. Believe I'm still digesting that steak."

"Sheil . . ."

She was still smiling. Squinting in the morning sun, but smiling.

"You don't have to do that."

The smile declined a degree or two. "Do what?"

"Pretend nothing happened."

Her smile vanished entirely. She bent and slid washers onto the bolts and began spinning wing nuts on behind them. It took a good half a minute for her to run the wing nuts down to the base of the exposed bolt threads, and when she finally spoke she did so without looking up. "And you don't have to do that, Greg."

I analyzed the gas in my own tanks. It came out 35.8 percent oxygen, within the margins for NOAA Nitrox 36. For a dive over a fifty-five-foot bottom, it was ideal—less nitrogen than air, so less chance of decompression illness on repetitive dives, but not so much oxygen that there was any risk of toxicity. I recorded the reading on the same slate as Sheila.

"What's that?" I finally asked.

She looked up, still squinting. "Tell me about it—unless you want to."

"You'll think I'm weird if I don't."

She glanced around and gave my hand a squeeze. "I'll think playing that music triggered something pretty intense. You'll tell me about it when you're ready. And as you have not, you are not."

On the fantail, Malibu and Mikey and a couple of the deck-hands were working in the early morning sun, sorting the PVC tubing into a weighted net. I started fitting my own backplate onto the double set I'd just analyzed. "I can tell you now."

"And I can wait."

This time, instead of squeezing my hand, she glanced to make sure no one was looking and then kissed me lightly on the cheek.

SIXTEEN

Ted put his hand to his cheek, brought it slowly away. "What did you do that for?"

Sally smiled. "Did you not like it?"

Ted touched again the spot where he'd been kissed. "Yes. Very much. But for what?"

"For courage," Sally told him.

"Courage?"

On the floor above them, the living space above the public room of the inn, heavy footsteps—boots—sounded, moving toward the head of a narrow set of stairs.

Sally smiled again, a half smile this time. "You'll see."

The footfalls became clearer, the boots themselves appearing on the stairs at their side. Wordlessly, Sally moved back a step, away from Ted. Then Oscar Emmons's body came into view, his tricorner hat under one arm, a black book—its flapped cover tied about it—under the other.

Ted peered at the book, and Oscar caught him at it.

"What are you looking at?" When the big man was irritated, his voice bordered on thunder. "Have you never before seen a man carrying a Bible?"

"Never so small. All the Bibles I have ever seen have been . . ." Ted used his hands to approximate the size of a family Bible.

"Oh? And you have seen your share of Bibles, have you?"

Ted met the older man's gaze. "I have seen a few."

Oscar hefted the book. "Seen them, or read them?"

"There is no 'or' to ask about, sir, as I have done both."

"You don't say." Oscar Emmons untied the cover of the black book, turned the pages carefully, and stopped when he had found what he was looking for. He held the Bible out. "Here—where the mark is penciled in the margin. Read me that verse."

Ted accepted the leather-bound book, glanced about, and walked to the window, its rippled panes presenting a distorted view of Road Town Harbour. He turned the book so the light from the window fell upon the pages. The pencil mark was curious—not just a mark but a small oval with a tiny vertical line pendulant from it. It was next to First Corinthians 13:12.

" 'For now,' " he read aloud, " 'we see through a glass, darkly; but then face to face.' "

His voice was strong, his cadence practiced and even, the reading voice of one who had read aloud often. He continued, " 'Now I know in part; but then shall I know even as also I am known.' " He looked up. "Shall I give you the rest of the chapter?"

Oscar glared at him, walked over and took the book back, the gesture rough and rude.

" 'And now abideth faith, hope, charity, these three,' " Ted said evenly, reciting from memory, " 'but the greatest of these is charity.' "

Oscar's brow furrowed.

"First Corinthians 13:13," Ted told him. He held a hand out, pale palm up, indicating the Bible. "It is the only verse remaining, sir, in that chapter."

Oscar harrumphed, tying the cover shut again. "Am I to be impressed because you memorized a bit of Scripture?"

"No, sir." Ted shook his head, tapping his hat against his thigh. "But perhaps it will better your opinion of me if you know that I have memorized much of the New Testament."

Oscar stood a little straighter, crooked his head.

"Well . . ." He opened the door of the public room, letting the sunlight stream in. "Nathaniel Winslow, the farrier, has a parrot that can recite the Lord's Prayer. It is a pleasant entertainment, but I seriously doubt that the ability has moved the bird any nearer to paradise. Let us go now, or we shall be late for morning services."

The older man settled his hat upon his head, and Ted did the same. When he stole a glance at Sally beneath his brim, she was tying the bow of a bonnet under her chin. She smiled at him and he smiled back.

They left the house and, to Ted's surprise, did not walk up the hill toward the houses of Road Town, but crossed the dirt road to the harbor. There, Sally turned and headed for the dock while Oscar ambled down to the stony beach.

Ted hesitated, and Oscar turned his way. "Well, man? Are you not going to help?"

"Sir?"

"With the skiff, man. Help me to launch the skiff."

"We're going by . . . ?" Ted squared his hat more securely upon his head. "Yes, sir. Of course, sir."

He followed Oscar Emmons down to the beach, where a small boat, tapered on either end, rocked, half-beached on the high tide. A brown pelican squawked, lifted its wings and lumbered off the tiller, wing tips tapping ripples on the sparkling water of the harbor until it had gained sufficient speed to arc up into the cloudless blue Caribbean sky.

Oscar leaned on the bow of the little boat to take off his boots and stockings, and Ted did the same, setting them inside the skiff, where the scent of tar lingered, a clue that the vessel had been very recently caulked. Indeed, the wood of the skiff gleamed with the soft, yellow sheen of tung oil and varnish. The hull was painted a flawless forest green, and the brass fittings shone with not even a hint of verdigris or tarnish. The mast was stepped far forward, just behind the first of three plank seats, and the jib was lashed to the boom with three lengths of manila rope, the stiff white canvas of the sail accordioned neatly between the two.

They both hiked their breeches above their knees, and then the two men lifted and shoved, moving the bow off the beach. Oscar climbed in first, and his weight grounded the skiff again, so Ted kept pushing, walking the little boat out until the harbor water had nearly reached the bottoms of his new breeches. Finally the boat came free and he clambered in as well, sitting in the bow as Oscar used a pole to move the skiff over to the dock.

At the dock, Sally waited, a line in her hand, which she tossed to her father, who passed it around a pin and handed it up to Ted, letting him hold the boat against the dock while Oscar helped his daughter to board. Then they cast off, and there was an awkward moment as Ted helped Sally to the bow, conscious every moment that Oscar Emmons was watching precisely where he placed his hands and for how long.

When that was done, Ted sat amidships, with Oscar poling them out to deeper water. In a minute or so, the older man was laying the pole lengthwise within the skiff while a gentle breeze moved the small boat aimlessly in the harbor.

"Would you like me to hoist, sir?" Ted put his hand on the line that raised the jib.

"I will thank you to lower the leeboard first, man, so you do not put us all in the drink in our Sunday best."

"Leeboard?" Ted looked around and saw that the skiff had a pair of blade-like boards lashed between lengths of oak on either side. He pulled the top of the one that was away from the wind and it pivoted stiffly into the water. Then he took the rope that ran from its top and looked about, trying to figure out what to do with it.

Bruskly, the older man took the rope from Ted and passed it around the rear seat, tying it off one-handed.

"You may hoist," Oscar said, doing little to hide the disgust in his voice.

Ted did so, cleating the rope around a wooden belaying pin. The sail filled, and the little boat began to porpoise gently across the harbor.

"You crew on Hatch's ship and you do not know of leeboards?"

Ted looked up. "The *Regent* does not have a leeboard, sir. Nor did the merchantman that I helped bring in. They were not like this craft at all. Not nearly so . . . diminutive."

If Oscar Emmons heard the slight concealed within the observation, he did not show it. He shifted on his seat, bettering the little boat's angle to the water, and took a visible breath like a man settling back into a favorite chair. He looked Ted full in the face.

"So," he said, his voice even and low, "what is it that you do on the *Regent*, man? Are you the loblolly boy?"

Ted bit his lip, blinked. A loblolly boy was a surgeon's assistant, someone who helped hold down a man having a musket ball extracted, or who brought soup to the sick, or who cleaned up the mess when a feverish man soiled himself. It was considered one of the lowliest positions on a fighting ship, the job given to a person who was otherwise useless.

"Sir," he finally said, "if I was needed to assist in a surgery aboard ship, I would do so and do it gladly. All work is honorable. But that is not my primary duty. Captain Thatch is training me to be a navigator."

"Navigator? An officer's post?"

"All of our officers serve at the will of the crew, sir, and my knowledge of mathematics and astronomy made me suitable to the post. Besides, most of the men are suspicious of navigation. They believe there to be magic involved. So they are happy to have someone else do it, and Captain Hatch says that it would ease his mind if someone other than he had the ability to see the *Regent* safely home."

Oscar Emmons put both hands on the tiller and pointed the little skiff at the open sea.

" 'All work is honorable,' " he said, half under his breath. "On a *pirate* ship . . ." He made a sound like a chuckle, but he did not smile. Then, looking out to sea, he grumbled, "In my experience, officers tend to be overdressed peacocks."

Ted stayed quiet and looked out at the water on the other side of the skiff: deep, cobalt blue under the morning sky. He pounded softly on the gunwale of the skiff, lifting and dropping his fist perhaps a quarter inch as he did so, a motion he hoped Oscar Emmons would not see. It didn't help, and he turned back to the older man.

"Sir." His voice trembled a bit as he spoke, and that riled him even more. "I am not shy about going into a topmast or out on a yard when the need arises. I have done so more than once, and that in a running sea."

Oscar shot him a glance. "The *Regent* is a schooner, man. Schooners have no yards."

"True enough, but our last prize did."

The older man harrumphed and sat back, both callused hands upon the tiller.

They sailed out of the harbor and then west along the coast, out past the shallows where coral heads rose so close to the surface that they could threaten even a vessel that drew as little water as Oscar's skiff. Ted looked to the bow, where Sally was sitting, her skirts drawn around her so they would not get wet as the bow bobbed across the sea. She met his glance and smiled. Seeing this, Oscar cleared his throat, so Ted gazed out at Tortola instead: green hills tumbling down to the washing sea.

A sea turtle surfaced a few feet from the skiff, lifted its head and gasped in a breath of air. Its eyes appeared ancient and wise, and it seemed to inspect Ted for the briefest of moments before sinking silently back beneath the surface.

Ted turned back to Oscar. "It's a good day for a sail." His words seemed empty and dull the moment he said them; a fool's attempt to fill the quiet.

"Good or bad, we would sail it," Oscar answered. The boom creaked against the mast. "It is the Lord's Day."

The wind lifted Ted's hat a bit, and he caught it with one hand.

"Is there no road to the church?" he asked.

"Of course there is a road. What manner of fool would build a church not reached by roads? But from Road Town it would be two hours around the hill by wagon. Each way. And a skiff does not eat of oats, nor need to be shoveled after."

Ted found himself looking at Oscar Emmons's pink-soled feet. Both men had left their boots and stockings in the bow after the boat had gotten under way. No sense in replacing them if they would just have to remove them again to beach the skiff at their destination.

"There was a church in town," Sally offered from the bow, "but it burned last spring."

"Some fool left a candle burning after Good Friday services,"

Oscar grumbled. He glared at Ted as if he believed that the young man might be the very fool in question.

Ted looked out once again at the sea and the passing island. There was no sign of the sea turtle. The creature had apparently put a fathom or two of water between himself and Oscar Emmons.

Bold Ted envied the turtle.

The little skiff rounded a headland, and four other sails emerged on the water beyond. In the bow, Sally lifted a hand in greeting, and from the nearest boat—still a quarter mile distant—a woman waved back, her hand white against the gray-green of a distant island.

Oscar leaned back, pulling the tiller toward him and leaning the skiff into a long, continuous, quartering landward tack. Ted looked toward the bow, doing his best not to allow his eyes to settle on Sally lest her father somehow catch him doing so. He gauged their heading, factoring in an allowance for the *crab*—how much the boat would move sideways as it sailed. Sure enough, at the end of that line, on a rise above a beach, people were walking by twos and threes up to a small gray-stone church, the tower above its gaping doors crowned by a squat, slate-shingled steeple.

The white line of a sand beach appeared in the curve of the bay beneath the church. Two boats were already beached there, and the boats on the water were all growing nearer as they headed for the same beach. Soon the skiff was crossing water so shallow that its shadow seemed to mimic it on the scalloped white sand of the bottom. Ted quickly undid the line and raised the leeboard so it would not ground as they neared the beach.

A few moments later it was the skiff's keel that was touching sand, so Ted moved forward and, being careful not to brush against Sally as he did so, hiked his breeches to his knees and swung over the gunwale.

The water very nearly reached the wool of his breeches, none-theless, and Ted grabbed the painter on the bow and pulled, taking exaggerated steps through the clear seawater. There was a double splash at the stern and then a muffled curse as the boat lightened. Sally giggled, and Ted, realizing the water had come over Oscar's hiked trousers, grinned back at her.

"Heave!" Oscar growled. "For heaven's sake, man, will you heave?"

Ted grinned at Sally again and, the gunwale under one hand and the painter in the other, pulled the skiff, using its momentum— and that of Oscar pushing from behind—to bring the bow of the little boat well up onto the sand. There was a limestone boulder there with a black iron ring driven into it; there were several such boulders at intervals along the beach. And although the tide was as high as it was going to be anytime before sunset, and the waves lapping the beach could be measured in inches rather than feet, Ted passed the painter through the ring and tied it off with a practiced bowline.

Still smiling, Ted turned to the bow and held his hands up.

"That will not be necessary," a deep baritone boomed next to his ear. "I can attend to my own daughter."

Chastened, Ted stepped back as Oscar swung Sally, her shoes in her hand, out of the bow and onto the sand. Ted helped beach the next boat in, and then the three of them walked up the beach to a set of stone steps.

Once the steps had ascended to the grassy rise above the sand, there was a wooden bench next to the steps. Ted turned and gazed seaward while Sally put her shoes back on lest her father think that Ted found Sally's bare feet somehow attractive, which he did. Very much so, in fact.

Ted continued to stand aside while Oscar put on his stockings, bringing them up over the bottoms of his breeches—he muttered as he did this, for they were wet—and then he fastened garters over hose and breeches both, in the style of an earlier decade. He put on his shoes, using a curved slice of ox horn to do it and, grunting as he stood, surrendered the bench to Ted, who quickly pulled his woolen hose on, rolled the tops, and fastened his breeches bottoms over them. Then he turned his attention to his shoes.

"Might I trouble you for the use of your horn?" When there was no reply, he turned and saw that Oscar Emmons was already halfway up the hill. Sally, glancing back, made a *come on* motion with her hand. So Ted used his fingers to guide his stocking heel into the stiff new shoes, pinched a finger, cursed, realized he was within earshot of the other congregants—one elderly woman tsked—and then took the steps two at a time to catch up with the elder Emmons and his daughter.

The church was even smaller within than it appeared without, the walls being built thick to resist hurricanes. The one-room building was dark, illuminated only by smoking tallow candles and the daylight falling through the open door and two side windows, one set into each of the opposing walls. It was unlike any church Ted had seen in Africa, and he would have wagered it was unlike any in the colonies of America as well, because black heads were sprinkled among the white, the two races mixed by family among the dozen or so long benches that served as pews. Accepting greetings from his left and right, Oscar Emmons walked to the front, where one end of a bench seemed to have been held open for him and his daughter. Given the deference accorded the older man, Ted took it that Oscar was an elder within the church, perhaps even one of its benefactors. It made sense; The Rose and Crown was easily one of the most heavily patronized businesses on the whole of Tortola.

Oscar guided Sally to the bench and then sat next to her. Ted stood, uncertain, until he saw Oscar patting the open space on the bench next to him—a space that would put Oscar between Sally and Ted. Ted bowed, head only, and then sat, his tricorner hat resting on his knees.

The congregants continued to trickle in, and Oscar made a show of untying the cover of his Bible, opening it, and laying it upon his knee, bending forward to scan the text.

Ted glanced over. The text Oscar Emmons appeared to be studying was First Chronicles, the sixth chapter: the numbering of Levi's descendants. In his education, Ted had read a history that included segments of the *Domesday Book,* the survey William the Conqueror had ordered of each man, woman, sheepcote, and ox in every shire of eleventh-century England, and he had found it roughly as memorable and readable as First Chronicles—the first ten chapters, at least.

Oscar glanced his way and then turned the page and resumed following the text with his finger: the seventh chapter, the descendants of Issachar.

Ted sat back and examined the altar—a simple stone platform with a small oaken pulpit, with a plain wooden cross on the wall behind it.

At length, an elderly man walked to the front of the church and stood before the platform.

"Let us now praise God," he said overly loud.

The man began to sing, and the hymn was not one that Ted recognized. At the very least he did not recognize it in its present form, so he stayed mute, as did most of the congregation. A few voices faded in and out, and when it became obvious that the last verse was coming to a close, every voice joined in for a thunderous "Amen!"

The process repeated for three more hymns. Then, when the fourth "Amen" had left Ted's ears only a step short of ringing, a man wearing the black robe and crossed white collar of an Anglican curate got up from the front bench and mounted the single step to the pulpit.

"Our . . . lesson . . . today . . ." The curate spoke with a measure of silence between each word, and Ted sank a bit as he listened. He knew the signs of an overlong sermon coming his way.

". . . is taken . . . from the . . ." the curate continued, "twenty-second . . . chapter . . . of the . . . book . . . of . . . Genesis."

He paused as if waiting for his congregation to turn there, which was a futile gesture as there were only two Bibles in the whole of the church—the tome on the pulpit and the Bible that lay upon Oscar Emmons's knee—and Oscar's Bible remained open to First Chronicles.

"I speak . . . of course . . ." the curate said, "of one of the most troubling passages of Scripture in all of the Old Testament. It is the passage . . . in which God . . . orders Abraham to sacrifice . . . the one thing in the world most dear to him: his beloved . . . son . . . Isaac."

Now Oscar Emmons began to turn the pages of his Bible, going back to the first book of the Old Testament. He searched it and finally settled on a page. But when Ted looked over, the man's finger pointed not to Genesis 22:1, but to Genesis 22:8. And about a thumb's width down on the left-hand margin was a penciled mark. It appeared to be a small, upside-down triangle, crowned by a shallow, cursive, inverted *w*.

Oscar, rather than focusing on the text, looked up at the curate, attentive.

"Our text," the curate said, "is a study not only in the obedience of Abraham, but even more important, the obedience of his son. For if Abraham obeys and fulfills God's command, he will be left within his grief. But if Isaac obeys and submits, and submit he must do, because he is a man easily capable of fending off an elderly man, then Isaac is allowing his beloved father to leave him bereft of life itself. It is a situation that would seem to you and me beyond understanding, and Isaac does not attempt to understand. And that is the true beauty of this story. It is a son's unquestioning faith in the wisdom and the righteousness and the love of his father. . . ."

Ted heard that last sentence, and he heard nothing further until the sermon had ended and the congregation had risen to leave the little church.

Sailing back to Road Town turned out to be downwind and swift, the little skiff settling into a heel and staying there, leaning against its leeboard almost the entire way. Ted had been silent ever since the sermon had begun, and Sally wondered about this. Had he simply fallen mute to avoid entering into another verbal sparring match with her father? Or had the truth of God's Word found him through the curate's message? Or was it something else?

The skiff was so small; there was no way to speak with Ted without her father overhearing them. And after sixteen years, she knew Oscar Emmons well enough to know that he would not simply turn a deaf ear to anything that passed between this young rogue, this pirate, and her. All she could do was hope that her father would leave them alone for a moment once they had reached shore. She needed only enough time for a question or two.

They rounded the last headland with Peter Island off to their left, and aimed the bow at the small congregation of buildings that was Road Town. There, Ted again went into the water first, and he and her father beached the little skiff, using the sail to drive it up onto the low beach and working harder to get it well up onto the sand, because the tide was out now and the boat, if not well beached, could be lifted by the evening tide. They had not let her off at the dock, and she did not begrudge that. The skiff was her father's only vessel, used to fetch vegetables from the small farms down the coast, and she knew that he had to beach it securely.

The Road Town beach was rocky, so she could leave her shoes on, but the men left theirs off and crossed the road that way, with their stockings rolled and tucked into their footwear. At the door of the inn, her father removed an iron key that he wore on a leather lace around his neck, unlocked the door, and let the three of them in.

Then he turned to her and said, "I baked bread first thing this morning, and there is a small ham to the right of the door in the smokehouse. Why don't you set a dinner for us?"

"Yes, Father." Sally stole a glance at Ted and then she left.

Ted waited until Sally had left the room before sitting at the bench beside the door to put his stockings on. Oscar set his own boots on the floor and stood, looking at the younger man, his big arms crossed.

"Your clothing is very fine," he said. "Is it taken off a prize?"

"No, sir." Ted shook his head. "It was purchased here in Road Town."

"Yet it is not the same suit of clothes that I saw you in the night you were here with Captain Henry."

"With Captain Thatch? No, sir. It is not." With one stocking on and one leg of his breeches fastened, Ted stopped and looked the older man in the eye.

"So you have more than one set of fine clothes?" Oscar asked it as a question, but he did not wait for an answer. "Men who throw away their money on finery have no character, if you ask me. They are only interested in appearances."

Ted leaned back. "And you are not, I take it."

"Not what?"

"Interested, sir. In appearances."

Oscar scoffed. "I am a working man."

"Yet you carry your Bible to church."

"What of it?"

Ted took a long breath, let it out slowly. "Are you willing to swear upon that Bible that you can read it?"

Oscar said nothing, but his shoulders fell ever so slightly.

"There is no dishonor in that," Ted said, his voice soft. "Many good men—many very good men—do not read."

Oscar tapped the black book against his open palm. "The curate gave me this when he came here. His thanks for being an elder to his congregation. Sally tried to teach me the reading of it, but the letters blur and run together for me. I did not want our pastor to know that he had given me a gift I was incapable of using."

He squinted at the younger man. "How did you know?"

Ted shrugged. "The pencil marks in the margins. At first I thought they were symbols, a code of some sort. Then it came to me: they are pictures. The oval with the tail is a looking glass: 'through a glass darkly.' And the upside-down triangle was topped with horns, a ram's head. The ram that God provided as a substitute for Isaac. So you can appear to be in the right place in the Bible just by finding the picture with the key word for that story or that verse. You cannot follow every reading, but you can do it often enough to preserve the illusion."

Oscar broke away from his gaze and looked out the window, at the harbor.

"These clothes, sir," Ted said. "My captain bought them for me."

Oscar glanced his way. "And why would Henry do that?"

"Because he tossed me into the harbor in my others. To keep me from shooting a man on the dock. Just after we left here that night."

Oscar scowled. "You were not that far into your cups."

Ted shook his head. "I was not. But I drew my gun because the man had said something that . . . something that impugned your daughter's honor."

Oscar straightened. "Do you not believe me capable of defending my only daughter's honor?"

"Without a doubt, sir, you are. But you were not there. And I was. And the man needed badly to be set in his place." Ted pulled on the other stocking and rolled its top. He cocked his head. "Sir, I swear. You have my word . . . I will not tell a soul about the Bible." He reached for his shoes.

"Here."

Ted looked up. The older man was offering the curved slice of ox horn.

"Use this," Oscar told him. "They will go on easier."

SEVENTEEN

I accepted the little squeeze bottle of baby shampoo, squirted a bit onto the inside of each lens of my dive mask, and handed the bottle back to Malibu. No wisecracks. No snide remarks. He was all business, double-checking that the valve was open on my cylinder, doing the quick once-over on my releases.

Which bothered me. Malibu cracked wise and made snide remarks to everyone. It was the nature of the insecure beast. I suspected Phil had spoken to him, and I really wished that he hadn't. I didn't want to be the guy on the ship with a Special Handling label on his forehead.

There was a bucket of fresh water hanging on the rail next to the dive gate, and I gave the mask a quick rinse—enough to keep it from smearing, but not enough to wash the shampoo out of it entirely. The mask still smelled of baby shampoo when I put it on. It reminded me of a girl I'd known in the program at Duke; she'd used mint toothpaste on the inside of her dive mask to keep it from fogging. It was harder to rinse off than the baby shampoo, and when I asked her why she used it, she'd said she preferred the smell.

Wearing a dive mask is like wearing blinders. You have to turn to see anything to your side, and I turned and saw that Sheila was rinsing her mask. I checked her valve, an empty gesture because, as divemaster for the watch, Malibu would have already checked it. But it made me feel good to do it, like I was taking care of her. She smiled when she felt the slight movement of the tank, so apparently it felt good to her to have me do it.

"I'll wait at the surface and swim the air lift down," I told her.

Another smile. "I'll give you a hand. You're the one who knows where we're headed, anyhow."

She put on her mask. The frame was neon pink, the one concession to color in her dive gear, all the rest of which was various faded shades of black. Her backup regulator was yellow, but that wasn't a fashion statement; they were all either yellow or orange, so another diver could locate them easily.

"Sounds good." My regulator was on a seven-foot hose, which I passed under my right arm and then around my neck before settling it into my mouth. It was yellow—a Poseidon Odin—which meant that an out-of-air diver had license to just snatch it out of my mouth, at which point I would move to my backup, an Air II integrated into my BC inflator. It was an arrangement that raised eyebrows on some dive boats, but no one had even commented on it on the *Peabody*. There are lots of cave divers in Florida, as well as wreck divers who have had cave training, and many of them "breathe the long hose."

Ladies first isn't necessarily the protocol when it comes to diving. The first one in the water has to swim out of the way so the next one in doesn't land on top of him.

And when seas are rough, you're apt to be breathing off your regulator and using up air. True, most women only use about half the air that a man would huff and puff during a dive, but there's this whole hair-shirt attitude about air consumption among divers.

I've known guys who consistently come out of the water with headaches because they've been skip-breathing—holding their breath between inhalations—in a vain attempt to come out of the water with more air.

I was under no such illusions. Sheila was an experienced diver, and with less body mass she'd use less air. It was simple physiology. But it was still polite to go in first and get out of her way, so I stood with both fins jutting out over the void in the open dive gate, then took one giant step forward.

The transition from air to water was the surprise it always was, the space around me filled with bubbles from the air pulled with me when I jumped, the weight of the equipment evaporating the moment I'd begun the drop.

Beneath my feet, I could barely make out the white nylon line marking the working grids on the sand bottom. Off to my right, a solitary southern stingray was winging its way out of the territory, no doubt startled by my splash.

Then the buoyancy of my vest began tugging me upward, and I kicked to help myself along. The surface broke, revealing sky, puffy clouds, a generator thrumming, and a dozen voices speaking to one another—the working sounds of the *Peabody*.

Touching my head with my right hand in the OK signal, I added a touch of air to my BC with my left and kicked to the side to open an ample clear space beneath the dive gate. I looked up to the boat and called, "Clear!"

Up on the boat, Sheila put a hand on her mask and giant-strided off into space. Three seconds later, she surfaced next to me, her blue eye and her brown eye beaming back at me from within the pink frame of the mask.

"You," I said, "are just about the prototypical water baby, aren't you?"

"Are you kidding? If it wasn't for the fact that I'd go all pruney,

I'd find a way to *live* in this. I'd never leave; Princess Ariel was daft."

I allowed myself an image of Sheila as a mermaid. Then a voice broke in, calling down, "Uh, you dudes, like, ready for the lift?"

Malibu, of course.

"Sure," I told him. "Send it down."

The business end of the air lift was a thick-walled aluminum tube: four inches in diameter, five feet long, and aluminum or not, considerably heavier than it looked. It had marine-grade stainless-steel handles mounted in six different places, and Malibu had looped a line around the rearmost of these to lower the head down to me. He did it slowly, timing his payouts with the rise and fall of the boat. I waited until the head was all the way into the water before calling, "Got it." Then Malibu slacked the line, and I took it off, filling my BC almost all the way full to offset the weight of the tube.

Attached to the tail end of the tube was twenty meters of what looked like heavy-duty dryer hose, most of it still up on the deck of the *Peabody*. On its very end would be fifty meters of line, tied off to an orange mooring buoy. The idea was that, hopefully, the current would be running in roughly the same direction as the surface current and that would carry the tailings plume—the light stuff lifted and ejected by the lift—away from our work area. It didn't always work; on some sites, the wind-driven surface current and the prevailing bottom currents run counter to each other, and you'd wind up working in an underwater sandstorm. But it wasn't very windy. Just a light breeze was blowing, so we were hoping for fairly straightforward working conditions.

"Okay," I told Sheila. "I'll swim the head down. If you can help feed from up here, so we don't get any air trapped in the tubing, I can get it down by myself, no problem. Then you can swim the hose down to me and we'll rock and roll. Okay?"

"I prefer bluegrass."

She meant it as a joke, so I forced a laugh.

"Cool," I said. I looked up at Malibu and Mikey. " 'Kay, guys. Taking it down."

Descending was not a problem. The head of the air lift weighed a good thirty pounds. All I had to do was vent a little gas from my BC and the air lift pulled me under. I aimed it in the direction of the square with the timbers, trimmed out my body so I was tagging along behind it, and steered with my fins, adding the odd puff of gas back to the BC to keep from dropping too quickly.

Down on the site, the salvage divers had left a weight belt with sixty pounds of lead on it, and I knelt to loop this through the two rearmost handles on the lift head. Sixty-six feet of tubing with air bubbles in it can get light enough to pull a diver right up off the bottom. I lifted my exhaust hose and vented all the gas out of my BC, leaning back and lifting my left shoulder to get it all out. The walking-in-space illusion of weightlessness left me. I was subject to gravity again—maybe not enough to make me feel as if I were kneeling back on the deck of the boat, but enough to give me a little more control over the air lift.

The gurgle of a second regulator sounded somewhere above me. I twisted and saw Sheila, her body spectral against the glare of the surface, drooping slowly toward me, the spider's thread of a three-eighths-inch air hose trailing behind her. She waggled her fingers in greeting and I waved back.

Sheila settled next to me and, sliding back the collar on the air-hose coupling, slid it onto the elbow valve on the lift while I held the tube steady. She gave the hose a little tug, nodded, and I opened the valve just a little. The tubing quivered, accompanied by the gurgle of bubbles colliding with its corrugated interior as they rose.

Now it was my turn to nod, and Sheila took hold of the center set of handles while I grabbed the ones nearest the open end. I cracked the valve a little further and we went to work.

Using an air lift is something of an art. First there's the air pressure. Use too much, and all it does is blast air toward the surface—the lift needs to send up smaller bubbles that can expand as the hydrostatic pressure lessens, fill the tube once they near the end of it and create a pocket of low pressure that pulls the water upward through the tube. Likewise, if you use too little pressure, the bubbles might not get large enough, or could do so intermittently, causing the lift to work in fits and starts.

But use the lift with a moderate flow of air running up the tube, and it will draw water—and sand, and algae, and grit, and silt, and just about any other sort of particulate overburden up off a site, both more quickly and more effectively than you could do it by hand.

Running such a lift looks a lot like operating an oversize version of one of those open-tube vacuum cleaners they have at coin-operated car washes. And the principle is pretty much the same, except the machine you put fifty cents in at the car wash isn't constantly trying to pull you toward the surface, which is why a lift the size we were using is generally run by two people. One helps hold it down while the other guides the mouth.

I ran it first, removing the sand with which Malibu and Panhead Mikey had re-covered the planking the day before. As I guided the head of the air lift five inches or so over the bottom, sand rose in a miniature tornado and disappeared up the tube.

A small school of cream-colored goatfish, their barbels drooping like Pancho Villa mustaches, began following the airhead at a distance of two or three feet, puffing at the edges of the cleared sand and feasting on the tiny crustaceans burrowed into it. Their bodies were each marked with a small dark rectangle right in the middle of their lateral lines, a bit of coloration without which the foot-long fish would be virtually indistinguishable against the sand.

A tiny brown damselfish began picking over the cleared wood as well and then—true to its reputation as one of the most ill-tempered fish in the sea—left off its gleaning to make little darting attacks on the goatfish, attempting to drive them away. They backed off at first. Then, the pickings being too good to resist, they ignored the smaller fish's furious inrushes, bobbing over the opened sand and puffing on it, like diner patrons blowing on their coffee to cool it.

The piece of decking was not overly large. Uncovering it took no more than five minutes. Once we had it exposed, I shut down the air lift. We waited until the suction subsided and set the weighted head off to the side, on the bottom, so we could have a closer look.

The wood was remarkably well-preserved, its grain clearly visible and only moderately eroded. We were looking at the upper surface of decking, which tends to look remarkably the same from sailing ship to sailing ship, whether the vessel was constructed in the sixteenth century or the nineteenth. I would know more once I saw its underside, and even more after we had gotten the wood back to the lab and determined the species: whether it was oak or teak.

Feeling at the edge of the wood, finding the boundaries of the piece, Sheila and I used our fingers to scribe lines in the sand about five or six inches away from the wood. When we'd circumscribed the entire piece, I held my hands about a foot apart to indicate the depth of the trench we'd need around it. Actually, in places, I figured we would need it far deeper than that, but a foot would be sufficient to start.

Sheila nodded. This time I took the back part of the lift head, and she would guide the mouth; the sand around the edges was compacted, not recently moved, and excavating it was going to take far longer than it had taken us to uncover the piece.

Sheila opened the air valve a crack, ran the mouth up and down over a little bit of the line we'd scribed, and then lifted the mouth, adjusted the air pressure and lowered it to the sand again. The goatfish rejoined us—the damselfish had apparently ceded the territory and left for parts unknown—and we settled into the work of making the trench.

When we'd stopped to inspect the decking, I'd had a moment to look around and take in the surroundings, featureless as they were. It was just sand in every direction, the nylon lines of the grids like the latitudes and longitudes of a map of the desert. But it had been a moment to register the fact that we were under water, that the sunlight was up there on the surface, too far away to dapple the sand, but enough to light it, and to see some distant garden eels poking weedlike from the bottom and the few fish that populated the sand-bottomed shoals.

But now that we were working on creating the trench, my attention was centered on what we were doing. The current, slight as it was, kept the tail of the tubing and its float angled away from us in a constant direction, and this had to be accommodated with the angle of the air-lift head. When we started, we were on the up-current side of the decking, and the head had to be held almost completely upright to dig a trench immediately adjacent to the wood. But as we worked away around to the sides, we could angle the head and do the job more easily. Then, when we got to the lee side of the wood, that steeper angle allowed us to not only excavate next to the decking but to undermine it somewhat as well.

Our movements fell into a rhythm. Sheila moved the head and I moved with her, able to tell, intuitively, where she was about to go. It was almost like dancing. It had the closeness of dancing. The air lift was tugging, despite the weight I'd added to it, and it was work to resist its buoyancy, to take that away so Sheila could do her work. But it was good to know that I was necessary to her task.

I was absorbed in this reverie of dancing and co-laboring when the sound of the air lift changed. The gurgle of the air and the *shuuush* of the sand being sucked up the tube behind me became a rattling sound—like popcorn, or like an engine pinging.

Sheila heard it as well. She turned and looked at me. I nodded and she shut down the lift. I pointed with my forefinger and middle finger at my eyes, and *she* nodded. She leaned into the lift head, nodded again to let me know she had it, and I let go and swam back in the direction the tube had trailed off into, adding a little air to my BC so I became neutral, a diver once again, rather than a mere bottom-plodder.

I looked up, following the tube. An air lift does not stop lifting matter simply because the air has been cut off. The suction will continue so long as there are bubbles rising within the tube, acting like moving seals. So the lift was still working, and I could clearly see, at its end far above me, a tannish plume of silt and sand being ejected into the current.

I got nearer and saw tiny glints of light dropping bottomward, slipping to and fro like flakes of snow or tiny autumn leaves, hundreds of them. I swam into their midst, held out my hand and caught several. They looked like bits of glass rod, like shiny, translucent pebbles mixed with flat-faceted shards. I took a dive light off the D-ring on my shoulder strap, turned it on, and played it over the pea-size objects in my hand. The dive light restored the sea-filtered spectrum, and they glinted back at me, a dozen or more shades of bright green and red.

Emeralds and rubies . . .

It was raining jewels.

EIGHTEEN

Sitting cross-legged on the deck of the *Regent*, Ted hefted the blood-red gem in his palm. It was heavy, and it shone in the sun, a deep fire glowing in its depths like a distant furnace, stoked and waiting for the crucible. He looked up at Captain Henry and Ben, the first mate. "Is it real?"

"A farthing to a fortune says it is," the captain told him. The pirate turned to the first mate and said, "Go on. Tell him, Ben."

The first mate shifted in his bare feet, like a schoolboy called upon to recite something in class. He cleared his throat.

"It's like this," Ben finally said. "Had you not wrestled that Spaniard out of the magazine on that ship over there?" He nodded toward a three-masted schooner half a mile off their stern. It was engulfed in flames, a thick column of black smoke rising from it. Beyond the doomed vessel, two longboats were dotted sparsely with men—officers of the burning vessel, together with the crew who had refused to join the pirates—pulling away and following the heading that Thatch had assured would take them to the island of Hispaniola. "Well, he would ha' blown his ship and ours to kingdom come," the mate finished.

It was true, and it was the reason Henry Thatch had gone to the drastic measure of ordering the burning of the Spanish ship.

The only thing that kept piracy even moderately safe was the widespread knowledge that resisting a pirate takeover was futile. To do so was to risk one's life. In this case, only the fact that the ship had borne a royal crest—meaning someone was a relative of the Spanish monarch—had kept the pirate from hanging the officers. Captain Thatch despised killing almost as much as he hated slavery; this was common knowledge among his crew. But he hated even more seeing his own men harmed, so he did what was required to ensure their safety.

"I saved myself as much as I saved any of you," Ted pointed out.

Ben grinned, revealing the gap where he had long ago lost a top front tooth.

"That fellow took a shot at you, he did. And he was going for his dirk when you grabbed him round about the arms. The size of you against him, a great thrashing bear of a man. But you know what they say about the size of the fight in the dog; you wrestled him down and done 'im proper. Anybody else, they'd have seen the torch in his hand and lit off for the deck, tried to swim for it. But you saved the ship. The ship and all souls, you did."

Ted rolled his eyes and shook his head.

The mate grinned at the captain. "You're right, sir. He's a bold one, this 'un is."

"Then tell him," Thatch said.

The mate folded his gnarled, leathery hands in front of him. "Well, the thing is, Ted, the men have had a talk, and afore we all split up the takings, we want you to have that there ruby. You know, as a present for that little lady of yours. For your savin' the ship and all."

Ted sucked in his breath and held it. The ruby was worthy of a monarch—the sort of thing one would mount atop a royal scepter. It was little wonder that the duke or baron or don, or whatever he was, had tried to send it to the bottom with the ship. To have it fall into common hands would be seen as an affront greater than its loss to the sea.

He pictured it mounted in gold and dangling on a chain from the ebony neck of Sally Emmons. That would be a thing of rare beauty, indeed.

Ted hefted the stone in his palm again.

"No," he said, carefully returning the ruby to the cask from which it had come, together with three dozen lesser stones, scores of gold coins, and several lengths of gold chain. "My share will suffice. I wish no more than that."

"Bold Ted," the captain said, his voice low, "the men have voted. It was unanimous: not one dissent."

The younger man gazed out at the empty sea on one side of the ship, at the burning vessel and the disappearing longboats on the other. He took off his hat, mopped his brow with his sleeve, and replaced his hat. He stood gracefully to his feet.

"Listen to me, everyone." His voice grew deeper as he called out; he was picking up the captain's tricks. From all about the ship—the bow, the stern, up in the rigging, and around the hold, where bolts of heavy brocaded fabric were being stored—pirates turned his way. Most were grinning, knowing what they'd voted upon. "You do me great honor," Ted told them. "But were I to accept this—this rare gift for the throat of my Sally—I know not where she would wear it. To church, perhaps, but even then, some scoundrel might decide that the taking of such finery is worth a young woman's life."

The men muttered and nodded amongst themselves.

"True, that," Ben said. "The world is full of dirty stinking thieves." And all around him, the crew groused like men who had never stolen a thing, who had not stolen the very gem in question.

"And besides," Ted continued, "this crew has already given me my life. Were it not for you, I would be dead these six months—dead or wishing that I was. So I risked naught when I took that man. I offered only what you had already given me. The share is sufficient. But I thank you for your kindness."

The men fell silent, as if taking time to consider Ted's words.

"Then three cheers," called a man in the rigging.

"Hip, hip . . ." Ben shouted.

"Hoorah," the crew thundered back. And they repeated the exchange twice more before returning to their work, with conversations resuming around the sloop.

"Well said," Thatch told Ted. He smiled. "For a moment there, you sounded like a gentleman."

"A man who sounds like a gentleman was my teacher," Ted told him, bowing slightly as he said it.

Thatch chuckled. "You may yet regret your equanimity, Bold Ted. That ruby is easily the price of a manse and a farm."

"I want neither," Ted told him. "Just a little house on Tortola will do."

"A house?" Thatch arched his eyebrows. "But you are all of what, fifteen years old?"

"I am sixteen come Saturday. And I know fellows my age who are in the ground already and will never see seventeen."

"Well . . ." The captain gazed at the square of patch canvas where the booty from the Spaniard had been heaped. There were cutlasses and dirks, three fine pistols, gold, silver, a pair of chalices worthy of a royal church service, and strings of fine white pearls. "I wish you would take *something*."

Ted looked down at the deck. He noticed a silver handle sticking from the mouth of a small velvet bag. Stooping, he drew the object out, his eyes bright. "This," he said, holding it up. "I would like very much to have this."

"That?" The captain furrowed his brow. "Are you sure? That's worth a couple of quid at very best."

"But, sir, it is what I would like."

"Then it is what you shall have," said the captain.

On the horizon, the burning ship erupted into a smoking orange fireball, barrels spiraling skyward and exploding as the schooner's powder magazine touched off. Just seconds later, the wind of the shock wave reached their vessel, followed immediately by the deep *BOOM* of the blast.

All around the sloop, the pirates cheered.

The voyage back to Tortola took three days. Captain Thatch ordered Ted to plot a course for the *Regent* that took them well north of the usual shipping routes, dropping down to sail into the Virgins from the east. By the third day, the fresh meat and vegetables had run out and they were down to eating salt pork and ship biscuit. But the Spanish ship had been fat with goods and gold, so no one complained. The sloop had the celebratory air of men coming home fresh from a victory in battle.

They reached port on a Friday, and the men drew straws to see who would stand watch and who would go ashore and start the revelries. Ted insisted that Thatch go ashore to his wife, while he stayed on the sloop for the night, sleeping next to the cask of treasure with a loaded pistol at his side, not leaving the cask until the next day when Thatch and a pair of merchants arrived to negotiate over the takings.

The ruby was a sticking point. Neither of the Road Town buyers had the cash to purchase it, not even at the greatly diminished price the pirates were asking. But one buyer put up his home and shop as surety and carried it away wrapped in cotton and secured in his purse, saying that he had a contact in St. Eustatius, a port so rich that it was known as the "Golden Rock." A fortnight was agreed upon as enough time for him to sail there and make a bargain.

Ted decided to remain on the sloop Saturday night as well. Then early Sunday morning, he roused the grumbling cook, and the two of them heated enough fresh water for Ted to wash and don his best clothes, and by dawn he and a few of the crew were in a longboat, pulling across the glass-still waters for the shore.

He walked from the dock to The Rose and Crown, the velvet bag clasped carefully in both hands, and tried the door to the public room. It was unlocked, and when he entered, after his eyes had adjusted to the darkness within, he saw Oscar Emmons at the bar at the far end of the room, trimming the wick on a lamp.

"Sally is upstairs, dressing for church," the innkeeper said by way of a greeting.

"Yes, sir," Ted said. "I thought that would be the case. I came early to see you."

"See me?" Emmons put the chimney back on the lamp and wiped his hands on a towel. "For what purpose?"

"To give you something, sir."

Emmons straightened up. "I can purchase my needs, and those of my house and my inn, as well."

"I have no doubt you can, sir." Ted walked to him, holding the velvet bag like a cushion upon his open palms. "But this is something I've not seen in Road Town."

"And what would that be?"

Ted opened the drawstring on the bag and drew out a saucer-size convex lens, mounted on a silver handle.

"What is that?" Emmons said, squinting at the strange object.

"It is a hand lens, sir."

"And what use have I of it?"

"Have you your Bible?"

Scowling, Emmons fetched the leather-bound book from a table near the door.

"Bring it here, sir," Ted said, moving nearer to the window. "To the light."

Emmons did as Ted asked, untying the book's cover. "I have told you that I cannot make out the letters," he said. "Is it your purpose to mock me, boy?"

"It is nothing of the sort." Ted accepted the Bible from Emmons and, turning the pages slowly and reverently, went to First Corinthians 13:12, the verse with the little crude drawing of a looking glass penciled into the margin.

"Here." Ted held the hand lens above the page, demonstrating its use, and then offered both book and glass to the innkeeper. "Have a look."

Still scowling, Oscar Emmons took the glass and looked through it at the finely printed page.

His scowl disappeared.

Ever so slightly, his mouth dropped open.

"The letters," he said, his voice barely audible. "They are . . . like when Sally tried to show me, when she chalked them on a piece of slate. I can—" He stopped, blinked, and handed the glass back to Ted. "I've no coin to spare for such niceties."

"Nor have I," Ted told him. "Fortunately for us, this cost me nothing. And the price to you is the same."

Emmons softened again for a moment. Then he squinted and said, "This is pirate booty—you stole it, did you not?"

Ted smiled. "I took it from the cabin of a Spanish prince's nephew. He was in the process of trying to light a powder magazine and send this glass, his ship, his crew, and himself to the bottom of the Mona Passage. So the way I see it, the fool was throwing it away. All I did was keep it from going to the sea bottom. And kept him alive in the process. I imagine he is swatting mosquitoes about four days east of Nativita about now."

Emmons looked at the glass in his hand, held it once again above the page.

"It is a wonder," he murmured. "Never in my days would I have thought that I . . ." He paused and looked up, but he no longer tried to hand back the magnifying glass.

"It is something you need," Ted offered. "To read God's Word. And once I knew that, it was laid at my feet. Does that strike you as a stroke of chance?"

"But you *took* it."

"When Israel came into possession of the land of Canaan, was it a gift?"

Emmons stole another look through the glass, stopped himself.

"I have very little Latin within me," Ted said, his voice low. "But these two words I do remember: *Dominus providat*. Do you know what that means?"

Emmons mutely shook his head.

"It means, 'God will provide.' " Ted touched the Bible. "Will provide what you need. To live. To care for your family. To worship Him."

Oscar looked at the words through the glass, his eyes moist.

"It is yours," Ted told him.

"It," Oscar said, "is a great treasure."

NINETEEN

I used to laugh at what people thought treasure hunting was like. Most people imagine a sunken shipwreck to resemble that little ceramic ornament you see in a home aquarium: a ghostly, skeletal hulk of a wreck with pennants still drooping from the mast tops. Truth is, most wrecks are half-buried in silt and sand.

Then there's the treasure itself. In popular imagination, it's always in an iron-belted, arch-topped chest, popped open and overflowing with scepters, tiaras, rings, jewels, and coins—gold coins, because silver's too pedestrian for a fantasy. But the fact of the matter is that much of the gold recovered from shipwrecks— when gold is recovered at all—is in the forms of flakes and nuggets: pieces so miniscule that they have to be sorted and separated from the sand with tweezers. One intact coin is a rare find. A dozen of them is a mother lode. To uncover a single bar of bullion, you might have to move hundreds of tons of sand and ballast stones, because most known shipwrecks got visited by salvors shortly after they went down, particularly if the wreck was shallow enough to free-dive.

But heaps of coins and jewels? That's a one in a million occurrence. Looking for treasure is like hunting for the proverbial needle in a haystack.

Yet there we were in the mess of the *Peabody*. Sheila and I were both in board shorts and T-shirts, our hair still wet from the showers we'd taken to rinse off the salt. Phil and Betty were there too.

And there on the table, in neat little squared-off piles on more than twenty sheets of white paper, were not hundreds of jewels but thousands of them: 4,736, according to Betty Rackham's count. In addition to emeralds and rubies, there were topaz, sapphires, even a few yellow diamonds. Several of the emeralds were as big as the first joint of my thumb, and a couple of the rubies were nearly as large and had already been cut in the pillow-like fashion of earlier times. Most of the stones were uncut and pea-size or smaller. Still, it was impressive as all get-out.

If anything, it was a bit *more* than what most people imagine when they think about treasure diving. It had taken both of Sheila's and my BC pockets—plus all four of our dive gloves and Sheila's hood, filled and zip-tied shut—to bring it all up. Yet somehow it looked like more out on the table, sorted and rough-graded, than it had looked scattered and pocketed on the bottom.

I checked my dive watch, an older Citizen Aqualand my mother had gotten for me about a month after I'd been certified as a diver. It was the analog model, recently discontinued back then, so she'd gotten it on sale. The history of the watch was a recollection that I'd tried without much success to distance myself from over the years, but I still wore it constantly. There was no way I could leave it in a drawer.

It had been about three hours since Sheila and I had gotten out of the water. Only Phil and Betty had handled the stones, and it was pretty impressive, how much they'd managed to do with them.

There was a quick double knock at the hatch to the mess. Jack Egan stepped in.

"Wow," he said. This was a man who rarely used the word. He looked at Sheila and me. "Do you think you got it all?"

I thought for a second. "Everything that went up the air lift, yes. That was all lying in a big teardrop pattern on the bottom under the outflow, and the sand there was pretty well compacted, so nothing sunk in. Then we went back to the decking and turned the lift on again but held it about a foot off the bottom, so there was only enough suction to lift sand, and we hand-fanned the spot we'd been working to clear the overburden, and found a second pocket. They were all very close together. It looked as if they had been sewn into sacks back in the day. Of course the fabric's long since rotten and dissolved away. But as to whether we got everything that's under the decking . . ."

I turned and looked at Sheila. She shook her head.

"There could easily be a third sack," I told Jack and Phil and Betty. "Maybe more. We won't know until we lift the decking. And now that we know there may be small items under it, we can't use the air lift to help bore the pass-throughs for the support piping. We'll have to dig by hand. Maybe put scoops on the ends of broom handles or something to be able to reach all the way under. It'll be slow going. But unless you want to risk destroying the decking, it's what we have to do."

"Do it," Phil said. "We don't throw curation to the winds just because there's a paycheck coming up. And take what time you need. That decking's probably been there almost five hundred years. It can wait a few hours, or a few days, if necessary."

He turned to Jack. "Crew know about the communications blackout?"

The captain nodded. "Cell phones won't work here; we're too far out. But I collected 'em all anyhow. They're in my cabin. Broadband's turned off and I locked the satellite phone in my safe."

"Good." Phil looked at the bulkhead, as if he could see through it and into the water beyond. "We don't want a circus out here." He turned to his wife. "What do you figure?"

"Lowball?" Betty consulted the calculator in her hand. She was a nice-looking woman, even in the galley's fluorescent lighting, and that's saying a lot. "I'm saying two million."

"That was my guess." Phil looked at Sheila and me. "Two million dollars. One percent of that is twenty thousand—ten thousand dollars for each of you. Not bad for a single dive."

Sheila blinked.

"For what?" I asked.

"Recovery bonus," Jack said. "Standard share. Divers get one percent of what they bring up."

"It'll probably be more than twenty," Betty added. "But we want you to know that's where we'll start you. We can do a check for each of you right here, or we can run a tab if you want. Just keep track and then pay you once it's all up and a certified gemologist has graded and appraised each stone." She paused, then said, "Then you'll each get your proper share at the end of the year, on top of that, of course."

Sheila and I stared at each other. I ran a hand back through my wet hair.

"But we didn't find the decking," I told Betty. "Malibu and Mikey found it. They stopped clearing because I told them to. Otherwise *they* would have found the stones."

"That just means everybody followed proper procedure," Phil said. "Fact remains, you two brought the rocks up out of the water, so you're the recovery crew. You get the bonus."

"We decided on this years ago," Jack chimed in, "because it solves the chicken-and-the-egg problems, with everybody thinking they have a claim. Even the guy back on the beach, who suggested searching the quadrant. So we've kept it simple. You bring it out of the water, you get the bonus."

Sheila made a come-here motion and I leaned toward her. She whispered in my ear and I listened. Then I nodded.

I turned to Phil. "If it's okay with you, we'd like to split the bonus. Half for us, half for Malibu and Mikey."

Phil looked at his wife. Betty put her hand to her chin. "Are you certain? We could be talking a fair amount of money here. Enough to put a down payment on a house."

I'm fairly certain my face reddened for a second at that last comment. I don't know if Sheila's did, but under the table, out of sight of everyone else, she squeezed my hand.

"We're certain," I told Betty.

"Well." Jack nodded. "Doesn't look as if we'll have to listen to any grumbling from the crew."

We all just stood there for a moment. The mess, big enough to seat twenty people, seemed cavernous with only the five of us there. The light green enameled walls, the distantly antiseptic smell of the spray the cook wiped the tables with, the buzzing of the fluorescents in the silence—all underlined the notion that we were far from shore. Above us, on the deck, a winch was running. Probably putting a RIB in the water to help ward off any curious boaters. As a vessel flying a Delta flag—the international symbol for a ship conducting diving operations—we were entitled to clear water for two hundred yards in all directions, and the recent find was just one more reason to insist upon that right.

The five of us looked at all the stones. Even under the flat fluorescent lighting, the few that were cut sparkled like items in a jewelry store window. And the rest of them gleamed like the precious jewels that they were.

Sighing, Betty picked up two sheets of typing paper from the stack lying at the table's end. Taking a pen from behind her ear, she handed them to Phil and said, "Here. Initial these, sweetie."

He did so without asking why—the silent compliance of a man long married to the same woman.

Betty folded both sheets of paper in thirds and reopened them. Then, picking up a long pair of plastic tweezers, she bent over the stones and, after puzzling over them for a moment, selected four stones: two emeralds and two rubies. There was a jeweler's scale on the table and she weighed them. Each was about four carats in size, uncut.

She put one ruby and one emerald in the center of each sheet of paper. Then she folded the papers in thirds again, the way I'd seen diamond brokers do it in the shops in New York, sliding one side into another to make an envelope that the stones could not fall out of. Phil Rackham's initials were clearly visible on the outside of each one.

"Here," Betty said. She handed one pair of stones to me, the other to Sheila.

"What's this for?" Sheila asked.

Betty smiled. "For being the sort of people that we are very proud to have serving on our crew."

Everyone smiled, and the room seemed to broaden, and Sheila McIntyre's hand was in mine. It was small and it was warm and I squeezed it and she squeezed back, and the room seemed to broaden even more.

TWENTY

I'd suggested scoops on the end of broomsticks for the next stage of the excavation, which shows why I'm a marine archaeologist and not a marine engineer. Broomsticks would have floated: not an ideal attribute in a tool intended to be used fifteen meters under water. Then there was the question of how the scoops were to be attached to the broomsticks; even duct tape has its limits when it's being continually soaked in salt water.

Fortunately, in addition to being a U.S. Coast Guard-certified captain, Jack Egan *is* a marine engineer. Which is why it took him all of about six seconds to press the button on the ship's intercom speaker on the mess bulkhead and ask for a deckhand to meet him up on deck with two six-foot lengths of three-quarter-inch IPS galvanized steel pipe and a TIG welder. Then he went to the tray of dishwasher baskets, where the cook kept the clean flatware, selected two soup spoons and turned to Sheila and me.

"I figure we've got a good nine hours of daylight left," Jack said. "You two up for another dive or two?"

I nodded. Sheila did as well.

"Start gearing up, then."

By the time we'd analyzed fresh tanks and put our gear together, Jack had turned the pipes and spoons into digging tools by first bending the spoons at an angle and then welding them to the ends of the lengths of pipe.

"Can't guarantee them unbreakable," he told us as he handed them to us. "But until Trudy starts locking up the flatware, I can always make more if these two break."

Once we got under water, the cobbled-together tools worked surprisingly well, slow but well. We began tunneling under the decking just by using our ungloved hands, and we actually found a few more emeralds that way. We put those into a fine-meshed bag that we'd brought along for the purpose. It's amazing how quickly something like finding precious stones on the seafloor can almost become routine.

Phil had come along on this dive and was shooting what we did with a camcorder in a submersible housing.

I suppose a person could view that as intrusive; the DVD would, after all, provide a video record against which our take from this dive could be audited and compared. But I doubted that was Phil's intention. Video such as this can be pure gold for investor presentations. There's no better way to show the viability of a treasure hunt than to show actual treasure being found. And I was already learning that Phil was just too ethical to do as many outfits did and salt the site with previously recovered artifacts so a cameraperson could record the salvage divers "discovering" them.

Making the tunnel for the first piece of pipe took forty minutes, and we found a dozen more emeralds, all near the place where we'd started the hole. To get the tool through and to keep it close to the decking we used the air lift, carefully digging out a basin next to the planking, which gave us room to work the long steel-pipe handles. I went up to ten feet, did a five-minute safety stop, surfaced to get the right length of PVC, then took it down so we could snake it under the decking.

Afterward we came up to swap tanks and take the hour of surface interval required by the rules of the boat.

Malibu handed cold bottles of water to the three of us.

"Mikey and I can jump in and keep going on what you're doing down there," he told Phil.

Phil shook his head. "Thanks, man, but research staff only for the time being. That wood is pretty fragile. We need to control who's working around it."

Malibu shot me a look that was ice cold. He'd seen the gemstones come out of the water on both dives. And apparently nobody had told him and Mikey that Sheila and I were splitting our bonuses with them. So from the way he probably saw things, we were eating his lunch and there was nothing he could do about it. I shrugged it off; he'd learn soon enough that we'd thought of him.

The third dive of the day was anticlimactic. No jewels showed up in the sand we were carefully spooning out from under the large, flat piece of planking. In fact, nothing came out but sand. I went back to the surface, making a brief safety stop before fetching another length of PVC pipe.

We slid it under the decking smoothly—no obstructions and no issues. Two pieces of pipe in place, with three to go.

By that time, an hour was up. The sun was low in the west and light was falling on the seafloor. Even the goatfish had left the site, swimming off to wherever it is that goatfish go at night. The little damselfish had come back and, having no other fish to hassle, burned off its excess calories by attacking us, nipping aggressively at our exposed hands. It felt as if someone was picking at them with a soft pair of plastic tweezers, so we ignored the little creature, which only seemed to deepen its fury. As I used Phil's homemade tool to ream out the PVC pipe and make sure it was clear, the tiny fish chomped down with its entire quarter-inch of mouth on the hair on the back of my hand. I remembered what one of my dive instructors had told me: *"If damselfish were four feet long instead of four inches, scuba diving would not exist, because nobody would ever go into the ocean."*

I checked the dive computer on my instrument console. We'd had plenty of surface interval between our three dives, and we even had a good reserve of air left in our cylinders. But we'd been in the water, off and on, for nearly three hours. Even the warm subtropical water off the Keys begins to feel a bit chilly at that point, and cold and tired divers are divers on the verge of making mistakes. I turned to Sheila and Phil, shrugged and showed them a thumbs-up.

Both nodded. We gathered our tools and headed for the surface.

Panhead Mikey helped Sheila and me break down and rinse our gear once we were out.

"Dudes," he said, apparently forgetting that the word is supposed to be gender specific, "Hans, like, told us what you two asked to do with the finder's bonus. I just wanted to let you know that that is totally righteous, man. I mean, really. It's heavy. Awesome, you know?"

Once he got his emotions going, listening to Panhead Mikey talk was more an exercise in sensing and interpreting biker aura than it was an exchange of ideas.

As for Malibu, he was rinsing down the air lift with a freshwater hose, his back turned to the three of us as he worked.

With only three divers working in the water on this particular day, Hans had rounded up some of the crew and ran them over in the RIB to a tongue-and-groove reef system for an afternoon of spearing, and that meant dinner was black grouper, amberjack and hogfish, served with potatoes and broccoli, all cooked with fresh-squeezed key lime juice and hot off the grill.

Sheila and I took our plates up to the bollard in the bow. She wrinkled her nose as I took a bottle of Tabasco sauce out of my pocket, dotted my slab of grilled hogfish, and capped the little bottle back up. "What? You like bluegrass but you won't eat food cooked with real Southern seasoning?"

"I tried a drop of it on my finger once. Made my eyes water, it did."

"That's because it's made to be put on food, not fingers." I uncapped the bottle again, sliced off a tiny white cube of fish, and anointed it with a drop. "Let it soak in a second and then try it. And if it's still too hot, eat your dinner roll. Water will just make the hot last longer."

She looked at me sideways—those blue and brown eyes— and used her fork to cut the little bite of fish in half. She tried it, chewing tentatively. Then she chewed faster. She took the other half of the bite of fish. Then, grinning, she motioned for the bottle.

"Another convert sees the light," I said.

Sheila glanced at me, opened her mouth to speak, then looked back down at her plate. She dotted her grilled fish with the red pepper sauce.

Knowing when I've crossed a line—at least *this* time I knew—I said nothing more, but launched into my dinner.

We ate for the next several minutes in silence. Maybe it was the overwhelming nature of it all, finding more gemstones in one day than I daresay either of us had ever seen in our entire lives. Maybe it was Sheila's hails-from-down-under discovery of Tabasco sauce. Maybe it was my mimicry of what I knew to be Sheila's faith. Okay—probably it was that last one.

There were low clouds on the horizon. Nothing ominous, just the sort of cumulus you see near the horizon when in or near the tropics.

Finishing her plate, Sheila said, "No green flash tonight."

"If we want a green flash, we can probably ask Jack for a peek into the safe. Green flash, red flash, yellow . . ."

Sheila stretched. "One time I was diving off Heron Island along the Great Barrier Reef. A wall dive, it was. And I was next to this great fold in the wall when a smallish spotted eagle ray comes flapping along, straight toward me. And I'm all, 'Look at this, a spotted eagle ray, and I can get a pic that shows the face and not the bum,' which is usually all I get of a spotted eagle ray. So I raise my camera and I'm just about to snap, when all of a sudden—BAM!—this absolutely huge hammerhead comes darting out of the fold in the wall, and he nails the eagle ray.

"It was so quick—no way the eagle ray ever knew what hit him. And this hammerhead is shaking his head like a dog with a rat, and there's little bits of eagle ray going every which way in the water, which I know sounds rather disgusting, but at the time it was just . . . this reminder, you know? That we—the ray, the shark, the divemaster I was diving with—that we were all right there, in that moment. Like watching one of those nature spectaculars, only this wasn't film. It was there in the water with us. I even got the shot. It ended up in a magazine, back in Queensland."

I took her empty plate, set it atop mine on the deck. "Must have been amazing."

"Oh, it was all that. It was astounding."

We could not see the sun, but the clouds on the horizon were rimmed in gold, rays of light streaming up from them in that effect that nineteenth-century painters used to imply the presence of the Creator. There's a name for those rays—not the "God rays" that everybody uses in everyday speech, but a term that's technically correct—and I tried to think of it. But I couldn't. Reticular rays?

"For years," Sheila said, her voice low, I imagine because the setting sun seemed to call for a lowered voice, "that was my very best day, *ever*, under water."

"But not anymore?"

She shook her head, smiling that small smile of hers. "Not after today."

She put her hand in mine, rested her head on my shoulder.

Then somebody behind us cleared his throat, said, "Uh . . . dude?"

We turned. It was Malibu. He had a banjo case in his hands.

"Listen," he said. "What you told Phil you wanted to do with the finder's bonus. That's . . . well, it's totally skeggin', you know?"

I wondered to myself what it sounded like when Malibu and Mikey were by themselves, talking to each other.

"It was our pleasure, Malibu," Sheila told him.

"Don't get me wrong." Malibu shifted the banjo case in his hands; he was holding it by the body, not the handle, and it looked awkward. "I mean, this might not be a cool, uh, precedent, you know?"

Precedent? I wondered where that word had come from. Obviously 'Bu had rehearsed this speech with a little help.

"In what way?" I asked.

"Well, you know. Like you find this stuff today, and you split it with Mikey and me, and what if we find this, like, really huge gold cross or altarpiece or something next week. Then, well . . ."

"There's no quid pro quo," I told him. He looked at me as

if I were speaking Greek, which I very nearly was. "I mean, we shared with you today because it's what you would have found anyhow if you'd kept on working the quadrant you'd been assigned to when we started working this site. So we wanted to be fair. But whatever you find on your dives, well, you're the salvage diver. It's your bonus. We don't expect any payback. Don't want it, in fact. It wouldn't be right."

"Oh." Malibu still seemed to be mulling over *quid pro quo.* "Well, uh, cool then."

He stepped forward and held out the banjo case.

"Here, dude," he said. "It's yours."

I smiled, found myself cocking my head. "Malibu, you don't have to give me your banjo."

"Yeah I do." Malibu set the banjo case on the deck next to me. "And not because you're, like, turning me on to the five grand and all. Panhead Mikey's right, dude. I stink at this. And you don't. So, like, enjoy."

He held both hands out as he said that, and I let go of Sheila's hand and shook his.

Malibu looked down between Sheila and me, at where our hands had been. "Were you two, like, holding hands?"

I didn't answer, but Sheila said, "We were."

Malibu looked at me. "Was she reading your palm or something?"

"No."

"Then why . . . ?" Malibu glanced back and forth at the two of us.

Sheila laughed. "I was holding Greg's hand because I'm fond of him, Malibu. Quite fond of him, in fact." She rubbed my shoulder.

"You're fon—" Malibu turned to me and his eyes grew wide. "Dude," he said, "you cracked the code!"

And with that he was gone, and it was just Sheila and me, and the bollard, and the banjo.

She was laughing.

I took both of her hands. Looked her in the eyes. "You're fond of me?"

"Well." She traced a fingertip on the back of my hand, then looked up at me. Her voice dropped to a whisper. "I wanted it to be just the two of us the first time I said that I loved you."

TWENTY-ONE

I love you.

Sally Emmons mouthed the words to Bold Ted as he handed her the dainty handkerchief she had dropped on the seat of the backless pew between them; dropped it in such a way that their eyes would meet as he retrieved it and returned the tiny lace-edged square of linen to her.

He didn't dare speak back, not even silently. Her father had relented and let them sit together, but he and two other elders of the church were on the selfsame pew, just on the other side of Sally, and all three were turned Ted's way, watching the exchange.

So he only nodded, but even that was enough to earn him a rumbling throat clearing from Oscar Emmons. Ted sat up straight, feeling vaguely like a schoolchild, and imagined what it would be like to steal a kiss from Sally, right there in the front pew of the little church, while the curate dispensed the biblical story of Balaam's ass from the plain wooden pulpit, one creaking word at a time.

He glanced again at Sally, but her bonnet hid her face. He could see the Bible open on Oscar Emmons's knees, could barely make out the tiny horseshoe penciled in the margin. And he noticed with satisfaction that Oscar was using the hand lens to follow along.

"'House . . . full . . . of . . . silver,'" the curate intoned.

"'. . . and gold,'" Oscar whispered loudly, finishing the phrase.

Up at the pulpit, the curate blinked. "'And gold,'" he confirmed.

Sally looked at Ted and beamed.

Her father cleared his throat again.

"Wait here," Oscar Emmons said to Ted. Sally had gotten up to speak to the curate's spinster daughter at the end of the service; it was only the two men left at the pew.

Ted stayed near the pew, on his feet yet not going anywhere, while the church quickly emptied, the congregants walking the few steps out to the stoop and then gathering on the cropped turf. He could hear women talking about which farmers had suckling pigs for sale, the men arguing politics based upon news gleaned from four-month-old London broadsheets.

At last, an elderly deacon hobbled out, leaning heavily upon his walking stick. Oscar and Ted had the little stone church to themselves, and the older man stepped up onto the platform.

"Come up here, son."

Ted hesitated and Oscar chuckled. "We aren't papists, boy. No one is going to excommunicate you for stepping up to the front of the church."

Grinning sheepishly, hat in his hand, Ted stepped up onto the platform.

"Now take the pulpit, son."

Ted turned. "Take it?"

"Step into it, son. Stand where the preacher stands."

"But . . . ." Ted glanced at the door of the church.

"Stop gawking and get up there, boy," Oscar Emmons told him. "I paid for a carpenter from Saint Thomas to repair that

182

pulpit. I imagine it gives me some say in who stands in it. Now stand in it."

Ted mounted the two steps to the pulpit. He stood in it, left hand gripping the side, right hand holding firmly on to both it and his hat, as if he expected the old pulpit to take off at any moment and go galloping around the room.

"Look out the front door," Oscar commanded. "Tell me what you see."

Ted looked. "I see the Drake Strait."

"How much of it?"

Ted squinted. "All the way to Virgin Gorda."

"And what does that tell you?"

Ted thought about it. "That nothing can pass through and leave the strait without first being seen from this pulpit."

Oscar smiled. "Excellent; now step down. You are no preacher."

Ted descended the two shallow steps, and the two men walked toward the door of the church.

"The situation of that pulpit is no accident," Oscar told the younger man. "The first preacher to pastor this church was a pirate. At any moment during his message he could call out 'Sail!' and he and the congregation would empty into boats at the very stones where my little skiff is now tied off. And they would race out and take the unfortunate merchant."

Ted looked up at him slowly. "A preacher?"

Oscar nodded. "A man of God. And I tell you this, son, not to bless your course but to tell you of one end to it. Remember I said that I paid to have that pulpit repaired?"

Ted nodded.

"Well, one Sunday morning some Spaniards came ashore up the coast, walked here, came to that doorway and emptied three muskets into that pulpit while the preacher was starting his sermon. He was dead before he could say 'Beloved.'"

They got to the door. Emmons looked out at the broad blue water of the strait and weighed the Bible in his big left hand. He took a deep breath and turned to Ted. "Tell me something, son. Do you love my daughter?"

Ted kept his hat off. "I do, sir. Very much."

"It is your intention, then, to someday marry?"

Ted worked his thumb on the edge of his hat. "When I can build us a house, sir. If she will have me . . . and you will bless us."

"And Henry Thatch," Oscar said, "he is your best friend, is he not?"

"Sir, I owe him my life. He has been nothing but kind to me."

Emmons looked at the strait again. "He has been nothing but kind to me also, and to my daughter, and to my neighbors. He is partner to half the businesses in these islands. Has lands in England and Carolina too, if what I hear is true. Yet he is a pirate."

Ted cleared his throat. "Sir, he is a privateer. I have seen the letter of marque with my own eyes."

Oscar put on his hat. "You have seen parchment, son. And yes, that is the Lord Governor's own signature upon it. And yes, I have heard the story Henry tells, and England does dispute the claims of Spain, and France, and Holland to these islands. As they do ours. But we have had no war with Spain for more than ten years now. We have had peace—uneasy peace but peace all the same—with the Dutch for fifty. And a truce was signed with France nigh on a century ago."

Ted looked up at the older man, waiting.

"King George has authorized no letters of marque, son," Emmons told Ted. "The parchment Captain Henry has is simply an instrument that adds the appearance of legitimacy to his arrangement with the Lord Governor and the captain of the garrison. Henry gives five percent of what he takes to the governor and half that to the garrison, and they give him safe haven and shield him from prosecution. But it is a sham, and the only reason it has worked thus far is because London is more than a thousand leagues distant. Yet George is building his navy, and distance is less protection with each day."

"But . . ." Ted took a step nearer to Emmons as he spoke. "But Captain Henry speaks of it as if there is no guile."

Emmons nodded. "Henry has told the lie for so long that now he believes it the truth."

Ted shook his head. "I feel certain you are misinformed, sir."

"Are you telling me that you have never heard talk of this from others in Road Town?"

Ted crossed his arms. "Road Town is full of gossips."

It was an insult, and obviously meant as such. But Emmons did not take the bait. He shifted his Bible from his left hand to his right, then rested his empty hand softly on the younger man's shoulder.

"There was news from London with my barrels of brandywine this week." He looked askance at Ted. "Brandywine that made it past you and Thatch, so I paid full price. Anyhow, there was news that King George has offered a pardon to any member of the brotherhood who will sign the pardon and offer to pirate no more. But it has to be signed before Christmas. That's six months away. A long time by some accounts, yet I would not believe that His Majesty would place credence in any document sent him by a Caribbean governor. That would mean a man would have to go to Carolina to sign it, and Carolina is a journey."

Ted squinted and put on his hat, an action that caused the other man's hand to slide from his shoulder. "Are you telling me I must take this pardon if I am to marry your daughter?"

Sally was already down at the water's edge with two of the

ladies from the church. Shaking his head, Oscar began walking toward his skiff.

"I am telling you," he said over his shoulder, "that I do not wish to see my daughter a spinster. But I wish to see her a widow even less."

TWENTY-TWO

Suspended in a dark-surrounded orb, the edges of the circle tinged the colors of the rainbow, the three-masted ship showed its stern castle and beat through the afternoon waves of the Atlantic.

"Why does he run?" Ted asked the question without taking the spyglass from his eye. "We are faster than him. We have gained more than a mile in the last quarter hour. He cannot escape."

"He is giving his passengers and crew time to hide the valuables," Henry Thatch said. Both men shifted their weight to keep their balance as the *Regent* completed the end of a leg. Their quarry kept trying to turn away from the direction of the Jamaica-built sloop's tack, trying to get enough space to come about and run with the wind. It was a futile gesture; under full sail, the smaller ship would only close the distance faster.

"We will have to take the entire ship," Thatch thought aloud. "That will give us time to find at our leisure the doubloons they are presently sewing into the mattress ticking in the passengers' cabins. And even then, these Dutchmen are prone to having their women tuck the wealth away beneath their skirts."

"That would stop a gentleman," Ted said, watching the ship.

"A pity that they are in short supply here," Thatch replied. He wasn't laughing.

Ted collapsed the spyglass, slid it into its leather case, and tucked it into the sash at his waist, next to a brace of loaded pistols. He put a hand on the rail to steady himself as the *Regent* lifted over the crest of a wave.

"What do you think of the king's pardon?" He did not look at Thatch as he asked the question but kept his eyes on the fleeing ship.

Thatch said nothing.

"There is talk in the town that our letter of marque is a sham," Ted said. "That the king will never honor it. But he will honor his own pardon."

Thatch smoothed his beribboned beard with his hand. "Were that true, that would make us innocent in London's eyes. But to Madrid, and Paris?"

He nodded in the direction of the three-masted ship. Men were running to and fro on its deck, and someone had climbed up to a yardarm and was staring back at them through a telescope. "And to Amsterdam as well . . . We would remain felons and thieves. No longer active, perhaps, yet guilty nonetheless."

"They could pursue us only by crossing your king."

"And cross him they have, many times in the past."

Ted turned, putting his back to the fleeing Dutchman, so he could look Thatch full in the face. "When the hare is pursued by the fox, he takes to his burrow, even though the fox can dig. He does it because to stay aboveground would be madness. And we could settle in an English country—in England herself, should we wish to be safest. We could stay on Tortola should the crown decide to garrison more troops there."

Both men bowed their heads as spindrift sprayed over the bow from one of the larger swells.

"This is odd counsel," Thatch said, "from a man who wants to have his own sloop so he can sail away to Africa, kill an old vicar, and no doubt face the gallows the next morning. Who would risk a life of leisure with a beautiful woman at his side, the prospect of children, of grandchildren, all for one minute's revenge."

More spray came over the bow, and both men held their hats and hunched as it passed.

"Your Anne and my Sally do more than read together, you know." Ted looked at the tacking Dutchman as he said it. "Sally says that oftentimes when we are out here on the sea, Mistress Anne weeps, afeard that she shall never see you again."

"And what of your Sally? Does she weep in my Anne's arms over your plot to kill the old Scotsman? Or have you not shared that particular madness with her yet?"

Ted said nothing and Thatch laughed. "I give you leave to work upon my reformation, Bold Ted, so long as you will grant me leave to work upon yours."

The Dutch ship turned as dark squares appeared in the side of its hull—four of them.

"The idiot," Thatch slapped the sloop's rail. "He is running out his guns."

One hand on his sheathed cutlass, he turned to face his ship.

"Ready these bow cannon," he called back. "Grease the rounds so the powder stays dry as we close, and plug your touchholes until we are ready. Ben, put us around in her stern quarter and then keep us there."

Four men raced forward and began loading the four-pounders in the bow of the sloop. The boom creaked against the mast while the sloop took a steep heel, turning to get into the one spot not covered by the Dutchman's cannon.

For the next half hour the two ships ducked and weaved, trying to place themselves at an advantage, into a position from which they could fire without being fired upon. Ted and Thatch watched the Dutchman run.

"It is exhilarating, is it not?" Thatch raised his voice to be heard above the breeze moaning through the taut lines supporting their mast. "Moments such as this, with the quarry at hand, the prospect of a bit of a fight. It puts the life back into you."

"It can take the life back out as well," Ted said.

Thatch folded his arms. "You have earned your share through your navigation. You needn't board this Dutchman if you haven't the heart for it."

Ted bit his lip. "I shall be first over the rail."

"A curious course for a pilgrim." Thatch stepped forward and clasped a gunner by the shoulder. "Loose one into her sails, would you, Tom?"

The gunner looked back at the helmsman and pointed to his right. The sloop changed direction slightly and then, as the *Regent* was lifting on a wave, the gunner took his hand from the touchhole and lowered a smoldering match to it.

The cannon boomed as hellish, sulfuric smoke rolled back across the sloop. A hole appeared in the Dutchman's mainsail, and the pirates cheered.

The three-master kept running. Thatch shook his head. "All right, Tom. Her hull this time. Well above the waterline, if you can."

The other cannon thundered. Two seconds later, splinters erupted from the Dutchman's rail, and men scattered on her deck.

"Run out all guns," Thatch thundered. "Vapors!"

The pirates roared and screamed like demons.

"Make hay while the sun shines," Thatch told Ted, shouting to be heard over the din. "That pardon will keep until Christmas. We can consider it later—if we can keep you and your hot blood on this side of the Atlantic."

TWENTY-THREE

The shot into the rails did the trick. The Dutchman closed its gunports, and no one resisted as the pirates pulled alongside the larger ship, tossed grappling hooks and hailing lines, and pulled themselves over the rail.

Ted was one of the first to step aboard, a dirk gripped in his teeth. As soon as he cleared the rail, he pulled both pistols.

The crew had for the most part backed against the rail on the far side of the deck. None held a weapon of any sort. One of the younger ones was wearing canvas trousers on which a large wet spot was slowly spreading. The boy was looking over Ted's shoulder, so Ted turned, and there was Ben, the first mate, in his size-too-small officer's waistcoat. Ben had painted his face bright blue for the boarding. He grinned at Ted.

"Splendid day for it—what?"

Near the mainmast, an older officer was crumpled onto the deck, a bloody sword next to him. A younger officer, his face almost childlike under blond ringlets, was standing over the body, wiping his hands. It was obvious there had been a disagreement in the chain of command about the wisdom of surrender.

Ted nodded to the young officer, and the officer nodded back.

Up on the poop deck, aft of the quarterdeck, a dozen men and women were kneeling in a circle, the women weeping audibly, the men praying in low, quavering voices.

A hand clasped Ted's shoulder.

Thatch.

"Cabins under the quarterdeck are where the gentry sleep." The pirate pointed in that direction with his cutlass as he spoke. "Best pickings will be there."

Behind them, the pirate crew was swarming onto the deck. Several already had a deck hatch open and were peering into the hold.

No one resisted as Ted and Thatch crossed the deck to the aft-castle cabin. Lifting the latch, Thatch kicked the hatch open and both pirates jumped back clear of the opening. No shot rang out, so Ted peered cautiously around the jamb of the hatch.

The cabin was spacious, and three people cowered inside: a man in a wig and frock coat, a woman in a silk gown, also wearing a wig, although hers was askew as if it had been donned in haste. Then there was another woman in a simpler cotton dress, obviously a servant, and quivering in fright. The man held a long-barreled dueling pistol.

"Either use that or set it aside," Thatch told him.

The man blinked.

"He does not speak English," the woman said.

"But you do," Thatch said. "And a Londoner's English at that." She smiled thinly.

"So." Thatch smiled. Ted always marveled at the pirate's rapport with the ladies. "What is a servant of King George doing married to a Dutchman?"

"We are not married." The woman kept her hands folded as she spoke, and her voice was steady, unafraid. "We are betrothed. My father made the match after his trading business failed. He kept losing his ships—to pirates."

Thatch smiled and made a little bow. "Then please ask him to set his pistol down before someone gets hurt."

She did, and the Dutchman grimaced and then put the pistol on a table. Ted picked it up, removed the flint from the lock, and returned the pistol to the table.

Two large trunks and a small cask stood in a little space at the side wall of the cabin, a wooden footer around them to keep them from shifting in rough seas. Thatch walked over and opened the cask. He shook his head and held it up so Ted could see it.

Empty.

Thatch pulled back the blankets on the bunks on either side of the room, lifted the goose-feather duvets.

Nothing.

He looked at the woman. "Tell him to take off his clothes."

Her mouth dropped. "Sir, I am a lady."

"Then you shall avert your eyes. Tell him."

She said something in Dutch and the man began complaining. Thatch tsked and chucked him under the chin with the tip of his cutlass, and the man took off his coat, followed by his vest.

Thatch motioned with his cutlass and the man removed his shirt. His skin was a pasty white, his belly ample, with a line of black hair leading up from his rather pronounced navel.

"What have we here?" Cutlass to the man's neck, Thatch tugged on the man's trousers, revealing a canvas money belt tied around the Dutchman's waist. Undoing the bows with one hand, Thatch removed it and hefted it.

"About fifty quid, from the feel of it," he told Ted. The older pirate turned to face the lady. "What did he do with the rest of it? Give it to you to hide upon your person?"

"It is all that he has."

"Fifty guilders to start a life in the New World? You seem too bright a young woman to cross the broad Atlantic with a fat old Dutchman who has only fifty guilders to his name."

The woman said nothing.

"We are pirates, you know," Thatch told her. "We are strangers to shame. Do you mean to make me search you?"

The woman cocked her head at Thatch, as if considering the proposition. Then she stepped behind a dressing screen. The shirtless Dutchman began shouting at her—curses, from the sound of it. Ted aimed a pistol at his belly, and the man subsided to a low grumbling.

"I never wanted this match in the first place." Her face was visible above the screen as she undressed. "He is ill-mannered and he smells. And now I see that he is a coward, to boot. My father told me that I had no home if I did not marry this pig."

"We can find you a very good farmer in the Virgin Islands," Thatch told her. "Young. Strong. One who knows respect and good lye soap, both."

"I would like that." She put the gown back over her head, redressing, then said something in Dutch and the servant woman went back and helped her. When they stepped out from behind the screen, the woman held a belt from which six leather pouches were hanging, like fruit dangling from a branch. She had it in both hands and it was obviously heavy. "And my girl too? Can you find us a farmer for her? She speaks very little English."

"A wife who cannot nag?" Thatch laughed. "I wager she would have her choice. Yes. We can find her a farmer."

Ted opened the trunks. Atop one was a heavily beaded dress made from dark blue silk.

"Have you worn this?"

The woman shook her head. "Only for the fitting. It was to have been my wedding dress. But he paid for it."

She nodded toward the half-naked Dutchman. "I would like very much to have it out of my sight."

Ted looked at the woman. "What do you say? She is about Sally's size, is she not?"

Thatch cradled his bearded chin. "She is her match in height and waist and hips. As for her . . . well, up there these London women do all sorts of things with underpinnings. Hard to say."

Ted held up the dress. "May I buy this from you?"

She laughed. "Sir, you are a pirate. Take it."

"No." Ted shook his head. "I will not. What would you have for it?"

She shrugged. She had taken the wig off, and raven black hair tumbled down to her shoulders.

"Tell you what," Thatch said. "What say we leave you half of what this coward here made you hang about your waist? As a dowry. Not that a woman as handsome as you would need a dowry to turn the head of any farmer on Saint John. And we shall transport you and your servant in safety to Saint John or any of King George's islands that you may like."

She smiled, the perfect coquette. Ted resisted the urge to roll his eyes. It was always like this with Thatch and young women. And yet he had never seen the pirate stray one iota from Miss Anne.

"Then that would reward me amply," the woman said. She turned to Ted. "The dress—is it a wedding gift?"

Ted dissolved just a little bit. "I hope so."

"Then I wish you health, wealth, and a long and happy life."

The three of them left the cabin, the servant woman skittering in their wake. On the deck, several members of the Dutch crew had fallen in and were helping the pirates unload casks of wine and barrels of salted pork.

Ben, blue face and all, responded to Thatch's motion and

helped the woman to the railing. Two of the crew called down to the *Regent* for a bosun's chair.

Up on the poop deck, the weeping and the prayer continued undiminished. No one on the pirate crew had yet approached the prayer circle.

"I daresay there might be a brooch or a snuffbox or two up there," Thatch said. "Shall we have a look?"

He and Ted climbed the stairlike ladder to the poop deck. The twelve people were huddled on their knees, facing inward, like oxen weathering a storm.

"Who speaks English?" Thatch asked.

No one answered. Thatch nodded at Ted, who drew one of his two pistols, pointed it into the air and fired it.

On the small square of decking, all of the women and most of the men flinched and shook visibly at the report of the gun.

"Now, I know that I heard an 'Our Father' from amongst all the wailing and gnashing of teeth up here," Thatch said. "So who was that? You are not *all* Dutchmen. Come on. Speak up now."

Ted eased the other pistol out of the sash at his waist.

" 'Be strong and of a good courage,' " quoted a deep Scottish baritone from the circle kneeling on the deck. An older man in black—black breeches, black coat, a broad-brimmed black hat—stood up, his wiry gray hair hanging unevenly about his shoulders. " 'Fear not, and be not afraid of them: for the Lord thy God, he it is that doth go with thee; he will not fail thee, nor forsake thee.' "

The man stepped forward and stopped.

"Sweet Jesus, my precious Savior . . ." He ignored Thatch and stared, mouth open, eyes wide at Ted. Tears began to roll down his cheeks. "How great is thy faithfulness. How marvelous thy provision."

He held his arms out to the young man.

"Captain Henry," Ted said, his voice low. "I shall not be needing the use of that sloop after all."

"What?" The pirate looked back and forth between his young African navigator and the aging Scotsman.

"No need for it." Ted ignored the Scotsman's arms and placed the muzzle of his loaded pistol against the older man's forehead. The man stared at Ted. He was weeping unashamedly, oblivious to the gun at his head.

"Ted?" Thatch kept his cutlass at the ready and looked about. "What are you about? What is this?"

Ted cocked the pistol.

"This," he said, "is the vicar . . . Bascombe."

TWENTY-FOUR

The look on Sheila's face was worthy of a picture. Then again, even though there was a camera on one of the tables, I pretty much had my hands full.

I'd gotten to the preservation lab a full hour early, setting my iPod in the Bose speaker system and getting the volume and tone set properly. I took the resonator off the Kay Bluegrass, adjusted the head tension, replaced the resonator, and tuned the banjo using a digital tuner I'd dug out of a box of picks and other junk I'd hauled down from Duke. Amazingly enough, the battery was still good.

Timing was sort of tricky. I knew about how long it would take for Sheila to get from the street up to the lab, but then there was the off-duty Key West cop the insurance company had insisted we hire to sit down at the staff entrance and check IDs, given the fact that we now had close to three million dollars' worth of precious gems in the big, heavy-as-two-engine-blocks preservation-lab safe. So I'd played the harmony track through twice the night before when I'd recorded it onto my PowerBook, giving me a good five minutes of wiggle room in the music I'd uploaded to my iPod via iTunes.

And I knew I'd be able to see her from the lab window when she rode up.

Sheila had a car, an ancient Ford Fiesta she said she'd purchased because it reminded her of the Ford Cortina that her brother had bought as his first car back in Australia. But that was sitting next to the house trailer she had rented, covered in yellowed palm fronds and seedpods, and while the tires still seemed to hold air, I'd never actually seen it running.

Around town, Sheila walked if the weather was rainy or she had a bundle to carry. And if neither of those things applied, she usually rode her bike, a big old balloon-tired Schwinn, the sort of bicycle that everyone refers to as a "beach cruiser," even though bicycle-able beaches are few and far between in the Florida Keys, and pretty much nonexistent in Key West.

And that was what she was on. I saw her coming up Greene Street on the old Schwinn, which had once been red and white, but had long since sun-faded to hues suggestive of a half-sucked candy cane. I smiled when I saw her, wanted to slap myself for smiling when absolutely nobody else was around, and then smiled again when she passed into a shaft of sunlight between buildings and her blond hair shone in the morning light.

She disappeared beneath the sill, and in my mind's eye I saw her getting off the bike, coming in the staff entrance, stopping in the hall to show the rent-a-cop her Florida driver's license (which she had conscientiously obtained for the Ford Fiesta she never drove), waiting while he checked it against the list on his clipboard, then coming into the offices proper.

The elevator was another tricky part. It was so old, I wouldn't have been surprised to learn that it was the actual model Otis used to apply for his patent. If it was on the ground floor when you got to it, it would groan and rumble and creak its way up to the third floor—assuming nobody short-stopped it for the records on two—in about forty-five seconds.

But if it was up on three, the round trip could potentially last even longer than my ten-minute harmony track; for some reason, gravity notwithstanding, the old elevator was even slower going down.

The way to be prepared, then, was to assume that the elevator was waiting on the ground when she got there. A forty-five second ride up, a stop to check her mail slot, and then maybe twenty seconds to walk down the hall . . .

I started the iPod and then joined in, playing a counter-picking harmony on the Kay. It was "Will the Circle Be Unbroken," originally written more than a century ago as a hymn, but later reworked with new lyrics and recorded by the Carter Family, then covered in the seventies by the Nitty Gritty Dirt Band. While that made it more country-folk than bluegrass, it was a very easy melody to 'grass up. Besides, it was spiritual, and while I had considerable baggage with that, I knew Sheila would like it. I kept on playing. Ten seconds later, when the melody was at its richest, she came through the door.

I didn't sing as I played. I'd rarely sung when I toured with my father, and on the rare occasions when I did, it was harmony. But I'd heard the song a thousand times, heard the lyrics in my head as I played it:

> Will the circle be unbroken,
> By and by, Lord, by and by?
> There's a better home awaiting
> In the sky, Lord, in the sky.

Sheila didn't say a thing as I played. She just stood there—she didn't even sit down. She had her gym bag over her shoulder and she rubbed the strap between her fingers and had this look that was half joy, half awe. My harmony track began again, and I played the song all the way through a second time, this time picking counter-melody with the melody, a process that requires you to think as if you are playing two separate instruments at the same time.

I had to look down as I did that. It's something teachers tell you never to do, but I was out of practice, and besides, when it gets that complicated, it helps me to see the frets. So I looked down, and when I'd finished, I looked up and saw the tears streaming down Sheila's face.

"Hey." The resonator was still ringing as I took the strap off and set the heavy banjo aside. I held my arms out and she came to me, half onto my lap and half into my arms. "What's this?"

"I thought . . ." She dabbed at her eyes. "I thought you didn't like . . ."

"I didn't." I fished out a handkerchief—thankfully a *clean* handkerchief—and offered it to her. "I had some bad connotations."

She held up the hankie. "Can I blow?"

I nodded.

She blew her nose and put the handkerchief in her pocket, saying, "I'll wash that." Then she asked, "What happened to them?"

"To what?"

"The bad connotations."

I smiled and ran my thumb lightly over her damp cheek. "I replaced them with good connotations."

She began to weep again, and I put my hand to her cheek, but she shook her head and said, "No. You needn't wipe them away. They're happy tears."

So I held her instead.

But that wasn't the real surprise. That was just the prelude to the surprise.

I pulled over a stool and patted on it. "Sit here."

She sat.

I picked up the banjo and began playing "White Pine

Breakdown." I played it slowly, because that's what you do when you want the music to be background and not the focal point. And I played it without the strap over my back, which is sort of difficult because even though a banjo may look skinny and diminutive next to a guitar, a resonator banjo is heavy, like holding three or four guitars all at the same time. But I played it that way because then I could stop midsong and hand Sheila the little jewelry box I had hidden on the lab table behind me.

"What's this?" Her eyes were wide.

"Don't freak. It's not a ring."

She raised an eyebrow. "What makes you think I would freak if it was a ring?"

That initiated a pretty awkward silence. Then I said, "Why don't you open it" at the same time that she asked if I would mind if she did.

She undid the bow, smoothed it, and set it aside as if she intended to save it, and I gulped just a little when she did that, because my mother had been a lifelong bow-and-ribbon saver, never reusing the ribbons, but keeping them in a drawer that I came across after she was gone.

I pushed myself forward to the present, happier place.

Sheila opened the box, took out the little satin-covered hinged box inside. She looked up at me.

I nodded twice. "Open it."

She lifted the lid. Gasped. Started crying again.

Inside the box was a pair of earrings, one brilliant green and one blood-red: an emerald and a ruby.

"Where did you . . . ?"

"Miami," I told her. "When we went up there so Phil could do that sit-down on the news, he introduced me to this jeweler who knows how to cut stones."

"Oh . . ." Sheila got up and began rifling through the junk

drawer where she kept lip gloss, hairbrushes, chewing gum and all the other junk that most women lug around in purses, because Sheila McIntyre was not a purse-carrying type of girl.

"What are you looking for?"

"A mirror. I want to . . . Oh, come here."

She took me by the hand and I followed her down to the ladies' room, where she poked her head in, sounded a very Australian and echoey "Hellooo," and then stepped in, pulling me after her.

People who say there are no taboos left in the world have never been in the opposite gender's restroom. Most guys still get that deep, guilt-ridden sense of wrong about being in a ladies' restroom. I'll bet even male janitors do.

Then again, it was sort of fascinating as it blew the whole gender-equality notion out of the water. I mean, the guys' restroom at Rackham's Key West Treasures looks like somebody took a hull sander to the walls and then quit the job halfway through. But the ladies' room was neatly painted. There was even a little shelf next to the mirror with a vase on it holding a plastic rose.

What would you put on a shelf in a men's room? A piston?

Sheila stopped for a second, shut the door and locked it. She went to the mirror and motioned to me. "Come here."

I joined her as she put on the earrings. Pierced ears on guys— that plus tattoos—is practically part of the dress code for men in treasure-hunting operations, but all the way through school I'd resisted the pressure to go that way. Even watching somebody put on a pair of pierced earrings has always had for me a queasy, unsettling feeling—like you get when watching the guy at the carnival sideshow push a ten-penny nail through his nose.

But it's different when the earrings are a gift to somebody you—well, somebody you care for. A lot different.

"Oh." Sheila turned her head to look at the earrings, one at a time. "I adore them. I am absolutely going to pitch every other pair of earrings I own and wear these every single day."

She stopped swiveling her head and looked at them both at the same time.

"Red and green," she said. "I love it. I mean you think they'd look Christmassy, and they could, I suppose. But they don't. Whatever gave you the idea? Using the two colors?"

I turned her to face me and touched her face lightly beneath each eye. "Blue. Brown. Two colors."

She melted a little and gave me a hug. I was seriously thinking of graduating it to a full-blown kiss when the handle jiggled on the door.

"Out in a minute!" Sheila called. She kissed me on the cheek—truth told, I was hoping for the lips. Then she unlocked the knob and led me out of the ladies' room, past a flabbergasted Marge—the lady who checks people in and answers the telephone in Records.

Like I said. The last taboo.

TWENTY-FIVE

I've never figured out why there seems to be this law of emotional equilibrium in the universe; that every poignant high has to be followed, in fairly short order, by an equally potent and effective buzz-kill. I mean, there's no physical reason it has to work that way. It's not like water seeking its own level, or action and reaction. Those I can understand—they *have* to happen. But emotional downs cancelling out emotional ups? That doesn't make any sense to me. We are creatures with free wills. We make choices. We choose, to a fairly significant extent, our own destinies. So why can't we just be happy all of the time?

The question is rhetorical, of course. The only possible answer is—because that's the way it is. And that answer is, unfortunately, right.

As I discovered later that day.

Sheila has this thing about "real American food." It had come up a couple of weeks earlier when we'd driven up to Miami to drop off the *Santa Maria* pearls.

Actually, we hadn't driven them. An armored car had. We'd followed along in one of Phil's pickups, listening to bluegrass and just enjoying the ride up the Overseas Highway, which is sort of like a boat trip, only you don't have to time everything to correspond with the rocking when you stop for a restroom break.

Anyhow, the firm receiving the pearls had been in Miami, not far from the Southland Mall, and she'd spotted a Johnny Rockets—a fifties-ish restaurant chain where the staff dances the Macarena and they draw a little smiley face on the plate with the ketchup when they bring your order of fries.

A Johnny Rockets is to the American diner what Main Street at Disney World is to small-town America—an idealized representation with considerable liberties taken. (Does Main Street in your hometown terminate at a seventeenth-century castle?)

To tell you the truth, I'm not that big a fan of the Johnny Rockets burger. I'm not sure if they spray the thing with butter or what, but I swear you could wring the thing out and lube a diesel engine with it. Their fries are okay, and the shakes rock, but the burgers . . . ? I could name you about ten places I'd rather go.

But when Sheila saw the white faux-tile exterior and the signage, straight out of *Happy Days*, she'd wanted to go. This was before the kiss on the dock. This was before any of that, when I thought she was . . . Well, you get the picture. But even though I'd pretty much pegged Sheila as an unreachable ideal by that point, I would still do just about anything to see her smile, and if a burger fried in 10W-30 was what she wanted, then a burger fried in 10W-30 was what she was going to have.

She'd been so happy. She kept searching her pockets for nickels to put in the little tabletop jukebox controls that they have in their booths (until I told her that the waitstaff will give you all the nickels you want, as they just recycle the same supply over and over again). She'd thought the smiley face with the ketchup was "brilliant," and there was absolutely no way I was going to tell her that our waitress had not thought it up just for her. And when the burgers and fries came, as she munched happily on her burger and I picked at my fries, she'd said, "So this is a real American restaurant, isn't it? I mean this is what you think of when you think of proper American food."

The answer to that, of course, is that it's nothing of the sort. I'm pretty sure the whole malt-shop thing is a Southern California idiosyncrasy that television and movie producers glommed on to in order to have a central set where they could film teenagers in something other than a classroom, and that any malt shop/diner in someplace other than L.A. was probably life imitating art. And I'm nearly positive that my grandparents never ate in a place like that, and if they ever did, nobody there ever danced the Macarena.

But are you going to tell Virginia that there isn't a Santa Claus?

So I settled for, "Yeah. They're all over. Lots of people like 'em."

Thank goodness there is no Johnny Rockets in Key West. And even a wide-eyed Australian like Sheila is hip enough to know that the Cheeseburger in Paradise is just an attempt to leverage a song lyric, and that the real Cheeseburger in Paradise that Buffet sang about is about a thousand miles away in the British Virgin Islands—on Tortola, if I'm not mistaken.

So she'd settled on the Hog's Breath Saloon as her go-to, lunch-on-Friday source for "proper American food."

The Hog's Breath burger is about a million times better than Johnny Rockets. Fact is, most Key Westers consider Hog's Breath to be a tourist trap with draft beer (a description that applies to pretty much everything on Duval Street). But by now I would pretty much go to the ends of the earth for the woman. Hog's Breath was a much shorter trip, and at least their food is edible.

That's not the buzz-kill. The buzz-kill came later, on the walk back to the lab after lunch. Sheila was holding my hand and humming in this happy post-hamburger-coma kind of way, and I was thinking about the fact that I really needed a microwave.

Because I did. The one in my apartment wouldn't even pop popcorn. It would warm soup, but that took so long that by the time the soup was reaching room temperature, you'd forgotten what kind it was and you took it out expecting chicken noodle, only to find that what you'd warmed up was beef barley.

But Key West is an island. An island connected to the rest of the Keys and ultimately the mainland by a highway, but an island nonetheless. Key Largo, at the top part of the Keys, is around a hundred miles away, and much of that hundred miles is two-lane. Moving companies hate it. And when people get jobs outside of Key West and have to move, and they discover how much Allied and Bekin and the rest of them want to charge to come load up all their stuff, they usually sell most of it—unless they're Navy, in which case the government moves them, and you and I foot the bill.

Which means that for people living on a shoestring—and that describes pretty much everyone in Key West under the age of thirty—other people's relocations off-island are sort of a bonanza.

Think of an antelope dropping dead from old age on a savanna somewhere. Think of a pack of hyenas. You've got the picture.

I know. I know. I wasn't really broke. Not if you count the bonus money—it was turning out to be nearer to eleven thousand apiece for Sheila, Malibu, Mikey, and me. Mikey was using his as a down payment on a Harley—a spanking-new Road King Classic. Malibu, I'm pretty sure, was planning on dispensing his in weekly portions to Paradise Ink and the Green Parrot until absolutely nothing was left. And while neither Sheila nor I had said anything to each other about it, I think we'd both heard Betty's comment about a down payment on a house, and we'd taken it to heart and just sort of set our shares aside in savings.

Still, needs are needs, and I needed a microwave. And there's one of those bulletin-board kiosk things over by Mallory Square where, if you look under and around all the stapled-up flyers for metal bands and massage parlors, you can sometimes find notices from people who are moving and selling off their stuff for a song.

So we crossed the street and, with Sheila still holding my hand and humming, I walked slowly around the kiosk thing, looking for those sheets of laser-printed paper with the rows of scissor-separated take-one phone numbers, like the buckskin fringe on Daniel Boone's sleeves. And there in the middle of it was a flyer from Boondocks, up on Ramrod Key.

Anyplace else in the world, Boondocks would just be a tourist trap. Don't get me wrong—it *is* a tourist trap. It has a miniature golf course on one side of the parking lot and a tiki bar on the other and, except maybe for Shell World, you can't get much further into the tourist-trap spectrum than miniature golf courses and tiki bars.

But Boondocks had been embraced by the locals, and this was largely due to the house tunes: Howard Livingstone and the Mile Marker 24 band.

Howard is an autoworker expat from Chicago, who these days fills the void left when Jimmy Buffet packed up and left Key West for the land of solvency some several decades ago. He sings about leaving the snow and the rat race behind and getting away to the islands and never coming back, which more or less describes the mind-set of anyone living in the Keys who wasn't born there.

Just to show how well they fit into the scheme of things in the Keys, Livingstone and his band have a 1951 Evinrude outboard motor that they've converted into a gasoline-powered blender. In between the first and the second set, they wheel it out onto the dance floor, fire it up, and make margaritas for the crowd.

That alone will pack Boondocks on Friday and Saturday nights. But I guess they'd decided that their Sundays were running too slow, because they had a notice up that they were starting up a series of Gospel brunches that would run on Sundays from eleven in the morning until two in the afternoon. And I was glancing over it when a name caught my eye.

"What is it?" Sheila asked. Maybe my hand had tensed and she felt it. I'm not sure.

She followed my gaze and read the name listed on the flyer for the second Sunday in September.

"Ted Rhodes," she read aloud. She turned me by the shoulder. "Greg? Is that your . . . ?"

"Yes," I told her. Even to me, my voice sounded flat. "That's my father."

TWENTY-SIX

"'. . . like unto treasure hid in a field,'" Bascombe quoted, "'which when a man hath found, he hideth, and for joy thereof goeth and selleth all that he hath, and buyeth that field. . . .'"

"Touching," Thatch said. "Poetic. But I am not so very certain that treasures and pearls of great price are apt metaphors if you *sold* the boy. And not to impeach your powers of observation, but have you noticed that he has a pistol to your head?"

Not moving his head, Bascombe glanced at Thatch.

"You have ribbons," he said. "In your beard."

"It is an affectation."

On the deck nearby, the kneeling men were watching with hangdog eyes, and one of the women had begun to wail, loudly.

"Be silent or swim," Thatch told her in his deep commander's baritone. A moment later the only sounds on ship were the laughter of the pirate crew and the soughing of the wind in the lines.

Thatch stepped nearer to Ted.

"Not to tell you your business," the pirate said, "but killing this old fellow may not be the proper thing to do. He does not seem at all right in the head."

"I am right in my head," Bascombe said. Both pirates squinted, regarding him. "But I am wrong in my heart and impoverished in my soul."

"Yes," Thatch told him. "Raising a child to sell him like a fatted pig will do that to you."

Ted pushed the pistol, forcing Bascombe's head up.

"Go ahead, son," Bascombe said. "Slay me if you see fit. I shall not blame you. I . . ." He stopped and, ignoring the flintlock muzzle against his forehead, turned to look Thatch in the eyes. "What was that you said? Did you say that I . . . ?"

He fell back to his knees, his arms around Ted's legs.

"Oh, my boy, my boy, my boy. I am a wicked man, a deceitful man, a sinful man. I have transgressed against my God and against my brother. I should not be suffered to live. But do not think that I, that your . . . that my dear wife, would ever, even in our most desperate of moments . . ."

Ted no longer had the gun to the older man's head. To do so would risk putting a ball of lead into his own foot. "You sent me," he hissed. "They knew where to wait."

"They had spies in the town." Bascombe kept his face pressed against the younger man's knees. "They saw you leave, saw the wagon, the barrels. They knew your errand, knew your route, knew where to lay in wait. We could not imagine what . . . We thought you had left us, had run, a woman perhaps. We didn't . . . And then one of the ones who'd spied let it slip in the tavern that . . ." He paused, then looked up. "By the time we got to the fort, you had gone. But then I saw, saw with my own eyes how the ships were loaded. How the . . . the people . . . What they did to them. So I came. I sold the house, the property, and I bought the passage and I came."

Ted tried to back away, but the older man kept his grip around his legs.

"You knew you were supplying slavers."

"I did. I knew they were carrying the people away to a Christian country. I thought the trade could save them. Could take them to a place where the Gospel would be heard. That they might be imprisoned, but this life is but a vapor, and then they would be—"

Ted pulled the trigger and the pistol boomed.

It worked. The kneeling man released his grip. Far off the stern of the drifting ship, a white jet of water shot up as the ball dropped harmlessly into the blue Caribbean.

Ted stepped back, the empty pistol in his hand.

"Do what you want with him," he told his captain.

The young man turned and dropped down onto the main deck, strode away toward the bow of the three-masted ship.

Thatch looked down at the sobbing Bascombe. "Where were you bound?"

The older man shook in his weeping and said nothing.

"This man here," Thatch said, directing his words to the kneeling passengers on the poop deck, "where was he headed? What is your destination?"

"We are bound for Willemstad," a young man answered. His English was clear, but possessed a heavy Dutch accent. "On the island of Curaçao. We are planters, most of us."

"And him, what is he? Has he people there? Family or friends?"

"He has neither." It was a woman who spoke this time. Like the one they'd met below, she was English, her accent more common. "He told us that he sold his business, bought this passage, and sent his wife to Scotland with the rest of his money. He has nothing. We have been sharing our food with him. He wanted only to find his son."

"His son?"

"That is what he said."

Thatch took a deep breath, looked down to the main deck. Ted was nowhere to be seen. He cleared his throat. "Ben—come up here, will you?"

The mate clambered up, grinning.

"Take this man." Thatch pointed to Bascombe. "Put him in our hold until we reach Tortola."

"Chains?" The mate eyed the kneeling man suspiciously.

"No chains. He is our guest. Our honored guest."

"Honored guest?" Ben glanced at the weeping Scotsman a second time. "In the hold?"

"Make him comfortable. But keep him out of sight."

"Aye." The mate bent to lift the man to his feet.

"Oh, and Ben?"

"Aye, Cap'n?"

Thatch pointed at the kneeling group. "None of these people are to be molested. Neither their persons nor their possessions. Take the consigned cargo, but leave their things and let them go on their way. Am I clear?"

"Aye."

The mate dragged the sobbing man off.

"Thank you," the Englishwoman told the pirate.

"Thank yourself," Thatch said. "Your charity was your salvation."

TWENTY-SEVEN

"I have always relied on the charity of strangers. . . ." Vivien Leigh's Louisiana accent was wistful, plaintive, the admission of an emotionally exhausted Blanche DuBois.

Curled up with me on the sofa, Sheila dipped her hand into the big bowl of popcorn on my lap and grabbed a few kernels. I'd made it the way I figured popcorn should be made for a movie: drizzled with half a stick of melted butter and topped with freshly ground sea salt—which I used not because I'm a gourmet chef or anything like that, but because sea salt and a grinder was the only salt I'd been able to find in the kitchen of Sheila's trailer.

Butter. Sodium. I could think of a lot of women who would have taken one taste and then given me the health-and-nutrition lecture. But Sheila had simply tried it, said "Brilliant!" and then snuggled in to watch the old film.

"Tennessee Williams," she said. "He lived here, did he not?"

I looked around. "This trailer? Is it that old?"

She jabbed me with her elbow. "In Key West, you silly cow."

"Yeah." I rubbed my side. "I think Captain Tony's got a barstool with Tennessee's name on it still. Then again, knowing Captain Tony, he's probably had about a hundred barstools with Tennessee's name on them, and he's probably sold every single one of them off to tourists."

"Captain Tony is a lecher," Sheila murmured. "First time I was in there, he asked me if I would marry him. Said he has thirteen children and he thought fourteen sounded luckier. Then I reminded him that he was already married, and he said, 'Sweetheart, there's always Vegas.' I'm not sure if he was talking about a quicky divorce or what-happens-in. Or both. And my goodness, his oldest son is something like, what? Seventy-two? But he wants another."

She nibbled another kernel of popcorn and added, "Then again, you think about it, that's rather sweet, really. Don't you agree?"

"Sweet?"

She nodded.

"The popcorn or Captain Tony?"

The elbow again. "This is a good movie, isn't it?"

"It's a classic."

"That's not a real answer."

I thought about the elbow. "It's okay."

Sheila sat halfway up, sipped some Coke from her can, and recurled herself. "Well, I think Tennessee Williams had rare insight into the feminine psyche."

"Tennessee Williams *had* a feminine psyche. He was a flaming homosexual."

She wrinkled her nose. That was weird. I could *feel* that she wrinkled her nose.

"Well, he knew how to write about women." She looked up at me. "Ever watch this before?"

I shook my head. "I read it in a sophomore lit class. That was enough for me. But I think I remember my mom watching it on TV one time. . . ."

I stopped talking.

"Fourteen kids," Sheila said. "What do you suppose Tony wants? His own football team?"

"That'd only take eleven." I was glad to go back to the subject. Any subject. "I don't think Tony cares about the sons. I think he just likes young wives. Or young women who act like wives."

"I don't know." She took just a single kernel of popcorn this time, chewed it. "Men like sons."

On the screen, Blanche DuBois was acting fadedly promiscuous.

"How come you didn't know?" Sheila asked me.

"Know?"

"That your father was going to be at Boondocks in September?"

"It's still a couple months away."

She looked up at me. "But still, he made the booking. That would have been a while ago. And he knows you're in Key West, does he not?"

I shrugged. "My father and I don't talk much."

She sat up. "Why?"

"Phil didn't tell you?"

She shook her head.

Oh, great. Phil knows how to keep a confidence. "It's complicated."

Sheila cocked her head. "And you don't think that I can follow a complicated story? Little old simpleminded me?"

"I'm not saying . . ."

"I know." She hit the remote, leaving Blanche DuBois and Stanley Kowalski and Mitch Mitchell to work out their own problems. She turned the light up to a higher setting—snuggling time over. "Greg, when I was twelve, my sister, the twin of my older brother, drowned in a watering hole on my father's cattle station."

"I know."

"My mother went into an institution over her grief. My father drank for a while. Nobody in the household swam."

"I know."

"I learned to dive even though I was afraid of the water at the time. I went to Queensland and took lessons one Easter break so I could show my mother that not all of her children were going to perish in the water. I did it because I wanted to make her well."

I took her hand. "Sheila, I know this. I know all of this. You've told it to me before."

"I have." She withdrew her hand from mine. "But you've told me nothing about your family, Greg. And I need to hear about them. I need to know about how you feel about family because . . ." Both eyes, the brown and the blue, were welling with tears now, and I reached out to her, but she pulled back. "Because when I dream about a family of my own, I dream about you, Greg. But it's frightening, falling in love with a mystery. You're a wonderful man. But you keep secrets."

I set the popcorn aside.

"Not to hurt you, Sheila. I don't talk about that because . . ." I searched for the words. "It hurts *me* to bring it up."

She curled her lips inward. They looked thin. She searched my face.

"You want to know," I said. It wasn't a question. It didn't have to be.

Sheila nodded.

"Okay."

So I told her.

TWENTY-EIGHT

The hold of the *Regent* had been filled nearly to full by the cloth and the barrels taken off the Dutchman. Only a small stowaway hole had been left by the first mate as they loaded, a place only big enough for one man to stretch at length or stand and walk a stride, yet now there were two men in it.

Henry Thatch had turned the lantern low. On the deck above them, the crew was stomping and dancing in celebration as they sailed through the night toward Tortola.

The pirate was dressed simply: breeches, bare feet, a muslin shirt, and a kerchief knotted over his close-cropped head. The ribbons and the little silver beads had been removed, the bottom of the beard tied with twine, a concession to the wind up on deck. He watched as the old Scotsman ate a plateful of hardtack and salt pork, then finished it with a pint of grog—a half cup of rum mixed with an equal measure of water.

"You must consider me beneath contempt," Bascombe said. He did not look up as he spoke.

"Sir," Thatch replied, "I began this work as a privateer, a minion in the service of my king. But now the only papers of authority I hold are those that I bought with bullion from the governor-general of the Virgin Islands, and those papers are of . . . highly questionable value. People may see me as a sea captain, or a colorful character—some Robin Hood of the seas—but the truth of the matter is that I am a thief. A common thief. Yes, I only prey upon ships from those nations that vie with my own for possession of this New World. But no monarch endorses my actions, so my behavior is no better than the wretch who lurks in alleys and takes men's pocketbooks at the point of a dagger."

Thatch uncorked a jug and poured the older man another cup.

"I have no children," Thatch told him. "But I have a comely wife, young and strong, and God willing she will bear me some children yet. And if she does—when she does—I do not wish them ever to know what their father did to earn his fortune. I say that and yet I took your ship today. Another man's goods, and I could not return it if I wanted to, because the main share is the crew's, and besides, were I to present myself to return, it would be the same as asking for the noose about my neck. It is an ugly, deadly circle, sir, and I have dragged the fine young man you raised into it."

Thatch paused, recorked the bottle.

"So do not speak to me of contempt," he said to the Scotsman. "If any is beneath contempt, it is I. You have come across this sea to try to undo the ends of your behavior, to rescue the young man you raised as your very son. You have no money, and you believed our Ted to be a slave. Had you found him in his bonds, how was it you intended to free him from his master?"

Bascombe looked up. "I was going to beg. I was going to offer to wear the chains in his place."

Thatch nodded. He looked up at the deck, where the tempo of the pirates' dance had increased by a beat or two. "I thought as much."

The ship rocked and they leaned with it. The creak of the

rudder turning, the helmsman correcting course, traveled up to them through the thick oak of the hull.

"Bold Ted tells me you were a vicar back in Scotland."

Bascombe chuckled and shook his head. "Ah, our Theodore. He never did get that clear. I was but a lowly deacon, and not a very good one at that. But truly, sir, I will tell you this: I love the Word."

Thatch rubbed his beard. "And what does the Word say about a man such as I? A sinner who speaks of repentance but has thus far failed to repent? Am I forever damned? Or is there hope?"

Bascombe's eyes grew clearer, brighter. "There is always hope."

Thatch pointed at the older man. "Then, sir, there is hope for you."

The ship creaked around them.

TWENTY-NINE

A table had been set on the deck of the anchored *Regent*, ahead of the single mast. Fine linen cloth covered the surface, and gilt-edged china had been set at all five places. A decanter of Madeira wine was left uncorked to allow it to breathe, and while he did not, like his captain, wear a wig, Ted had put on his finest clothes, the tricorner hat on his head in the setting sun.

"When Captain Henry told me that you would be coming to sup, I was quite surprised," Ted said as he pulled back a chair for Sally.

"I have always had Bridget and Kathleen to help me serve," Oscar Emmons said. Like Ted, he generally shunned wigs but wore a hat instead, his shaved head golden brown beneath it in the dying light. "They had been at my inn since before Sally was too small to reach the tables. And of late I have hired a man to help. I am growing no younger, and besides"—he gestured at Thatch and Anne, at his daughter and Ted—"if I do not take the time, from time to time, to have time with my friends, then what use have I made of the time in my life?"

"There was more 'time' in that last sentence than there is in a clockmaker's shop," Thatch said as he lit the candles. Everyone laughed. "But I am honored that you came, Oscar. And, Sally, with your face here, next to my Anne's, the *Regent* is a brighter ship than ever I have seen upon the sea."

"And there is more honey in that last sentence than there is in all of Elder Gladson's beehives," Anne told Sally. The two women giggled, the three men grinning as they sat with them.

The sloop had no galley in the proper sense of the term. Cooking was done mainly on an open brick fire-square well aft of the sails, and even that was modest: suitable only for heating stews and porridges. The *Regent* was designed as a short-range vessel, rarely away from land for more than a day or two, and its crew was accustomed to digging fire pits on a beach and roasting a wild pig or whatever fish they could catch, and then taking their meals under the shelter of overhanging palms. Meals aboard ship were of necessity simple affairs, and for this occasion a baker in town had been persuaded to make the use of his kitchen—with Oscar and Sally as guests, the use of the kitchen at The Rose and Crown had seemed less than appropriate—and the courses were being rowed out to the *Regent* in order by longboat.

Even now, Ted could hear Ben telling one of the crew, "You drop that hen, and by my eyes I shall have your guts for garters," as they used lengths of line to lift warm baskets up and onto the deck.

Ben himself was serving. The captain of the Dutch vessel had been more the first mate's size, and with that gentleman having no further need of his wardrobe, the mate had appropriated the better parts of it, right down to a fine, powdered wig.

"Benjamin, a queen's footman could look no more dashing," Anne told him.

"I thank you for noticing the effort, m'um." The mate poured Madeira all around. "Truth be told, these shoes squeeze me feet something awful. But I'll break 'em in proper, given time—shoes or the feet, one 'a the two."

This too got the laugh it deserved, and the dinner began.

There was pheasant raised by a farmer on Peter Island, followed by a standing rib roast—until that week, part of a milch cow that had been bound for a dairy in Venezuela via the island of Curaçao. A Christmas pudding had been baked, not because it was yuletide—that holiday was still five months away—but because the baker was known for them, and it added a festive air. Leeks and scallops and parsnips and peas accompanied every dish, and the bread was warm and moist and as hot as bread could possibly be after a quarter-mile row in a longboat.

Then, when the pudding had been presented, Captain Henry excused himself and descended to his cabin, emerging later with a fine wooden box twice as broad as his shoulders and tied with a golden silk bow. He came and stood next to the table while Ted rose and removed his hat.

"Deacon Emmons," he began. "Miss Sally. May I make you a present?"

Thatch actually dropped to one gartered knee so Sally could untie the bow. She opened the hinged box and put her hands to her mouth.

"Oh, Father, it is stunning!" She looked at him. "May I?"

Oscar Emmons nodded, and she lifted the fine gown from its box.

"I am told this is the work of the finest dressmaker in all of old Amsterdam," Ted said. "A gown worthy of a beautiful bride."

Sally's eyes grew wide.

"Miss Sally, if you will have me, and your father will permit me, I would like to present you before the curate for that purpose. Will you do me the great honor of being my wife?"

Sally looked at Oscar again. "Oh, Father—may I? May *we*?"

Oscar Emmons worked his lips and looked down at the remains of his pudding.

"He did not take the dress, if that is what you are thinking," Thatch told Emmons, leaning on the table as he said it. "He paid— even overpaid, truth be told. But I was there. I saw the transaction transpire, and it produced a smile on the face of each party."

Emmons received the information dispassionately. He lifted a napkin from the table and wiped his chin.

"What night is this?" He directed his question at Thatch. "Is it Thursday evening? Thursday? Is that correct?"

"I do believe you are right, dear friend."

Oscar pushed back his seat.

"Right, then." He clapped his hands on his thighs. "The morrow is Friday, and this week we shall roast a pig at my tavern. As I have eaten a fine meal at your table this evening, I would like to invite you—the three of you—to come to The Rose and Crown and give me the opportunity to return the favor. Can you do that?"

"Gladly," Thatch said.

"Very good." Emmons rose. He walked around the table and considered the young man before him. Sally folded her hands and, lips tight and twitching, watched her father closely.

"Come at seven," Emmons told Ted. "Seven at Captain Thatch's table in the dining room of The Rose and Crown. I shall give you my answer then."

THIRTY

" 'Come to my inn at seven.' " Ted groused as the men pulled at the oars. "Who does the man think he is?"

Thatch smiled and leaned back a bit. He'd donned a white wig for the evening. It made a shocking contrast with the various dark hues of his beard, but it lent him a certain dignity nonetheless. He rested both hands upon his knees.

"Well, you needn't put up with it, if you've no mind to," he told Ted. "The solution is absolutely simple. Marry another. So, my friend, does that strike your fancy?"

The boat fell silent, except for the creaking of the oars in their locks and the sound of the water falling off the blades at the end of each stroke. Ben the mate was minding the tiller, and he coughed, but it was an odd cough: the sort of cough a man might conjure up to hide a chuckle.

"Well, then." Thatch slapped Ted lightly on the knee. "That's done, then. Oscar Emmons *thinks* nothing. He *knows* that he is the father of the only woman in the whole wide world that you wish to wed. And he can dictate pretty much any terms he pleases. Now, that is an exceedingly hard place for a pirate to be, on the short side of surrender. Yet surely that is where you are. So you may as well face it with a smile on your face, Bold Ted, for you most certainly will face it, smiling or not."

Supper at The Rose and Crown tended to be an early affair. Sailors ashore usually have one thing in mind when they visit a tavern and—except as a ballast upon which to pour copious quantities of ale and rum—dinner is rarely that one thing.

Even the ale and rum would have to be sought elsewhere that evening. A hand-lettered plank declared *Taps Closd* at the door of the public house, and the peg-legged old salt who had sold Ted his bath on his first night ashore on Tortola was standing on the stoop, explaining the situation to those visitors who could not read, which was the vast majority of them. As Thatch and Ted approached the tavern, a couple of sawed-off plugs of sailors tried to argue with the old doorman, and he clubbed the largest one smartly with his walking stick and waved it at the pair of them as they fled down the hard-tramped dirt road.

"Evening, Edward." Thatch lifted his hat.

"Cap'n." The old salt bowed, a remarkably deep bow for a man who had a castoff furniture piece for a right leg. Then he straightened up and opened the door to the pub. "Splendid night for it, sir, is it not?"

"That it is."

The main room of the tavern had been transformed—swept and washed clean, and every table carried from it, save one. The windows had been thrown open, admitting the evening air, and candles burned and flickered on the table and on the windowsills, giving a fairyland feel to the low stone room.

"Remarkable," Thatch said.

"Miraculous is a bit more like it," said Sally Emmons. She and Anne Thatch entered from a side parlor, first one and then the other through the narrow door. "In all the days of my life, I have never seen The Rose and Crown shuttered, save for Sundays. Not even Christmas Eve closes my father's taps. Only the Lord's Day. For him to give a meal is a rare enough thing. When he gives the entire evening . . . why, sir, my powers of speech desert me."

"I believe my daughter is accusing me of . . . parsimony—is that the word?" Oscar Emmons laughed as he asked it. He was not in his usual homespun and apron, but wore woolen breeches and a waistcoat nearly as fine as those he had worn on the *Regent* the night before, polished shoes ornamented with large silver buckles, and a white wig that was startling on his huge, ebony head.

"Come, friends, come." Emmons shook Thatch's hand, even shook Ted's hand, and offered his large, fleshy saucer of a cheek for a kiss from the captain's wife. "Come to your table, and rest assured that I have lost my slate and my chalk for this evening. Your supper will be a gift from this hearth and from this house."

Ted stole a glance at Sally. He choked back a laugh as she rolled her smoky, dark eyes.

The dinner was . . . Well, Ted had no idea how the dinner was. He remembered that a suckling pig was brought to the table, complete down to the apple in its mouth. He remembered the "oohs" and "aahs" all round the table; Thatch even led the small group in a round of applause.

And Ted remembered wondering just who was in the kitchen. Oscar Emmons had been vocal on more than one occasion with his contention that cooking—"real cooking, as one does in an inn, and not just the Sunday after-meeting brisket"—was a man's job, incapable of being performed by a woman. Perhaps dinner for five did not fall into that category, but Ted did not see Emmons, under any circumstances, ceding control of his domain to the fairer sex. Then again, the landlord had mentioned that he had taken on a man to help him, some islander, no doubt. Perhaps this new man could find his way around a kitchen.

Perhaps, but it would not be proven by Ted. He ate. He drank. But he would not, for his life, be able to report later on anything other than the pig, and that only for the seeing of it. Ted was like a guilty man waiting for his sentence to be read. He had asked for Sally's hand, and Oscar Emmons had told him that there would be no decision on that matter until the conclusion of the dinner. So what should have been a festive meal was more like the condemned man's final repast.

Ted ate his meal without tasting it. He drank the toast to the landlord with not a clue as to what had been in his cup. At Thatch's advice—"a gentleman waits"—he did not press Oscar Emmons for a decision. But he longed to.

At last, Bridget and Kathleen, Emmons's two Irish serving women, had cleared the table, leaving only brandy and cups in their wake.

"Ted," Oscar said. "How did you find your meal?"

Ted blinked.

"I wager that he found it upon his plate and was fortunate to do that," Thatch observed. This got laughter from two of his companions. Ted and Sally remained somber, their eyes on Sally's father.

Emmons lit a clay pipe and leaned back in his chair, tobacco smoke rising in lazy rings to the dark recesses of the timbered ceiling.

"My Sally will be seventeen come Christmas," Emmons said. "Tender, in my eyes, yet my own mother bore me when she was but fourteen. And certainly it is good that a woman wed long before she is twenty. The bearing of children requires strength, after all."

When her father said "children," Sally began to smile. Then she averted her eyes.

"And I have long wondered what manner of man my only child should wed," Emmons continued. "Would he be an innkeeper? Someone who could carry on the custom of this house? Or perhaps a farmer, a man of the soil?"

Ted's heart sank.

"Then again, there is much to be said for a learned man as a husband," Emmons observed. "One who can read and write, do ciphers, and navigate a fine ship upon the broad and open sea."

Ted lifted his head.

Emmons turned to Thatch. "Henry, although I have done custom with you, I have never approved of your choice of profession. I hope I do not offend you when I say that."

"Hardly." Thatch sipped his brandy. "Most days I do not approve of it myself."

"It does my heart good to hear that," the big man said. "I live in hope that all my friends who fly the black ensign shall retire it ere Christmas and make their livings in a peaceful fashion."

Neither Thatch nor Ted said anything in response to this. But at the same time, neither objected.

Emmons turned to look Ted in the eye, and Ted, despite what was at stake, returned the look, coolly.

It was Emmons who broke off. He turned to his daughter, at his side. "Sally, do you believe you would be happy with this man?"

She nodded.

Emmons turned back to Ted. "Son." It was the first time the landlord had ever addressed the young pirate publicly in that fashion. "I know that you expect terms from me on any betrothal. I know that you expect that I shall insist upon your taking the king's pardon."

Ted opened his mouth to speak, but Emmons lifted a pale-palmed hand.

"That would not be my place, Ted. Even though I strongly

suspect that you have not the heart for a pirate's life, and you continue it now out of loyalty to those who saved you. But your reasons are yours and should be yours. A man who takes a wife should be his own man. I was when I wed Sally's mother. I remained so until the typhus took that good, strong woman. I remain so to this day. I call no man 'master' but my Savior, and I wear neither chains of iron nor the chains of another man's desires."

Ted nodded slowly as the older man spoke.

"Our Sally will tell you that my respect is not easily given," Emmons continued. "It is a failing of mine, I admit it. Yet you have earned my respect, Ted. You are wise beyond your years, and I trust you to make good decisions. You are the sort of man to whom I would entrust the light of my life, my only child."

Ted began to smile.

"Still . . ." If Emmons saw the look on the younger man's face, he did not show it. "This is not the sort of decision that one father alone should make. Before the bride's father gives permission, I think it only right that the groom's father should be in agreement as well.

The smile faded from Ted's face.

"Groom's father?" Ted cocked his head, that affectation he had when pondering something. "Sir, my father has been dead these sixteen years. He passed when our village burned."

Emmons nodded. "True enough of your father in fact. But I speak, son, of your father in deed." Emmons raised his head and looked to the doorway leading to the kitchen. "What says he?"

"He says well met and twice blessed," returned a Scottish brogue.

Every muscle in Ted's body seemed to tense. He turned, knowing what it was that he was going to see.

Sure enough, there stood Bascombe in the doorway of the

kitchen, an apron around his waist and a ragged towel in his hands.

"Theodore," the old man said, "my heart lifts up."

Ted stood. Everyone around the table was watching him expectantly. He glared at them, grabbed his hat, and stormed out—past the crippled doorman, out into the night.

THIRTY-ONE

Orion was riding high in the subtropical sky, Betelgeuse glowing brightly beneath it. These were heavenly bodies that had barely cleared the southern ridges back home in Black Mountain. But here in Key West, you had to crane your head back to look up at them.

Does the heart form calluses from its scrapes, the way a hand does? Or does a hurt simply become more bearable with each telling of it? I cannot say which is true; I can only say that, even though Sheila and I were close enough now that tears could pass between us with no one feeling shame, tears had not come this time.

Still, once I'd told the story, I needed air, more than Sheila's little trailer could provide. Outside her back door, several old wooden pallets had been arranged and leveled to form a very Key West sort of deck. There were two patio chairs that did not match, a table that was a stranger to both chairs and missing its umbrella, and a view across an empty road to the Gulf of Mexico. And there was night air, a bit cool now, because it was getting late, and a sky absolutely jam-packed full of stars.

Fingers brushed against my palm, and I opened it, accepted Sheila's hand—smaller, warmer—into mine.

"Less than four thousand," Sheila said.

I left Orion alone and looked down at her. "How's that?"

"That's how many stars they say you can see with the naked eye at any one time." She was looking at the night sky, not at me. "I learned that in an astronomy class in college. And yet when I look at all that"—she raised her free hand to trace the smudge of the Milky Way—"it seems to me like millions. Billions. Less than four thousand seems like far too few."

"Four thousand, one billion," I said. "They're both big numbers."

Sheila nodded and looked at me. In the starlight both of her eyes looked the same color, the same dark shade of brown.

"Greg . . ." she began.

I looked at the sky again. "Don't try to tell me it wasn't murder. Fact is, in most states, taking a life while driving impaired is homicide. Maybe not first degree, but a murder just the same. Might be in North Carolina too. Tell you the truth, I'm not sure. Even if it was, Ted Rhode—Ted Rhodes—had too many cronies in the county to be charged. I guess they figured he lost his wife, lost his unborn daughter, so he'd suffered enough."

"But you don't think he has."

I looked at Sheila again.

"Suffered enough," Sheila said.

Her hand was still in mine. It felt odd now. Foreign.

"And you do?" I asked.

She squeezed my hand, held it tightly for a long time, finally relaxed.

"I think that you lost your mother." Her voice was barely a whisper. "I think you lost a little sister you never saw. And your father can never do anything about that."

"But—"

Another squeeze of my hand. It was clear she was not finished.

"But you lost two people in that accident: your mother and your sister. And your father . . ."

"Yes?"

Sheila sniffled, once. "Your father lost three. He lost *you* that night as well."

As gently as I could, I released her hand.

"Greg . . ."

"Sheila." Of all the people in the world, the one that I least wanted to get hot under the collar with was her, yet I was getting hot under the collar. I walked to the edge of her improvised deck, and the wooden pallet creaked beneath my feet. "Have you ever had an addict—a junkie—in your family?"

She said nothing. Maybe she shook her head. I couldn't know; I was looking across the road at the sea, at phosphorescent wavelets curling onto the stony shore.

I turned. "I have. And they are beyond selfish. They only live to get high. They'll swear to you that they've kicked the habit, that they've changed. They have reprioritized their lives, and they can be so convincing. They seem so sincere. And then just when you trust them, they fall off the wagon and they're high all over again. Now I ask you, how many times is a person supposed to put up with such a thing?"

She replied, but she was weeping now, so I couldn't hear her. "Pardon?"

"I said . . ." Sheila took a breath. " 'Seventy times seven.' "

I looked skyward in exasperation, took a step back from her, and walked into the darkness, off the edge of her wooden-pallet deck.

It wasn't a big drop, maybe six inches to account for the thickness of the pallet, and another eight for the cinder blocks it was resting on. But you know how it feels when you step in the dark off a ledge of indeterminate height? That empty, creepy, off-into-the-void sort of feeling?

And of course I turned my ankle when I finally touched ground. Not broke it, not even sprained it, but pronated it far enough for it to be painful, and set me firmly on my rump, which was also painful.

My gentility abandoned me as I cursed, grabbing my ankle—not wanting to grab my backside. Then Sheila was on the ground beside me, and her arms were around me, and she was rocking me back and forth as I shook with anger, and my impotence when it came to curing my sick excuse for what was left of a family. I felt the hot wetness of her tears in the part of my hair as I reached up and touched her face, and she went on rocking me. She began to hum, and once the shakiness had gone out of her voice, she began to sing, softly, her voice a whisper. It was the tune I'd played for her on the banjo, the old hymn "Will the Circle Be Unbroken."

> There are loved ones in the glory
> Whose dear forms you often miss.
> When you close your earthly story,
> Will you join them in their bliss?

It calmed me. I had grown up in a household where I had been sung to all of my childhood, and the words she sung were the ones my mother had once used—not the Carter Family version but the original words of the old Ada Habershorn hymn—and it calmed me.

How could Sheila have known that music would soothe me so?

Then again, how could she have not?

When finally my shaking subsided, she stopped rocking and simply smoothed my hair with her fingertips, sighing one of those shuddering sorts of empty-it-all-out sighs.

And that's when Sheila asked, "Greg? Do you believe in God?"

I pulled my head back and looked up at her. "God? Sure. Sure I do."

"I mean the God of the Bible. Jesus. The Trinity. Love. Salvation. All of that."

"Yes." I have to admit—it took me longer to answer that time.

She kissed me on my head.

"Your mother," she said. "Her child . . . do you think they're with Christ right now, right at this very moment?"

I stopped breathing for a moment, realized that I was doing it and took a breath.

"Yes," I told her. "I hope so. Yes."

She kissed my head again.

"I know what you mean," she whispered. "My brother? The one who drowned? I heard him say he was a Christian, and everything I saw about him—well, most of the things I saw about him—led me to believe that what he was saying was the truth. He believed in God. He trusted Jesus—I hope he did. And I want with all my heart to believe he is there right now. I do believe that. I really do."

I nodded, my head still cradled against her.

"When I am convinced of that, Greg—really truly convinced, as I am at this very minute—then I have to wonder why I get so sad when thinking about my brother's passing. I mean, it wasn't sad for him. It isn't now. He is alive forever, in the presence of eternal love. And nothing we have on this earth, not even this—" she hugged me and held the hug for a long moment—"not even this can compare to what he's feeling right now. Wouldn't you agree?"

"I suppose," I said. "Yes."

"Then it begs the question, Greg." She released me, lifted my chin so we were eye to eye. "Who are we bitter for? The ones we have lost? Or ourselves? And if it is us we are bitter for, then who really is it?"

"Is it?" Her eyes still looked the same color.

"Who is it," Sheila asked, "that's being selfish?"

She turned away and looked up at the sky, and I looked with her, at Orion, at Betelgeuse, and at their thousands or billions of cousins, burning coldly, light-year upon light-year away.

THIRTY-TWO

Orion, Ted remembered from his lessons, was The Hunter, holding aloft the carcass of a freshly slain lion.

Ted stood at the edge of the harbor and looked up into the night sky at the familiar constellation. He wondered, as he had since he was a boy—not so very long ago—why someone had decided to call it The Hunter. After all, the most distinctive feature was the back-slanted T, the belt and the sword. It seemed to Ted that a more apt name would be "The Warrior."

"I suppose you believe that I have ruined your evening for you."

Ted did not turn at the sound of Oscar Emmons's voice. He continued gazing at the sky. "And what would you believe, landlord?"

"Oh, I am 'landlord' now, am I?"

"It is what you suggested, sir, when first we met."

"Then if you are so obedient to my wishes, would you turn to face me as we speak?"

Ted turned. Emmons had left the inn without his hat. Only the white wig covered his head.

"Your wig does not become you," Ted told him.

Emmons reached up, grasped the wig by its crown, and pulled

it off. The effect was remarkably like that of a man scalping him-self. And when he had finished, he looked about and then held the white horsehair wig in both hands, his bald head rimmed by starlight.

"Mr. Bascombe was penniless," Emmons said. "He gave all he had, save the cost of his passage, to his wife when he sent her back to Scotland."

Ted nudged a rock on the thin beach with the toe of his boot. "Oh, sold his chandlery and took his bloody profit, did he?"

Emmons turned the wig in his hands. "He told me that he burned it. Burned it to the ground and prevented his neighbors from saving it."

Ted squinted at him in the dark.

"He did not wish it to be an enterprise of that trade any longer," Emmons said. "He did not wish to step aside, only to have another take his place. So he burned his chandlery, his stock, everything. The only thing he sold was his house and the land his business had stood upon."

"And he just happened to come to you?"

"Captain Henry suggested the arrangement."

Ted felt his eyes go wide, despite his efforts to appear detached. "Henry?"

Emmons parted the wig with his thick fingertips. "Your fa— Mr. Bascombe needs work to buy his passage back to Scotland. I needed the help. And, Ted, he is a most contrite man."

Ted pulled a leather pouch from his broad belt, opened it, began to count sovereigns, and then stopped. He held the bag out, entire, offering it to Emmons.

"What is this?" The older man asked.

"His passage." Ted shook the bag, the coins ringing solidly against one another within it. "Take it. Buy him passage, food for the voyage. Send him back to Scotland and out of my sight."

Emmons ignored the offered bag. "He is frail from the voyage. He needs time ashore. To be fed up. To regain his strength."

Ted dropped the bag and held his hands out to either side, looked up at the cold, distant stars. "Is everyone against me? Do you plot to keep me in torment? Yes, I agree that he may not have put the chains upon me, but he helped to put them on hundreds, on thousands."

Emmons picked up the bag and held it out. Ted did not take it.

"I do not have your experience, son," the older man said. "I was not taken into slavery."

Ted nodded, his mouth a straight line.

"I was not taken," Emmons repeated. "I was born into my bonds."

The younger man looked the older in his eyes, searching them.

"On Saint Lucia," Emmons said. "My mother herself was second-generation slave. My father—the man I called my father—was a slave from the next plantation over. They married secretly, but he did not father me. Our master thought it sport to bring in big brutes of men—his 'stud stock,' he called them—and let them force themselves on the women while he watched. I owe my size, my strength, to the pain that was forced upon my mother."

Ted found himself putting a hand to his mouth, then stopped himself.

"My father's master was kinder, or as kind as a slave driver could be. He allowed my father to plant cotton on some land he cleared himself, and to work his field in the dusk, after he had worked his master's fields. It took him seven years to make enough money from cotton to buy his own freedom, and that of my mother and me. And then he brought us all here to Tortola, and he started this inn—named it after a public house a sailor had told him about, because he liked the name. He said the rose reminded him of my mother, and the crown reminded him of what he would one day cast at his Savior's feet. But that was not before I too had worked a man's fields, for naught, and while still a child felt the lash against my back."

"You were a slave?"

"For seven years," Emmons said.

Ted beat his hand against his thigh. "You were a slave and you do not hate a man who filled his pockets from the slave trade?"

Emmons leaned down, set his white wig upon a low boulder, and put the pouch full of gold coins atop it. "I hate what he did. But for him I feel only pity."

"Pity?" Ted nearly shouted the word. "How can that be?"

Emmons looked out at the dark waters of the harbor, then he glanced at the younger man. "When you told me that you have memorized much of the testament of our Lord, was that the truth or an empty boast?"

Ted straightened. "It was truth."

Emmons nodded. "The fifteenth chapter of Luke, there is a story about a young man, and a verse that reads, 'And when he came to himself, he said, How many hired servants of my father's have bread enough and to spare, and I perish with hunger!' Do you know the passage of which I speak?"

Ted nodded sullenly.

"Then give me that which comes next," Emmons told him.

Ted stood, mute.

"Come, boy," Emmons said. "What comes next?"

Ted cleared his throat. " 'I will arise and go to my father, and will say unto him, Father, I have sinned against heaven, and before thee, and am no more worthy to be called thy son: make me as one of thy hired servants.' "

"That is it," Emmons said. "Keep going."

" 'And he arose, and came to his father. But when he was yet a great way off, his father saw him, and had compassion, and ran, and fell on his neck, and kissed him. And the son said unto him, Father, I have sinned against heaven, and in thy sight, and am no more worthy to be called thy son.

" 'But the father said to his servants, Bring forth the best robe, and put it on him; and put a ring on his hand, and shoes on his feet: And bring hither the fatted calf, and kill it; and let us eat, and be merry: For this my son was dead, and is alive again; he was lost, and is found.' "

"Exactly," Emmons said. "And the next words are what?"

" 'And they,' " Ted concluded, " 'began to be merry.' "

"That is so," Emmons said. He leaned down and picked up both the pouch and the wig. "They began to be merry, as we have been tonight. This man who had been so deeply wronged, with the man who had wronged him. Because the one wronged showed grace to the other's contrition. And if there can be a prodigal son, is a prodigal father so difficult to imagine?"

Ted said nothing.

"I think not," Emmons said. "This is how our Savior views repentance, and who are we to view it elsewise?"

Emmons handed Ted his pouch. This time the younger man took it.

"And now . . ." Emmons set the white wig back on his head. "Let us make merry."

It went against every fiber of Ted's nature, but he followed the older man: back to the inn, and back into the darkened doorway.

THIRTY-THREE

The doorway to the trailer was in shadow, a stark contrast to the September sunlight. The sun had been up for only a couple of hours, and already the air was warm.

I went back into the trailer. I didn't go back in there *for* anything. I just went in, stood at the sink in the kitchen. I turned on the water. The noise of it running seemed to help.

"Greg?"

Sheila stood in the open doorway. Behind her was a resurrective miracle: the Ford Fiesta, idling smoothly in the Key West sun, seedpods cleansed from its exterior, although the imprints of several leaves remained, the Fiesta having once been white. *Peabody* had been in port the week previous, and during her reprovisioning, our divemaster, Hans, had proven to be not only an able mechanic but exceptionally malleable when presented with an Australian accent and a smile. He'd even seemed more than satisfied when his reward turned out to be lunch at the Hog's Breath.

Truth be told, I'd hoped he would run into a jam—some rare Ford part from the Pleistocene era that would have to be ordered in from Detroit via Miami. But he hadn't. He'd just cleaned the spark plugs—"sparking plugs" to him, as he was Dutch—removed the mouse nest from the air cleaner, charged up the battery, and sprayed about a quart of Gumout into the carburetor. Next thing you know, the old Ford was ready for a trip to Miami, if we put our minds to it. And Ramrod Key—where Boondocks was located— was a mere twenty-four miles away.

"Greg?"

I'd had a couple of months to get used to the idea. You'd think I would have done so by now. I hadn't.

"Greg?"

I turned the water off. "It's just not a good idea, Sheila."

"We don't have to talk to him. He might not even see you. Let's just go."

I waved a hand at the window. "It's broad daylight, Sheil. It's a Gospel brunch, not a dark theater. He's going to see *everybody*. And if he sees me, he's going to think I'm there to offer the olive branch."

"That, or pull the timber from your eye."

I sagged. When Sheila began regressing into Bible-verse short-hand, I knew we were entering territory from which there was no escape. We went out and got into the Fiesta, myself in the driver's seat, because I'm from North Carolina, and as progressive as I like to think I am, I occasionally regress and view driving as a gene-linked activity.

Sheila happily took the passenger's side. She loved to sightsee, still getting a kick out of the fact that in America you could sit in the front seat on the right side of a car and not have a steering wheel in front of you.

"Perhaps," she said as I started the Fiesta, "we could swing by your apartment before we leave."

"Sure." I put the car into gear. "Why?"

"To get your banjo."

I put it back in neutral, shut off the engine.

Sheila laughed. "Oh, come off it, mate. I'm having you on."

Was she? I glanced her way, started the engine again, and we were off.

It wasn't much of a road trip. Even with RVs ahead of us, lumbering along at ten miles per hour under the limit, and slowdowns for those suicidal few who seemed to believe that the Overseas Highway was a bicycle path, we made Ramrod Key in just forty minutes. It was ten forty-five. The flyer had said the music would begin at eleven.

I have to admit that I looked for my father's Ford Econoline van, the one he'd been using for his touring when I'd last seen him. And I had this moment of hopefulness when I didn't see it. But then I saw a tan Chevy van with North Carolina plates parked near the kitchen entrance, and I realized that he'd probably bought or leased something new. He was like that—he held on to that old motorcycle and his pickup for decades, but when it came to what he toured with, he traded in and bought new every four years, because what he used for work had to be dependable.

My mom's car too. He traded hers every five years, and the dealer was always waiting for it, for she never racked up that many miles.

Through the open windows of the old Ford—it lacked air-conditioning, a glaring omission in the Keys anytime, but especially in the heat of mid-September—I could smell bacon, roast beef with a hint of garlic, and barbecued something. Maybe chicken.

I shut off the engine.

"Ah." Sheila stretched. "I'm famished."

Now that we were no longer moving, subtropical heat was beginning to creep into the car.

I pulled the key from the ignition, pocketed it. "I think I'll just sit here a bit."

"Not hungry?"

"No."

Sheila ran her fingers through the hair on the back of my head. I think it was starting to feel a little damp, but if she noticed she did not say.

"Thank you." Her voice was very soft.

I looked out the windshield at the palmetto bushes that line the back of Boondocks' gravel parking area.

"I know how difficult this is, Greg."

"Do you?" I looked her way.

She nodded. "When my mum went nutters—her expression, not mine—well, the way it started was that my dad came in at breakfast time and she'd overfilled the grease fryer for the crullers she was making, and it had run onto the burner and flames were leaping up, all the way to the ceiling. A week after the funeral, this was. And my mum wasn't doing a thing. Just standing there, weeping. The shelf above the stove was already starting to singe. My dad actually had to lift her up and set her aside so he could use the fire extinguisher. So she went from there to hospital, and from hospital to . . . to the place where they finally put her."

It was now warm enough in the car that my neck *was* damp. Yet Sheila didn't seem to notice the heat.

"And before I went to visit her there the first time, my dad had a talk with me. Told me not to be frightened, but that my mum was not herself. That she rarely spoke, and she fussed when they tried to wash her, and the one time he'd come in he'd found that she had soiled herself and she had taken the poo and smeared it on her arms."

"Wow."

"No joke. And I'd known my mum was ill, but this just freaked me out, you know? Because, I mean, she was my *mum*. The person who'd raised me, who dried my tears. Always the strong one in our family. The rock. And when you come to think of someone like that, to think of them as capable, and dependable, and unshakable, it is very, very frightening to discover that they are not. I made it all the way to the door of her room on Dutch courage, but then when I got there I found I could not reach out to take hold of the door, could not open it because I did not want to see what was on the other side."

Sheila stopped talking. Outside her window was another palmetto bush, and on one of its saber-like leaves a small lizard sat, the wattle beneath his throat expanding and then contracting as he proclaimed his territory.

"What did you do?" I asked.

She put her hand on mine. "I told myself that it was not forever. That my mum had . . . fallen, that she had gone to this terrible secret place out of desperation, but that it would not last, and that one day soon she would return, and she would be whole again. She would be my mum again. And you know what? I was right." She brightened, gave my hand a squeeze. "So, shall we go in?"

"I'd rather wait until the music starts."

And right then, as if a celestial cue had been given, we heard the quaint and intricate sound of a bluegrass banjo.

Boondocks had been built as a couple of big decks, a main floor that fronted what served as the dance floor when Howard and Mile Marker 24 were jitterbugging, and an upper deck where the bar was located. They had steam tables set up on both levels, and the main floor was already full. The hostess, a girl in a long skirt and a buttoned blouse—not the short-shorts and midriff tee one would expect at Boondocks when Howard was playing—showed us upstairs. We got a table above the stage and to the side, out of my father's sight line, unless he looked up, which I knew he eventually would.

He was opening the way he always opened when he played

for dinners, doing what he called "seating music"—no vocals, and nothing tricky or intricate. Just some background music for people to get settled by.

He was maybe thirty feet away, as close as we'd been in five years. The funny thing was that he didn't seem to have aged at all. His hair was a little shorter, and he wasn't bleaching it anymore, so there was some gray showing among the light brown. He still had the thin vertical strip of beard just beneath his lower lip that made him look like a movie pirate, and he appeared healthy. He had a tan and was wearing an Aloha shirt, no doubt out of deference to Boondocks' tiki-hut décor. I wondered if he was back building houses with Habitat for Humanity. Before the accident, it had been one of his favorite ways to spend a rare weekend off.

He was playing the old song "Down to the River to Pray," and he was playing it exactly the way he'd taught it to me, complete with the parts that sounded like improvisation but were actually carefully rehearsed, put together through trial and error years before and kept intact once they'd been perfected.

He was looking up from time to time, saying "Hello" and "Good morning" and "How you doing" to people as they passed the band-stand. Even that had a purpose, I knew, as he was looking at the readouts on all his sound gear, checking levels, and exchanging greetings was a lot more cordial and less sterile than doing the "Check one-two-three, check, check," which amateurs resorted to through a microphone.

I knew the song well enough that I could tell when he was about to wrap it up. That would be a natural time for him to scan the crowd, and when he did it, I wanted my back to him.

"Let's get something to eat," I told Sheila. She lifted one eyebrow—just a little—but then got up and followed me to the steam table.

"Good morning." Even over the sound system the voice was

familiar, the voice I'd heard at breakfast nearly every morning for nineteen years. "I'm Ted Rhode."

Like that. Not "Ted Rhodes." Maybe the family name was fit for performance after all. Then again, it was printed as *Rhodes* on the concert flyer.

"Boondocks has graced us with quite a spread this morning. I wonder if you'd mind if I just went ahead and said grace for us all?"

We were at the steam table as he said this, and Sheila immediately closed her eyes and bowed her head. That irritated me a bit. It irritated me even more when I did the same.

"Gracious heavenly Father, we thank you for the bounty with which you have greeted us on this beautiful morning." The voice on the PA sounded genuine, sincere. He always had. "We ask you to bless it to our bodies, and to bless us to your purpose. In Jesus Christ's name we ask this . . . "

The amen rippled all around the restaurant, and when I opened my eyes, I was trembling—not enough that you would notice it, but enough that I had to rest my plate against the bar on the steam table so it didn't rattle.

I hated him. Part of me did. Hated him as the selfish thief that he was, the taker of my mother's life. And part of me wanted to run down there and throw my arms around him, and for that I hated myself.

"Um, excuse me?" A tall young woman, who looked as if she put on her makeup with a picture of Gwen Stefani next to the mirror, was standing next to me, plate in hand, nodding at the poached sea bass.

"Sorry." I stepped back and let her through. I hadn't put anything on my plate yet, so I got some scrambled eggs and biscuits and gravy and went back to our table, where Sheila was smiling over rare prime rib and mixed grilled vegetables.

His sets had changed. Or maybe he had mixed them up for the brunch, but some of the picking was different too. Much as it vexed me to admit it, he'd gotten even better since I'd last heard him.

He started with some old favorites, inviting people to sing along on the last verse of "Amazing Grace," and doing a long improvisation—one I'd never heard before—on "When the Roll Is Called Up Yonder." Then, as he played the opening bars of "Smoky Mountain Prayer," one of the singles that had gone gold off his second album, everyone in the place applauded.

Everybody but me.

I had a roommate in college who was an amateur magician and always wanted to be a better magician, so he was always dragging me off to shows when The Amazing Blackstone or Daniel Chesterfield or David Copperfield were in town.

And the thing about a great magician—a truly great magician— is that, even though you know how the trick is being done, that the performer himself is doing nothing, but his assistant is contorting herself so she can fit into that tiny space and the spin of the box is being done, not to show you that there are no contrivances, but so she can stick the mechanical legs out of the hole in the box for the sawed-in-two trick, he sells it nonetheless. You know it's fake, and you know the legerdemain behind the illusion, but you believe it anyhow, and you are charmed.

A really good musician is that way as well. I think it was Don Henley of the Eagles who said the key to touring successfully was an exceptionally high tolerance for rote repetition.

Put somebody talented onstage, and they can make you think that you are watching their first concert, and yet they are performing it perfectly, not missing a single note. They can make it look as if they are enjoying it as much as you are and in fact they often are.

You would never suspect that they had already played the same music, in the same order, and cracked the same between-set jokes fifty times that month.

It takes a rare individual to pull that off. My father could do it, though. When I looked across the table at Sheila, she had set down her knife and fork and was just sitting there, nodding, smiling, enthralled. And then when I looked down at the stage again, my father was looking up as he sang.

He was looking right at me.

The nod was so imperceptible that I doubt anyone there except me, and possibly Sheila, noticed it. It was the nod he used to give at an event when he'd look out into an audience and see my mother and me, a secret acknowledgment just among family. He never stopped playing. And then he played eight songs more, until he reached the end of his first set, when he said something about needing to pick at some bacon before he picked at any more banjo. He started a DVD of some set musician friends of his that I recognized—fiddle and mandolin and dulcimer—and he left the stage.

It was weird, waiting for him to come up. Of course, it would have been weirder if he hadn't. And when he did, he was pretty civil about it all: a handshake for me, and a "Thanks for coming," and then he turned to Sheila and said, "Hi, I'm Ted," and that was all it took for her to envelop him in a hug as she gushed, "I am Sheila, and you are *fabulous*."

Then, as if he saw us every weekend, he said, "Well, I'm going to get a bite, okay?" And he left for the steam table.

"I'm sorry," I told Sheila. "I should have introduced you."

"Not to worry." She put her hand on mine. "I daresay this is passing odd for you, what?"

I can't raise one eyebrow like her, so I raised two. "You just got *very* Australian on me there."

She sipped her sweet tea. "It's passing odd for me too."

I was glad to have her there. Not just for the moral support, or for the fact that just about anything, up to and including a root canal, would be better in the company of Sheila McIntyre, but because she kept things cordial. Having a third person there had a moderating effect, like the zinc plate you put on an outboard motor so the salt water won't corrode the other metals. My father didn't ask me where I'd been for the past few years, and I didn't ask him why he wasn't dead yet.

Like I said: cordial.

We talked about the Keys, about some bluegrass players we both knew. He ate to fill the silences, and when he'd finished his breakfast—mostly fruit and just a little protein, because he was playing—he looked at me, cocked his head, and said, "So . . . want to sit in on the next set?"

"No, thanks." I shook my head. "I haven't touched an instrument in years." Then Sheila shot me a look, and I added, "Not really."

My father shrugged. "They say it's like riding a bike."

"And I wouldn't want to try riding a bike right now," I said. "Not in front of an audience."

He laughed. "Okay." Turning to Sheila, he said, "But you should twist his arm sometime. Guitar, banjo, mandolin. You name it; this guy's great."

"Well, it's easy to see where he got it from."

And we let that oil rest upon the water for a while.

He was just getting up to start the second set when Arvin, the owner of Boondocks, swung by. My dad introduced us by name as "my son" and "his friend," and Arvin said, "If I had a friend like that, I'd marry her," which got everybody laughing. Then Arvin said to my father, "Hey, Ted, I know this is short notice, and you're probably booked, but do you have anything on for next Sunday?"

"Sunday?" My father dug an iPhone out of his pocket and checked its calendar. "No. I don't have a gig at all until a week from Tuesday—Atlanta."

"Great!" Arvin clapped him on the back. "I had a cancellation. Can you do this again next week? I'll make it worth your while. I got a friend who can take you sportfishing every day if you want— my treat. And I'm sure we can find you a room."

"He won't need it," Sheila said.

Arvin glanced her way. "He won't?"

"No." She smiled. "Greg has a sleeper sofa in his apartment." She turned to me. "Don't you?"

"Um, yes."

"You local?" Arvin asked me.

"Key West."

"Oh yeah?" He crossed his arms. "Where do you work?"

"Treasure Hunters," Sheila told him. "Phil Rackham's operation."

"No kidding?" Arvin laughed. "Well, tell Phil thanks."

"Thanks?" I asked it, but I was still thinking about the sleeper sofa idea.

"For recommending your dad," Arvin said. "If the second set's like the first, and word gets out, we'll fill every single table here next week."

Then I was looking at Sheila, and she was shaking her head as much as she could without making it obvious, and then Arvin was gone, making the rounds with his customers.

"Listen." My father took a last sip of ice water. "I can crash in a motel. I'm in one right now and couldn't be out until tomorrow, earliest, anyhow. I don't want to be on top of you."

He looked at the two of us, Sheila and me, as he said that, and maybe that's why I said, "No. Really. It'd be fine. My pleasure."

"You sure?"

"Positive," Sheila said. She smiled at me as she said it. A sweet smile.

"So," I said after he'd left. "The fine hand of Phil Rackham."

"I swear," Sheila told me. "I didn't know a thing. Scout's honor."

"You were a scout?"

"Girl Guide."

"Well." As the music began again, I wondered to myself what there was that I could be doing on the *Peabody* for the next seven days. "It should be an interesting week."

THIRTY-FOUR

"One week?" Thatch asked. "Are you certain?"

Ted looked from the pirate to the sea captain he was speaking with. He had just stepped into The Rose and Crown, and his eyes were still adjusting to the light, but he was certain that the captain—for his waistcoat and fine hat identified him as such—was no one he had ever seen before.

"Today is Thursday, and that makes it one week to the day," the sea captain said. "We were on the Golden Rock, unloading, when in comes this Spanish commodore, bold as you please, his ship o' the line moored just outside the breakwater, longboat standing by at the dock. And when the captain of the garrison asks him his business, he says that a nephew of the Spanish royals had been robbed in the Mona Passage, and that they had it on good authority that a large ruby taken in the event had been sold by a merchant on Saint Eustatius the month before, and he meant to find out where that merchant hails from. Garrison captain calls for his sergeant to ride up the hill with orders to load guns, and it wasn't until then that the Spaniard backed down. But they are on the hunt, sir. They are most certainly on the hunt. I will wager we have not seen the last of that swell of a Spaniard."

"We should have cut it," Thatch thought aloud. He took two gold sovereigns from his pocket. "For your kindness."

"Very gracious of you," the sea captain said. He did not touch the coins. "But if it's all the same to you, Cap'n, sir, I've a three-master called the *Tulip*, and she don't always sail under the same ensign, if you catch my drift."

"I do," Thatch said. "You have my word that she will not be molested. Not by me, or my company, or any company we keep."

"That is kind of you." The sea captain accepted Thatch's offered hand. "Well, sir, I would steer clear, were I you, of any gunships flying Philip's standard. Fact of the matter is, I will steer clear of them myself. And a very good day to you."

With that, the man drained his tankard and left.

"What was that about?" Ted asked as the inn door closed again.

"We must call a parlay," Thatch told him. "All hands. The women too. And Oscar Emmons. And your . . . Vicar Bascombe. We must call him too. As soon as we can muster, we must talk." The pirate shook his head. "It is the height of the storm season. I'd hoped to wait later . . . until November."

Ted's heart began to pound. He had never seen Captain Thatch so agitated. "Henry," he said. It was the first time he had ever addressed the pirate by his Christian name. "What is it?"

"We are betrayed," Thatch told him. "Not yet, but surely very soon. And when we are, it is not Wapping Old Stairs that we must worry about. Some Spanish commodore's sword will cleave our heads. Time remains, but very little. The fuse is lit. Gather the men."

Ted found Ben, and together they spread the word, a daunting task because Thatch's company of pirates was not a crew in the classic sense of the term, but a very fluid organization. Some of them planted during the season, and pirated only over the dormant months of midwinter. Others alternated between benders ashore and raids at sea. Still others sailed with whatever crew was leaving the harbor, and a few practically lived on the Jamaica-built sloop.

Only those last were easy to find. The rest took a full afternoon of hunting, and when all of those had been summoned, and Anne and Sally and Emmons and Bascombe told as well, it was coming on evening. The gathering could not be held in town; there were too many ears, and the group was apt to prove riotous if gathered near an open tap. So Thatch called the parlay at Sopper's Hole, an anchorage just west of Road Town, where any lights or fires would be shielded from passing vessels by the low, wooded mass of Frenchman's Cay.

They sailed the *Regent* there at sunset, arriving in a throng of some four dozen vessels: everything from dugout canoes and dories to single-masted skiffs and another sloop, which was well past her oceangoing years. A large pit had been dug on the beach, and several wild boars were already turning on their spits. When the *Regent* dropped anchor, a cheer went up.

"We shall see," Thatch said as he and Ted swung down into the longboat, "if they love me so much once they hear what I have to say."

"My friends . . ." Thatch's voice rolled across the two hundred people assembled on the beach, then echoed back from the vessels moored off Frenchman's Cay. "Very soon I go a-pirating!"

Another cheer roared back from the crowd.

Thatch waited until the noise had subsided. "And very soon after that, I shall pirate nevermore."

At that, no noise at all was heard from the crowd. The only

sounds were the wind in the palms, wavelets on the beach, the sputtering of the fires. Two torches stood to either side of Thatch, their flickering orange light playing over his face. Around him stood the great semicircle of pirates—not pirates only, but their wives as well, some with babes in their arms.

"Philip," Thatch said, "that lisping coward who sits on the Spanish throne . . ." Boos erupted and subsided. "He has bankrupted his nation to build a navy, and now that navy is hot upon our heels."

"Let 'im come!" The shout went up from the edge of the crowd, and everyone laughed.

"That is the spirit of a pirate of Tortola," Thatch agreed. "But the mark Philip has placed is on our heads in particular. Just last week, a Spanish ship of the line tested the resolve of His Majesty's garrison at Saint Eustatius, and he was there in pursuit of the *Regent*."

The crowd fell silent again.

"We are our own men," Thatch declared. "Each free to do as he chooses. But the pirating that I will begin soon will end in the Carolina colony, and once I am there I intend to take King George's pardon."

Ted looked at his old friend, his eyes wide. A hundred conversations erupted at once, until a pistol was loosed into the air, silencing the crowd.

"What good does an English king's pardon do against the navies of Spain?"

Much grumbling showed that some of the crowd was of the same mind.

"None whatsoever," Thatch admitted. "Unless one flees to a well-garrisoned holding of the crown. I myself intend to take to London."

"We've farms here," shouted someone in the crowd.

"And you may farm them if you wish," Thatch said. "These

many years I have urged you to share no family names aboard ship. None has been called to our quarry save mine, and it is my head in particular that Madrid craves. I can guarantee no man's safety, but I strongly suspect that only my close associates will share my peril."

After he said this, Thatch looked at Ben and Ted, and at Oscar Emmons, who stood, large arms crossed, with his daughter and Anne Thatch.

"But he who takes the pardon, infamous or not, regardless of any . . . questions regarding his letters of marque, shall be safe from His Majesty's courts," Thatch continued.

"No pardon!" another man shouted.

"Let the captain speak," cried another. And at that, four or five brief fistfights broke out.

Thatch let them quell and then raised a hand.

"The pardon is each man's decision," he said. "But I sail in three days' time, and I shall need a crew. If you sail with me to Bath, in the Carolina colony, tell me by the morrow."

"Three days?" The questioner was an older man who wore a coat, despite the warmth of the evening. "Cap'n, not to say you are not wise in the ways of the sea but, sir, this 'ere is the Caribbean, and it's coming up on the top of hurricane season."

"Thank you, Joseph," Thatch replied. "I have considered that."

"But the Carolinas, Cap'n. If a storm takes you on the open sea, you'll 'ave no place to go."

"I know that. But if the Spanish can best our garrison here and take me—and I believe they can—then the gallows is the *only* place I'll go."

All up and down the beach, the pirates grumbled.

"Three days' time?" Oscar Emmons asked.

Only a small group—Emmons, Thatch, Bold Ted, Ben, Sally, and Anne—was gathered on the quarterdeck of the *Regent*. Bascombe was aboard as well, but he lingered in the shadows near the bow, respectful of the fact that Ted only spoke to him rarely, and only when there was a need.

"Why so soon?"

"I am going by my gut," Thatch said. "And my gut says we must leave this island as soon as possible, and three days' time is the minimum I can countenance for men, for families, to wrap up their affairs and depart."

Emmons nodded, the skin of his head reflecting the watch lamp hanging from the boom. "I can understand that. Were I to have to leave my home? My inn? I can scarcely think of all that would need to be done. I doubt that I could do it."

"But, Oscar . . ." Thatch's voice was as gentle as Ted had ever heard it. "You must. Anyone close to me is in peril. They would take you to try to get to me. I know it seems much to ask, but I have much set aside. I can sell some of my holdings, buy you a new inn in Dorchester."

Emmons shook as if he had been punched. "No. Feldman, the baker, has been approaching me with offers on my inn for many years. And you think it is necessary for the safety . . ." He looked at Sally, and Thatch nodded.

"Even then, it shall not be entirely safe," Thatch explained. "There is the weather, as Joseph told us. And some of us must sail upon prizes."

"Prizes? You mean to take more ships on your way to Carolina? Haven't you taken enough?"

Thatch laughed. "Wealth? I daresay I have enough for several lifetimes. But I must take prizes because I need the ships." He gestured toward the pirates gathered, eating and drinking, on the shore in the warm summer night. "I know these men, and I daresay most will elect to go with me. But the *Regent* is only a sloop, snug for fifty and impossible for all this company. I need the ships to put deck beneath their feet."

THIRTY-FIVE

"I need to be at sea." I pled my case.

Phil Rackham leaned back in his chair. "I admire your enthusiasm, Greg. But *Peabody*'s reprovisioning, and those new engines are being re-torqued. We won't be back on-site again for three, maybe four days."

"Don't you have anything?"

"What's the hurry?" Rackham put his hands behind his head. "Isn't your father in town?"

I crossed my arms. "Don't play coy with me, Phil. I talked to Arvin."

Phil was not a blusher, but he reddened a bit. "Nobody put a gun to your head and said you had to go to Boondocks. And before you ask, I never said a word to Sheila. I only projected the possibility."

"Phil . . ." I sat without being invited. "This evening, that 'possibility' is crashing on the couch in my apartment. Can I at least stay on the *Peabody* while you reprovision?"

He shook his head. "Exterminator is making a pass this morning. Food's off. Linens are off. Everybody's on the beach for the night. I'm afraid you're on your own for the evening. Check back with me again in the morning."

THIRTY-SIX

The morning came clear and cool, a steady breeze blowing—perfect sailing weather, rare for high summer.

The *Regent* was under sail an hour before dawn, her deck and hold crowded with nearly five times the number of men it took to crew her. They sailed southeast, toward the Dutch and French Indies, and a dexterous thin fellow was sent aloft, shinnying up the single mast to stand atop a deadeye and scan the horizon in all directions. At the bow, both Thatch and Ben peered through spyglasses, trying to coax sails from whitecaps.

At sunrise, sails were spotted, and the sloop gave chase. Then Thatch got a clear look at the stern. "T-U-L-I . . ." He collapsed the spyglass. "Leave off, lads. She is a friend."

It was late in the afternoon when they spotted the next sails: two masts and upbound. She turned away, toward the Atlantic, as soon as *Regent* began tacking toward her. She rode middling low in the water, and when they had come within a mile, closed gunports could be made out upon her sides, a Dutch flag flying at her stern.

There was an odd air upon the *Regent*. The captain was plaiting his ribbons within his beard, the mate painting himself blue, the men donning their tarred vests, and yet the mood was muted. They were doing this for one of the last times, possibly *the* last time. Soon every man aboard would be a farmer, a ferrier, or perhaps a merchant sailor—a man who would begin his stories with, "Back when I was a pirate . . ."

The flag of winged death was run to the mast top, the warning shot fired—well across the bow. Vapors were commenced. Their quarry opened her gunports.

"Jack," Thatch called to the gunner on the bow cannon. "Can you whistle her deck without touching her?"

The gunner nodded, pointed this way and that to communicate with the helm, nearly touched his match to his weapon several times, then stopped, regauged, and finally fired the shot. On the ship they were closing upon, men scattered as the iron shot screamed past, touching neither rail nor mast nor sail. The quarry came about, sails sagging as they lost the wind.

Her gunports were shuttered and remained so as she was boarded. A sullen young captain said something when he saw Thatch, and a crewman who spoke Dutch translated for him: "He says that he is a hired captain and he should have fought you, for he will lose his job for surrendering."

Thatch peered down into the hold that six of his men had wrested open. The ship was carrying cane sugar, sack after sack of it.

"Tell the captain that he chose well," Thatch said, "because by surrendering he lost only his job. And before any of the crew say something, tell them we shall take no volunteers for the brotherhood. We shall put them all off at first landfall."

He looked about as his men rounded up the prize's crew.

"Leave the cargo where it is," he called to Ben. "We shall sell it in Carolina. I have a buyer in mind as we speak. Ted, pick your crew. You shall sail this prize back to Road Town."

Ted took to the quarterdeck of the merchantman, the *Adelaar*, which the Dutch-speaking crewman told him meant "eagle." They dropped the prize's crew on the less-populated side of Guadeloupe, then set a course for Tortola. En route they flanked and took an unarmed schooner with two raked masts, her French master protesting that she carried nothing, and baffled when the pirates seemed pleased at that. Her crew was taken to Anguilla, the pirates pausing in the harbor long enough to winch cannon from the *Regent*'s hold and lightly arm the *Dauphin*, their new prize. Then, navigating by the stars, Ted led the little three-ship fleet to Road Town, where they reached the harbor just as dawn was breaking, a long day done, with much of the crew asleep upon the deck.

From the quarterdeck of the prize, Ted glassed the harbor that had been his home for a little more than seven months. Up on the hill, Thatch's house was already shuttered, the place closed up as if Anne had known this day would one day come and had long been planning for it. In front of The Rose and Crown, workmen were loading a cart with a small collection of trunks. From up the hill, people were walking with bags and boxes, carrying only what was necessary, a small exodus of pirates, leaving their homes as soon as they had seen the *Regent* enter the harbor.

A longboat pulled alongside, and Thatch came aboard, easily climbing the rope dropped to him, wiping the salt from his hands once he was on the deck.

"Odd times," he said to Ted, and Ted nodded. "I am sorry, Bold Ted."

"For what, Captain?"

"For pulling you into this." Thatch made a small sweep of his hand, taking in the crowded dock, the flotilla of boats being rowed out to the three pirate ships.

"Henry, you pulled me from my chains and introduced me to the woman I shall wed. No apology is necessary."

Thatch wiped his brow with his sleeve, an odd gesture for him.

"Lad, I made a good man into a thief."

"And now we repent." Ted looked over his rigging; the men had lashed the sails as efficiently as if she were a naval vessel ready for inspection. "But, Captain, once we are under way to Carolina, I do have one favor to ask."

Thatch looked at him.

"Say it, my friend," he said, "and it shall be yours."

THIRTY-SEVEN

The ships had been sailing all day, their course west by northwest, their departure timed so the winds would put them within sight of the North American coast at dawn the next day. From there, navigation would be simple: follow the coast north to where the great knuckle of the Carolina colony jutted out into the broad Atlantic. The sun was low, just off the port bow, sinking toward water that gave no hint of the great continent that lay before them.

Ted ran a finger under his collar. It felt odd to be dressed in his finest with the *Regent* under way, odder still to see Oscar Emmons in his white wig and his tricorner hat, Sally on his arm, breathtaking in the exquisite blue dress.

"I had long thought," Thatch said from his place at the stern rail, "that we would celebrate this event ashore. And celebrate it ashore we shall, but not this night. This is the first time ever I shall perform this rite as captain, and it pleases me to no end to do so for two dear friends."

Anne Thatch sniffled, smiling, a gloved hand to her eyes. Even Ben, the first mate, gave a snort and blinked a bit.

"But before we begin," Thatch said, "let us hear a word about this occasion."

Bascombe stepped to his side. He was dressed in a waistcoat too large for him, the best that could be found in the *Adelaar*'s wardrobes, and he was carrying Oscar Emmons's Bible.

Ted felt his shoulders tense. He had not anticipated the event as taking place on this day, but Sally had asked for it, and Sally had asked for little else.

" 'Husbands,' " Bascombe read in his Scottish brogue, " 'love your wives, even as Christ also loved the church, and gave himself for it; that he might sanctify and cleanse it with the washing of water by the word. . . . ' "

Ted listened to the words, words he had heard on so many Sundays in the cool parlor of the house in Axim Town. He had heard the blessed assurances of Scripture, unaware that the man who read them to his—*family* was the word that came to mind, but it seemed deceptive, foreign now—that the man who read them to Ted and Mrs. Bascombe was outfitting, the other six days of the week, ships that stole freedom and dignity and life.

And yet this was a joyous occasion. A day to celebrate. And they were on their way to a pardon. Those two things—the celebration and the pardon—reminded Ted of something he had once heard: that when the king celebrated a joyous occasion, such as a birthday, or a holiday, or a wedding, one of the things he would do was to pardon someone who had been judged, so those beyond the king's circle would share his joy.

Ted was fairly certain he could not do that. Could not pardon Bascombe, not from the bottom of his heart. Not forever. But to keep this day bright for his Sally, he thought that perhaps he could do it for one day. So he looked into her eyes and he let the old man speak, and when the reading of the Scripture had ended and Captain Henry stepped before Ted and Sally, when Ted looked up, there was a smile upon his face, and it was genuine.

"Who gives this woman in marriage?" Thatch asked.

"I do," Oscar Emmons replied.

And the ship was filled with a golden glow, the sinking sun kissing the small sloop with the last yellow light of the day.

THIRTY-EIGHT

The sun was painting the docks and the buildings in shades of pink and gold, but the crowd gathered on Mallory Square, while ostensibly there for the sunset, was not looking to the west. Instead, they were watching the tightrope walkers, straitjacket escape artists, jugglers, and a French-Canadian man who had trained house cats to jump through flaming hoops.

As far as I can tell, the Sunset Celebration in Mallory Square was originally just that: tourists and locals gathering at the westernmost square in Key West to watch as the sun went down, and then, when it did, they would applaud.

Then somebody—I think the first one was a piper, as in a guy in a kilt, playing bagpipes—got the idea that as long as there was a captive audience of tourists standing around the square waiting for the sun to set, he would play on his bagpipes and make a little tip money off them.

As it turned out, he was able to make *a lot* of tip money. And word got around so that pretty soon the jugglers and the sword-swallowers showed up. Some of the locals began to complain about the carnival atmosphere, but then the mayor—and if I'm remembering this correctly, the mayor at the time was Captain Tony—stepped in and saved the celebration.

Today, Mallory Square is bigger than it used to be: They expanded it so they could dock cruise ships there. And while by law the cruise ships must be gone half an hour before sunset to allow a clear view for spectators—or as clear a view as one can get with Sunset Key in the way, which it is from most parts of Mallory Square and on most evenings—Sunset Celebration has become a sort of arts-and-crafts fair and circus. Performers and tradespeople rent space from the city, and competition is fierce for the spots near the water and the center of the square. There's lots of banter as the jugglers try to coax the crowds away from the tightrope walkers. Only a handful of diehards applaud the sunset anymore.

So you've probably already guessed it by now. Mallory Square? Sunset Celebration? Not my favorite parts of Key West, although the Captain Tony story is sort of cool.

Yet there we were: Sheila, my father, and me. On Mallory Square, waiting for the sun to set.

The thing is, you learn when you have an addict in the family that, even though there might be separate organizations like AA and NA, there really isn't any such thing as a drug addict as opposed to a narcotics addict. Alcohol and narcotics can be threshold drugs—the drugs of choice, what the person most desires when gripped by the need to get high—but for the addict, just about anything can serve. Clinics let patients chain-smoke and chew gum and eat candy to feed their cravings. When my father was in rehab, he smoked, which he had never done before and has not done since. But put an addict under stress, and he or she will drink aftershave or squeeze Sterno through a sock to take the edge off.

That being the case, and although he was singing in a bar that week, taking my father to a bar did not seem wise for his first night in Key West. And once Hemingway House and the lighthouse and the usual sightseeing spots are closed, bars are mostly what Key West has to offer.

So, since I couldn't take him to a bar, and I sure wasn't going to sit in my apartment with him and invite the cordial father-son talk, we were watching the sunset in Mallory Square. And I hadn't even asked Sheila along as the buffer. We'd swung by and picked her up—no discussion on the matter at all.

He was laughing and chatting up a lady selling seashell-studded souvenir picture frames, and I swear she was ready to hand over her entire inventory for free. Have I mentioned that my father can be rakishly charming when he wants to?

And Sheila was holding my hand and giving it a lot of reassuring squeezes. She coaxed us over to the cat guy, because she really likes the cat guy, and the cat guy really likes her. Most evenings, when she succeeds in dragging me down here, he picks her out as his assistant, to hold the hoops, knowing that a pretty girl can help him draw a crowd.

But this time when he looked her way and smiled, she gave him a little headshake. He flashed her the OK sign and instead picked out a long-legged blonde wearing a pink T-shirt with *I'm With Sugar Daddy* printed on it, all in rhinestones, and soon the cat guy drew his crowd.

Then the sun set, and a lady in a wheelchair applauded, and so did Sheila, and I was left wondering what to do next. The Hog's Breath isn't far from Mallory Square, and just about any night she can talk me into Sunset Celebration, Sheila knows she can talk me into getting a Hog's Breath burger. But I'd whispered to her about the bars.

And obviously the Green Parrot was out. So we wound up walking all the way down to Kelly's Caribbean, because even though the full name of the place is Kelly's Caribbean Bar, Grill, and Brewery, you can sit outside in their little fenced courtyard, where you don't even see the bar. Or the brewery.

I don't recall what we ate. I'm pretty sure we drank sweet tea, because Kelly's makes it with key lime juice, which Sheila and I both love. I do remember Sheila saying something about a headache. But that's about it. My father got the check, because he's always been a pick-up-the-check kind of guy. And I let him pick it up, figuring his total assets were higher than my own, and it was irritating enough just to have him there, let alone have to pay for his dinner.

After leaving Kelly's, we walked and walked and walked some more, up and down Duval and Whitehead, then finally saw Sheila back to her trailer.

"What's on for tomorrow?" Sheila asked on her doorstep.

"Phil needs me," I said. "On the boat."

That got a look from her.

"Well then," she said, recovering quickly. "It looks as if it is just you and me, Ted."

He smiled and shook his head. "You don't have to entertain me."

Good.

"Yes, but you must entertain me," Sheila said. "Particularly as your son has steadfastly refused to take me to the Little White House."

She gave me a little pout. It was playacting. I'd actually offered to take her there once, and she'd said, "Are you daft? It's just a summer house. It doesn't even have its water view anymore, because they built the Navy Annex right in front of it."

But now she was simpering, saying, "Can we go? Please?"

Say no. Say you have to practice.

But of course my father said yes, and she smiled.

"Brilliant! I shall come by for you at ten—wear your walking shoes."

Then she kissed me good-night, a sisterly kiss on the cheek as my father stood right there next to us. She pecked him on the cheek as well, which I viewed as a sort of low treason. And then we walked back to my place, my father and me. It was better than half a mile and neither of us said a word the whole way.

I finally spoke to him when we got to my apartment. That is, I showed him where the light switches were, and where to get an extra blanket if he needed it.

He was the only one who said anything of substance. Just before I shut the lights off, he said, "Thank you, Greg. You're a better man than I."

I pretended not to hear him. I got into bed and I looked at the clock on my night table. Half an hour later, I was still looking at the clock.

THIRTY-NINE

The Roman numerals on the clock, high above the entry to Bath's Government House, showed the time to be just shy of eight. Ted checked it, and checked it again, when Henry Thatch squeezed his shoulder.

"I thought," the older pirate said, "that pining was the duty of the *bride*."

Ted checked the clock a third time. "We've only a handful of our men crewing the *Regent*, Captain. I don't trust hired seamen."

"We needed them because so many of us are taking the pardon," Thatch told him. "Besides, I paid them but the tithe of what they'll be owed. The rest will be given them in Boston. So, rest assured, they shall take our brides safely to Boston. Every mile they are farther from Spanish waters is a mile gladder to my heart. We shall join them ere they have been there two days. And Oscar is with them; our ladies are safe as houses."

"Houses burn," Ted murmured. "I shall feel better when Sally and Miss Anne are at our sides again."

"Soon enough," Thatch told him. "But now the clock says it is time. Come, my friend, and let us have our sins forgiven us."

"Pirates," a captain of the guard grumbled as they entered the building, Thatch and Ted at the head of the throng. "Had I my way, we'd shoot the lot of you before you see the magistrate."

"Henry," Ted said, "will it be covered by the pardon if I murder this foul-breathed lout before we reach the governor's chambers?"

The captain of the guard stepped aside and let them pass.

The governor himself was sitting, wig slightly askew, a cup of tea before him, at a table. He beamed when he saw Thatch.

"Henry!" the man said. "Three ships, I believe it was I saw as you entered the harbor. Anything of interest to me?"

"Enough sugar to sweeten your tea," answered the pirate. "And all the tea in Carolina for many years, I daresay."

"Cane sugar?" The governor asked hopefully.

Thatch nodded. "We found the ship adrift off the Indies. Imagine that. I claimed her for you and brought her here. I'll have my men unload and put it in your warehouses."

"Thank you, Henry," the governor said. "And please, take the vessel as your reward. A fifty percent finder's fee, of course. For your trouble."

"It was no trouble, but that is very gracious of you, Your Excellency."

Ted watched the exchange and realized that he was breathing through an open mouth. Thatch had said they would sell the cargo in Carolina. But Ted had never dreamed that the governor would be the buyer.

"Well then." The governor straightened his wig. "That's settled, and I must say, Henry, I shall miss these occasional little meetings of ours."

He glanced at the heap of rolled parchments before him. Several had been set to the side. "Down to the business at hand, I suppose."

He handed the first parchment to a bailiff, who opened it,

glanced down his nose at what was written there, and cleared his throat.

"Oh-yay, oh-yay, oh-yah," the bailiff called. "The court of the governor-general of the Carolina colony is in session, His Excellency the governor-general presiding. Let Henry Thatch approach the bench."

The pirate stood.

"Henry?" The governor tapped the rolled parchment against the table, next to his tea.

The pirate stepped forward and placed his hand upon a Bible proffered by the bailiff.

"Henry David Thatch, His Majesty King George has in grace and wisdom offered you royal clemency for all crimes whatsoever, whether upon the high seas or in His Majesty's waters, against ships of His Majesty's flag or any others. Do you accept the king's pardon, and do you promise to pirate no more?"

"Aye," Henry said, "and on my honor and by God's Holy Word do I swear it."

"Done." The gavel fell and Henry accepted his scroll. The governor nodded to the bailiff.

"Theodore Bascombe," the bailiff intoned.

"Bascombe?" Henry whispered as he returned to his seat.

"It was that," Bold Ted said, rising, "or Smith, or Jones."

The governor provided a carriage for his former business partner, and Thatch stretched his arms as he alighted from it at the dock.

"It's remarkable, is it not?" Thatch turned to Ted, a broad smile on his face. "I feel as if a weight has been lifted from me. Is this what repentance feels like?"

"This," Ted told him, "is what freedom from prosecution feels like."

"And yet the result is the same." Thatch clapped his young friend on the shoulders, and they started up the gangplank.

"Captain?" Ben approached Henry on the quarterdeck of the *Adelaar*. "What would you have us do with this?"

He held out the black flag, the crowned and winged death's head with crossed bones and the hourglass. "I took 'im off the *Regent* afore she left this morning. Didn't figure you'd want it aboard, what with the ladies and all. Don't want them to appear to have gone a-pirating."

"Good thinking," Henry told him. "Put it in the cabin for now. We shall give King Death a proper pyre when we arrive in Boston."

"Aye, sir." The mate gave his captain a proper salute: the salute of a seaman, not a pirate.

Two hours' sail took them out through the inlet in the Outer Banks and into the great Atlantic beyond. In another six hours they were passing Ocracoke. And half an hour beyond that, a sail appeared on the horizon, drawing nearer, heading toward them.

Ted looked. Then he looked again. And his stomach sank.

"Captain," he said to Henry. "Have a look at that vessel."

Henry peered at it through his spyglass.

"Sweet mercy," he told the younger man. "It is the *Regent*."

It took twenty minutes to close on the Jamaica-built sloop, and as they did the smaller vessel turned away from them. Henry called for the helm to correct course to head them off, and when the smaller ship turned yet again, Henry called for the first mate.

"Open gunports, Ben. Run them out."

The mate's eyes went wide. "You mean to fire, Captain, on our own sloop?"

"No. But I doubt that whoever is on her helm will know that. Have the men arm themselves. I smell trouble."

The sight of bared cannon was enough to bring the sails down on the schooner. *Adelaar* swung alongside and half her complement poured down onto the smaller vessel. There was blood on the deck, and Oscar Emmons was slumped, hands over his abdomen, against the mast.

"Henry," he called, his voice labored. The hired crew cowered against the far rail. The few pirates that had been aboard were nowhere to be seen.

"It was Spanish," Oscar gasped. "A ship of the line. Your men tried to man the guns, but these cowards here killed them. We could have outrun them, but they dropped our sails, put a sword to my throat."

"We weren't hired to fight no navy," one of the hired crew protested. "He 'ad the guns and the flag. We hove to. We did as what was proper."

"He was a Spaniard in English waters, you imbecile," Henry shot back. He looked around. "Oscar, where is your daughter? Where is my wife?"

"He . . ." The big man gasped for air. "I tried to stop him, but he put a sword in my belly. That Spanish captain. And then Bascombe stepped between them but . . ." He pointed weakly to the great splash of blood upon the deck. "He clove his head from his shoulders and put him over the side." Oscar closed his eyes. Reopened them. "He knew who Anne was, Henry. He said, 'Tell Captain Henry Thatch that I shall hang this woman in the Castillo at San Juan in one week's time, unless he appears at the gallows to take her place.' He thought Sally was her slave, and he took her as well."

"How long ago was this?"

"Six hours. Maybe less."

" 'Ere, 'ere." The hired mate stepped forward. "You ain't about chasing him with us aboard. You 'ave to put us ashore. It's the law of the sea."

Henry looked up to the deck of the *Adelaar*. "Ben, put a longboat over the side."

"Launch a longboat, aye, sir."

"No!" Henry's voice was sharp. "Don't launch it, man. Throw it. Over the stern."

"Aye."

The men groaned as they lifted the longboat and heaved it over the side. It fell into the sea astern of the Dutch prize, the small boat's hull splintering as it hit.

"You sniveling coward," Henry hissed at the hired mate. "You killed my men. You were ordered to run and you hove to. 'Law of the sea . . .' I am well within my rights to have you shot, but I fear I may need the powder."

With that, Henry grabbed the startled man by the belt and threw him over the side. The rest of the pirates shouted and did the same with the hired crew. There were screams as the frightened seamen splashed for the listing longboat.

"We are faster than any ship of the line," Henry told Ted. "And we saw no sails, so he has bellied far to sea so as not to be sighted from shore. He will not harm the women; he needs them alive to lure us. And we can catch him." His voice rose to a shout. "Make ready both ships. South away as fast as we can run. We must catch this Spaniard before he makes San Juan. Ted, see to Oscar."

"You, my son . . ." Oscar breathed, "are no loblolly boy. Love your wife and tell her that her father blesses her."

He closed his eyes.

Ted bent to the big man's side. There was no breath. He looked up to the blood-soaked deck, where Bascombe had made his stand. Tears began to course down his cheeks, and he glanced from the dead man at his knees to the place where the only father he could remember had died in defense of his wife.

"Henry!" Ted called to his captain. "I want the man who did this. I want the man who killed my . . . I want the man who killed them."

The captain nodded. "Make haste!" he shouted to his men. "We must cover water here."

FORTY

The water flew beneath the RIB's hull, the blue Bimini top fluttering above our heads. Hans was at the hull and I was at his side. I
held a plastic chart flat against the console as we ran.

"The wreckage we are currently working, the jewel wreck,
is right here." I showed him the spot on the chart, and he nodded. "And the place where you found the flintlocks and the other
eighteenth-century items was up here."

He nodded again as I grease-penciled a second dot on the
chart.

"Wood and small items would tumble farther in a storm," I
shouted over the sound of the screaming twin outboards. "Follow
them back and they point to a line that runs southeast-northwest
just north of Fort Jefferson. The heavier items would be on the
bottom right about where the wreck first rolled, assuming this is
all one wreck."

I tapped the pencil on the chart and indicated the National
Monument waters surrounding the Dry Tortugas. We couldn't work
the Park Service area—not without a ton of paperwork—but the
waters adjacent to it were open. Shallow, but open.

"I'd like to run the fish through here."

"Makes sense," Hans agreed. He punched the latitude and

longitude for the bottom of our search area into the GPS and began following the digital lubber line.

I'd wakened that morning to strange scents in my small apartment: bacon and eggs, coffee. Of the three, only coffee had been present in my kitchen the night before. It was doubly strange because my father had never been an early riser; like most musicians, he tended to be more of a night owl.

But he'd had bacon and eggs and coffee ready, orange juice too, as I padded into the little kitchen.

"Morning," he said. "Why don't you go ahead and dive in while I catch a shower?"

Just that. I never got to say a word in reply.

So I ate, and then when he came out, I used the shower and got dressed. No conversation. He made up the sofa bed and closed it.

"Well." I glanced at my dive watch. "I need to get down to the docks. Sheila's off, though. Lab's closed. Tell her I'll call late this afternoon when I know what my schedule is, okay?"

"Sure thing," he said.

Relatively painless. And that had been my entire morning with my father.

Rackham had been resistant to my taking anything out into the Gulf at first. Then I made my pitch.

"All you've found from this wreck so far, whatever it is, is the light stuff. No ballast stones, no anchors, no cannon. If she went down in a storm, she might have tumbled for miles. And side-scan sonar won't tell us a thing because it's all sand bottom and sea grass out there—nothing standing in relief, so whatever is there is long buried, just like what you're working right now. If we can find the heavy stuff—the ballast, or the guns, or both—we'll have a starting locus. And if we find that, we can just connect the dots, work from there up through the parts you've found this far, and that way we don't miss anything."

"We don't even know if the flintlocks and the decking are from the same wreck," Rackham had pointed out. "If the decking is Spanish treasure galleon, then it's too early for flintlocks—that would be a matchlock period. Might be two different sites."

"Might be," I agreed. "But Hans and I are on salary. And the magnetometer is already in the RIB. All it'll cost you to find out is gas."

Rackham looked at me, his hand on his chin. "You really don't want to spend time with your old man, do you?"

I shook my head.

"Okay," he finally said. "Get out of here."

Hans went back and readied the "fish"—the towfish that we would pull through the water to pick up magnetic readings—while I took the helm of the small boat. I picked up the microphone for the marine radio.

"Rackham RIB to base."

"Base here." The return was faded and laced with static. "That you, Robin?"

"Hey, Greg. Where are you? Sounds like you're calling from the ends of the earth."

"We're pretty far out," I told her. "And we're on the RIB, so the antenna's pretty close to the water. We're almost out of radio range. Hans and I are heading up north of Fort Jefferson to run a grid. Be there through most of the day. I'll call in when we get back in range."

"You do that." Robin's voice was barely audible. "Stay safe."

The arrow blinked on the GPS, cuing me to correct my heading. I did so, and the lubber line reappeared. Ahead of the bow, blue water showed all the way across the horizon.

FORTY-ONE

For hours on end, there had been nothing but empty ocean. Late in the afternoon, sails appeared, but they were square-rigged, not a fleet naval warship and not running for the Spanish Caribbean. Unable to keep pace, the *Adelaar* and her crew had fallen farther and farther astern until even her mast tips were no longer visible.

Then, when the sun was low and shadows long, the lookout atop the single mast sang out, "Hard port, sail!"

Henry and Ted both trained their spyglasses on the eastern horizon. They were too near the water to see a sail, but after a minute of searching, Henry found it: a long, thin pennant, fluttering from the whisker of a mast tip. Following his direction, Ted found it as well. And then something else.

"Just ahead of it, Henry. Look."

Ted blinked to make sure he had seen correctly. And he had. A second whisker of mast tip almost overlapped with the first, and yet the pennant neither grew nor shrunk in size, so the Spaniard was neither going away nor coming toward them. And that meant the second mast could be only one thing.

"There are two ships," Henry said. And then he cursed. He

turned to the helm. "Port a quarter, Jack, and keep an ear open, man."

"Aye, sir."

"You are closing?" Ted asked him.

Henry nodded.

"But they'll see us. Soon as we clear their horizon."

"No, they won't, Bold Ted. Have a look at our shadow."

Ted looked. The shadow of their mast tip seemed to point directly at the two warships.

"We are coming out of the sun," Ted said.

"Aye," Henry agreed. "Now pray for a bright sunset and quick dark. If we have that, they'll stay blind."

For the next hour, the *Regent* closed on the warships. Sails appeared, followed by their ensigns, then the thin lines of hulls. Then the small shape of a longboat in tow behind the vessel with the bright pennant.

"That pennant is a commodore's ribbon," Henry said. "If they have taken women, they would hold them there, on the ranking officer's vessel. Easier to control the crew. She's the one we want."

With that, he called a parlay.

As night fell, Henry turned his vessel head-on toward the two warships and dropped sail so no shadow appeared against the setting sun. Then he hoisted again and urged the mate to get ahead of the two Spaniards.

Lights glowed in the stern castles of the two big warships, on the decks and at their bows.

The *Regent*, by contrast, was dark as night. No lights, not even matches aglow for the guns, and no man smoked, much as many longed to.

As Ted watched, their little ship drew ahead of the two Spaniards. Soon the sidelights to the Spaniards' stern castles were visible to either side of the ships—the Spanish warships were directly astern of the sloop. That was when the *Regent* dropped sail and used her boom to put her last longboat in the water.

Ted and Henry and Ben and five others slid down lines to the bobbing boat. Then, with the barest flap of canvas, the *Regent* took sail again and disappeared into the night like a ghost.

"Any noise shall kill us, lads," Henry whispered. And that was the last thing said aboard the longboat.

The men used the oars like paddles to scull to one side or the other, keeping the approaching warships dead astern. Glowing phosphorescence, two mustaches of it, appeared in the water— the curl of the two ships' wakes. The men in the longboat sculled a bit to the left, and then, just as it seemed the bow of the commodore's ship would cleave it, the longboat lifted on the bow wave and was pushed aside.

The men used their hands to noiselessly fend off the passing ship of the line. In the bow, Ben extended a gaffing hook, its point shrouded and silenced with a knot of rag. The stern of the big ship passed, and he hooked the empty dinghy as it came by. Moments later, the two small boats were fast together.

No one wore boots. No one carried swords. Their pistols were wrapped in waxed muslin under their vests, and each man had a dirk within his hand. Henry leaned close to Bold Ted, his mustache touching the other man's ear.

"Right, lad," Henry whispered. "You're the darkest of us. Hardest to see, so up you go."

Both hands on the painter, Ted had his knife in his mouth. He slipped into the water and began pulling on the rope.

FORTY-TWO

I pulled on the line to get the towfish oriented, lowered it into our wake, and watched the depth gauge. The bottom was only thirty feet—too shallow even for oceangoing vessels of the eighteenth century, if they wanted to be comfortable. But with storm surge and winds, it was feasible that they could have come here. I leveled the fish off at fifteen feet, as Hans began "mowing the lawn," pulling the towfish in parallel paths, each about two miles long, following our progress on the GPS.

I went up next to him.

"I'll let base know we're on the grid," I said. But when I keyed the microphone and called, all we got was static in return.

"I would say that we are off the grid as far as that radio is concerned," Hans told me. "No signal from base until we are nearer to shore, do you think?"

He waved a hand toward Fort Jefferson, a low redbrick smudge on the distant Dry Tortugas, to the south of us. "If we are in trouble, we can contact the Park Service, so it is all right, yes?"

Knowing it would be even weaker, I tried the backup radio, a handheld. Nothing.

That felt odd, being out of contact.

I went back to check the towfish, stepped onto the swim step with one foot, and looked down into the passing sea. We were running steady, the fish level in the clear green water.

I looked at the magnetometer readout. In the old days, this would have been a paper printout, but now it's a rolling display on a computer screen. There's a navigation bar at the bottom so you can go back and review anything you've done so far, and the unit was wired into our GPS and our bottom sonar, so latitude and longitude and depth readings could be constantly updated. Just by hitting the space bar, you could place a bookmark—the digital equivalent of marking an X on the printout. And the device automatically backed itself up onto a portable hard drive every ten minutes. It was a very cool toy.

Right then, our cool toy was showing us empty sea bottom. Everything was greens and blues, not the reds and oranges and yellows we would see if we overran anything metal. I adjusted the sunshade on the unit and, being careful not to unplug anything, brought it forward so I could sit within earshot of Hans while he piloted the RIB.

"It is working, yes?"

"Working just fine. Your speed's good, right where it is." I looked up as I spoke and checked the line running back to the towfish. It was taut and stable, sloping straight back into the receding water.

FORTY-THREE

Soon Ted's body was out of the water to his waist. Then his knees. And then his ankles. He lifted his feet high so they would not splash, but the wake of the warship hid any noise. Hand over hand, he climbed the slanting rope. Briefly, through crazed windows, he saw lights in the stern castle, the shapes of two women in dresses. Then he was at the rail and, silently, his bare feet were over and flat on the deck.

A sailor in uniform was at the helm, one hand on the wheel, using his other hand to light a pipe with a coal.

Ted hesitated. He had never before killed a man who was not about to kill him. He thought of his wife and Miss Anne, one deck below him, and he stepped forward. Then, in the dim light of the lamp swaying next to the helm, he spied the belaying pins in their holders in the port rail. He waited until the helmsman was concentrating on his pipe, crept over, and slipped a pin into his hand.

The sailor with the pipe fell with a single blow to his head, and Ted caught his limp body as he slumped. Laying him on the deck, Ted watched the rise and fall of the man's chest—still breathing, but no longer conscious. He grabbed the helm to maintain the ship's heading, holding it there until a hand closed on his shoulder and Ben took the wheel.

Henry was last aboard, a satchel of oiled canvas high on his shoulder. He opened it and began handing round, apple-size iron balls with fuses to the men—grenades.

"Marines will be in the forecastle," Henry whispered. "Gunners on the two decks below. Remember, these are men who wish to hang us, so give no quarter. We were in retreat to England, they could have left us be, yet they have brought this on their own heads. Make the signal, Ted."

Ted took the lantern from its stand next to the helm, went to the stern, and swung it three times. Ben held the ship on its course while the other seven men slid down to the decks below, like water silently seeking its own level.

For five minutes, nothing happened. For five minutes it seemed as if nothing would *ever* happen. Then cannon fire erupted on the far side of the second warship, outlining it in puffs of orange smoke, and the night lit up as men aboard the *Regent* uncovered lanterns and she continued passing the other Spaniard, firing her broadside.

One.

Two.

Three.

The door to the forecastle flew open, and Spanish marines, most of them shirtless, began pouring out, carrying muskets at quarter arms. Ted lit a grenade from the coals of a deck lantern and threw it into the wardroom behind them. It exploded with a thud amid screams as Ted's companions subdued the few marines who had made it onto the deck.

Belowdecks the muffled booms of more grenades erupted. Taking swords from the fallen marines, Ted and his allies ran to the stern castle, found handholds, and held on.

Seconds later, the great ship groaned as it heeled into a sharp turn to starboard, away from its companion vessel. Ted threw open the cabin door and ran inside.

Lights were burning from swaying lanterns, and both women had been thrown to the floor by the sharpness of the turn. An orderly was sitting next to them, holding his head, and an officer in a yellow wig and blue waistcoat was holding on to a mantel with both hands. Seeing the officer reach for the pistol at his waist, Ted threw his dirk at him. It buried itself in the man's throat as Ted's allies fell upon the stunned orderly.

"Ted!" Sally reached for him, but he put his hand out.

"Stay here," he said. "And douse those lights."

Then he was out again onto the darkened deck.

FORTY-FOUR

The sun was beginning to set when we got the hits: three in a row. Cannon probably, because they were fairly regularly spaced and there was an extremely strong magnetic return, the kind you'd only get from steel or iron. Hitting the space bar, I turned the screen, showing the display to Hans. He broke our grid and ran back over the same spot. Three strong returns again. Just to be safe, I punched in a waypoint on the GPS and glanced at the latitude-longitude numbers, fixing them in my head.

Hans ran us farther south, where we could clearly see the Dry Tortugas on the horizon; they looked near enough that a strong man could swim to them.

Hans took us parallel to the line we'd had the hit on, and four more bogies showed up, all oblong, two of them forming a rough X. I compared them to the positions of what we'd found earlier.

"I'd say cannon," I told him.

"You think?" His eyes were wide.

I backed up the display and looked at it one more time. "I'm almost positive. They aren't in a perfect line, but if they were deck guns, on a ship rolled either by a storm that sunk her, or one that followed, they could easily fall in this pattern.

The sun was getting lower, and I looked at my watch.

"Let's break off," I told Hans. "We can come back tomorrow and concentrate here if Phil wants us to. But I'd say we found the alpha on our wreck; assuming these are deck cannon, right here is where she rolled. Draw a line from here to where we're working, and you should have our debris field."

I brought the towfish in while Hans punched in a course for the dock. Fort Jefferson and the Tortugas came up on our right and then receded in our wake. I'd just locked the magnetometer case when the radio began to crackle.

" . . . -sure Hunter base to Rackham RIB. Do you read?"

Hans was busy balancing out the outboards. I stepped forward and grabbed the microphone.

"Hey, Robin. What are you doing? Working late?"

" . . . -eg. I'm glad we -ot you. You ne- . . . -ack here."

I looked at Hans. He shrugged.

"Say again, Robin? You're cutting out. Did you say we need to get back there?"

" . . . -firmative."

"What's up?"

"Sheila . . . -ushed . . . -ospital."

My heart sank.

"Did you say . . ." I remembered to key the mike. "Did you say that Sheila has been rushed to the hospital?"

Hans and I were staring at each other now.

But for the next three minutes, all the radio delivered was static.

FORTY-FIVE

Perhaps three minutes had passed since *Regent* had fired her running broadside. And in that time, more than fifty Spaniards had fallen.

The captured Spanish warship came all the way about, the only lamp burning a single lantern, hung on the side away from its companion vessel. Minutes later, the similarly darkened *Regent* was pulled alongside. Crew began climbing up grappling hooks linking the two ships. Belowdecks, pistol fire erupted occasionally as the fight continued with the Spaniards' dwindling crew.

On the deck, Ted and Henry held their wives.

"The *Regent* is crewed only by our men now," Ted told Sally. "Just a skeleton crew, because Captain Henry needs every man we can get to sail this warship. But be brave and go with them. *Adelaar* is behind us and you shall sight her ere dawn. They'll put more men on *Regent* and they will take you straight to Boston. We will draw the Spanish away, then break off and come join you. I swear we shall be together again, and soon."

She nodded, looked down, and then looked up again, peering over the side where the *Regent* waited in the darkness. "My father. Is he . . . ?"

Saying nothing, Ted held her.

"I love you, Bold Ted," she said, tears running down her cheeks. And then she was lowered away toward the waiting schooner.

Henry Thatch watched as Anne's yellow hair disappeared into the blackness below. When the bosun's chair reappeared, a black bundle was lashed to it. Thatch opened it and looked at the crowned and winged skull grinning whitely back at him. He stopped a passing deckhand.

"When every Spaniard is cleansed from this ship," Henry told him, "take Philip's rag off our staff and run this up."

"Aye, sir." The hand accepted the flag.

"And, boy?" Henry stopped him again.

"Sir?"

"Strip that commodore's pennant from my mainmast."

"Aye, aye."

The ship, the *Valeroso*, according to her bell, grew quiet as the fighting ended. After giving *Regent* time to slip away, Henry called for all sail and had his men light every lamp they could find. He edged nearer to the other Spaniard, fired a broadside, then heeled away, heading south, a fox for the Spanish hound.

"He is more apt to chase us," Henry told Ben, "if we are running toward his home."

All night the two ships raced. The former pirates carried the Spanish bodies to the deck and tossed them overboard, like phosphorescent bread crumbs upon the water. But the following ship never slowed: not out of fear, nor to retrieve its dead comrades. Yet it did not fire upon them.

"Save that commodore's body," Henry told Ben. "When he goes over, I want broad daylight. Perhaps they will slow to recover their commander."

As dawn approached, they saw the lights of St. Augustine, home to enough of a Spanish population that Ted assumed their chase would turn to port for help. The sun rose and fell full upon the pirate standard flapping at their stern.

"All right, here we go," Henry called. "Up and over with his lordship."

The men dropped the commodore's body into their wake. On the other ship, a full mile behind, they could see men pointing into the water. But their pursuer never turned. She stayed her course, and the officer's blue-coated body disappeared beneath her bow wave.

"That," Henry said, "is one coldhearted brute of a ship's master."

"If they are so hot to pursue," Ben said, "why do they not fire upon us? Have they no powder? No shot? Those are the last thing a navy runs short of."

"We need to lighten," Henry said to both Ben and Ted. "Take some men. Anything not needed to sail this Castilian horse trough, put it over. I want speed."

They began with the longboats, throwing them over the side. That was followed by the anchors, along with all their chain. Ted led a crew into the stern castle, where they knocked out the side-lights and began tossing chests, a wine barrel, and a harpsichord into their wake. As they were leaving, a bit of canvas caught his eye—something stuck above the lintel of the hatch. But it looked too small to be of any weight, so he left it.

They went below, and Ted put a crew to work, winching the spare cannon barrels out of the bilge and dropping them into the sea.

He found the magazine, copper-lined and surrounded by bales of tight cotton, but he left it; powder was something they might need. Then he found a second magazine and opened it, expecting more of the same. But when he lifted his lantern to peer inside, he was stunned.

Within, stacked in tidy piles, were bars of gold.

Night had fallen again and, certain that the *Regent* was safely out of their pursuer's range, Henry had ordered all lamps extinguished. But he lit one, a small one, to examine what Ted had brought him.

"This bar bears the broad arrow," Henry said. "That identifies it as property of the British crown. And I strongly doubt that Philip is carrying these as a favor to a Protestant king. Our friends here, the commodore and his lackey, who are presently pursuing us, have been taking English ships. Sinking them, no doubt, and then blaming it on pirates. No wonder they need to hang us. They want no story abroad that contradicts their own."

"One moment," Ted told him. He ran down to the stern castle and felt above the lintel, found one of the sacks secreted there. The heft of it seemed to confirm his suspicions, but he carried it out to the deck and let Henry illuminate the interior with the small bull's-eye lamp.

Rubies, emeralds, topaz, diamonds, and more glinted back at them.

"Apparently taking King Philip's own mine ships, to boot," Henry said. He looked astern. Their pursuer was showing lights and had fallen behind, but not by much. "Lose every other deck gun. We need to be lighter still."

Ted took the stones back and re-hid them where he had found them. In doing so, he discovered a wooden box. Opening the box, he found a navigator's instruments, finely made and accurately marked. He put it up along with the precious stones.

By morning, their pursuer was farther back still. The wind was freshening, coming from the east, and the sails strained, full, as they tacked.

Thatch was not watching their pursuer. He had his spyglass trained upon the shore as Florida proceeded past them, a slow parade of mangrove, saw grass, low trees, and white sand beaches.

"There is nothing but bush and jungle on that shore, Henry," Ted told him. "There are no settlements on this stretch of the coast."

"I know that, lad."

"Then what are you looking at?"

"The birds."

Ted peered at the shore, squinting his eyes. "Captain, there are no birds flying."

Thatch handed the younger man the glass. "Look at the trees."

Ted did as he was told. He glanced at his captain. "The birds are all sitting. None are aloft. Why is that?"

"The weather, lad. The air has thinned. A storm is coming."

Ted looked at the sky, turning in a slow circle. "But, Captain, I see not a cloud in the sky. Not one. In fact, I've never seen the sky so blue."

"That is because you have never before lived in this part of the world." Thatch pointed shoreward. "When birds are alight, and the wind's afresh and no clouds show, that is the time to seek a harbor—or better still, a river, one that runs deep and broad and far inland." He looked at the sails astern. "But we cannot. We need to catch every breath of wind that we can, and take the slack out of that mainstay."

FORTY-SIX

Night fell, and the stars came out, twinkling brighter than Ted had ever seen them. The wind shifted, strong out of the east now. Both ships made progress in fits and starts, running fleetly southwest, then tacking laboriously out to sea again so they could begin the next fast leg.

Dawn came, oddly red, because still there was not even the barest hint of cloud, and the shore drew away on their right. Soon it was nothing but a green line on the horizon, and half an hour later even that was gone. Everywhere he looked, all Ted saw was ocean.

An hour later, the sea was alive with whitecaps. The ship, large as it was, began to buck amongst the waves. Half an hour after that, strange tongues of cloud, the gray fog of rain beneath them, began to reach toward the two vessels from the northeast.

The crew, small for a ship of the line, had been working all night without rest. Stays were constantly being adjusted to better angle the sails for the changing wind. Every few minutes, Ted would peer back over the mounting waves at their pursuer.

Finally, he saw not the single column of sail that he expected but three distinct masts. As he watched, the display of sail widened.

"Captain!" Ted cupped his hands to be heard over the rising wind. "He is turning!"

Thatch glanced back, gave the wheel to a helmsman, and crossed the pitching quarterdeck to join Ted at the rear rail.

"Look." Ted pointed at the ship of the line, now in full profile. "Is he giving up?"

Thatch shook his head. "He is not giving up; he is heading us off. He knows we shall turn as well."

"Why?"

"Because of that," Thatch said, pointing.

To the left and ahead of them, the sky was boiling with clouds, the sea below obscured by the fog of distant rain.

"I was wrong," Thatch told Ted. "What I felt when we left the governor's house? That was not repentance. That was relief. *This* is what repentance feels like, lad, because I fear that all these years all I did was leading us here, to this moment. And what I am doing now is leading all of us to our doom."

The ship bit a wave and spray washed the length of the ship, wetting the two men.

"We have room," Ted said. "We can run, Captain."

"Only west," Thatch replied. "These are Spanish waters; he knows them far better than I. When we turn, to the north of us are a string of islands, from Largo, which we passed at dawn, to Cayo Hueso, far to the west. And two or three leagues to the south of them lies a reef that would take the bottom out of us. If I come about and tack north, he shall see me and head me off. So I can only run west, and that reef will fence our escape. It is simply a matter of time."

Ted searched his captain's face. "Then take us south. Or east. Take us out to sea. We have sailed in storm before."

"We have," Thatch agreed. "But that is no mere storm, Bold Ted. That is what I have feared since yestermorn; that is a hurricane, and no small one. It kills ships."

Ted looked again at the clouds, and his heart sank.

FORTY-SEVEN

There were clouds ahead of us—a summer squall, and something we would usually make an effort to run around. But Hans had the throttles all the way to their stops, so we barreled straight for it.

In my board-short pocket my cell phone vibrated. I dug it out and saw that the text message symbol was flashing. I flipped open the phone to view the message screen.

SHEILA IN LOWER KEYS MEDICAL CENTER
EMERGENCY ROOM. COME FASTEST.

Sheila.

My father.

No! Not again . . .

Just then, we entered the squall as rain began beating against the gray rubber tubing of the boat, the Bimini top, the Lexan windscreen, our faces.

Hans aimed the little boat at the heart of the strengthening rain.

FORTY-EIGHT

Rain lashed the deck of the ship. Men were aloft, braving the wind and the swaying of the tall vessel in order to trim the sails and keep the rising gale from capsizing them. On deck, the crew were tightening the stays, and every few minutes a wave would wash over the deck, sweeping men from their feet and sending them careening to the opposite rail.

Thatch was at the helm, with Ted at his side, helping the captain to keep the ship head-on into the waves. It was like wrestling a giant beast. As waves would pass, the helm would turn, and it took both men to maintain the ship's course. It had been that way for four hours.

"This is just the start of it," Thatch said, his voice raised so Ted, who was standing right next to him, could hear. All around the ship, the taut ropes and lines were sounding like the strings of a great musical instrument, like tormented souls keening for a moment of peace. "The hurricane sends fingers of rain before it. This will pass, but then the storm itself will overtake us, and it will be ten times worse. Waves as tall as houses. Wind so fierce that a man cannot stand."

He glanced to the north. The rain made it impossible to see more than a hundred feet beyond the ship.

"He is out there," Thatch said. "Close, no doubt. The Spanish have sailed these waters for more than two centuries. He will not break off until the storm itself forces him to seek harbor. And we cannot hide in this rain forever. When we come out into the clear, we must be ready." He shook his head. "I fear that I have killed us, boy. We are stuck between storm and cannon, and I have put us here. Were it me alone, it would be just. But I have pulled you down with me."

Aloft, a man slipped from a rope as he worked to make fast a sail. Both men watched as the crewman swung a leg back up to the line, clambered upright, and resumed his work.

"All these good men," Thatch said. "I have killed them too."

Ted looked at him and laughed.

"You find humor in this, lad?"

"I think," Ted told him, "that you look awfully quick for a dead man."

Then Thatch was laughing too, the two men nearly convulsed with it as they clung to the helm.

Thatch spun around on his heel, and his soaked beard swished back and forth like a horse's tail. "Ben!" he called.

The mate appeared at the top of the ladder leading up to the quarterdeck. He clung there as a wave broke over his back and ran, half a foot deep, across the deck.

"Aye, Captain?"

"We will need gun crews, Ben. Starboard side only if we've not the crew to put men on both. Bring down those men aloft; they've done what they can up there. Use the cannon belowdecks—anything we load up here will just foul in the rain. Grease your shot and your wads to keep the powder dry. When we come into the clear, we'll have a fight on our hands."

The mate grinned. "Aye, sir. Could use a fight to warm us up, we could."

He dropped down the ladder and disappeared.

"And so it starts," Thatch said. "What do you say, Bold Ted? Ready to go from bad to worse?"

FORTY-NINE

"How bad is she?"

Malibu took the corner coming out of the old sub base, going fast enough that the tires squealed.

"I said, how bad is she?"

Malibu shot me a glance. "Dude, I just don't know. They just said, 'Go get Greg.' I'm not, like, in the loop."

We bumped over some old railroad tracks and both of us went temporarily airborne.

"Malibu, answer me! Is she dead?"

"Dude, I *don't* know." He looked at me again. "I hope not."

Palm trees rushed by. Tin-roofed houses rushed by. Malibu laid on the horn, and some tourists in one of those gumdrop-looking econo-vehicles, halfway between a golf cart and a car, swerved and nearly struck a line of parked Harleys. It began raining again, pouring down on us for the next several blocks.

Finally we got to Lower Keys Medical Center, and it looked small—too small to be a real hospital. But it had an entrance marked *Emergency*, and a Navy SUV was parked cockeyed in front of it.

I Dukes-of-Hazzarded it right over the SUV's wet hood and ran toward the entry, rain beating down on me.

Seconds later, I pushed through the emergency room doors.

FIFTY

The rain was lessening, and it seemed to Ted that the wind was
dying.

"All right," Henry shouted down an open hatch to the gun
deck. "All loaded? Stand lively."

A shout came from below. Ted peered in; the men had spread
sand on the gun deck to give them footing and soak up the blood.
Two former pirates grinned up at him; one winked.

The *Valeroso* emerged into sunlight, and some of the men in
the bow sent up a cheer. Soon a form appeared from a patch of
fog and rain not two hundred yards away.

It was the Spaniard.

"Open starboard gunports," Thatch shouted.

A great creaking showed that his command was being
obeyed.

"Run them out!"

Shouts of "Heave!" came up from below as gun crews winched
their heavy cannon into firing position.

Ted blew the moisture from the lens of his spyglass and
raised it.

The other ship had men in all of its rigging, men clustered on
its deck. Heavy thuds, like hailstones striking solid ground, erupted

around them, and then Ted heard the sound of musket fire and saw the smoke from the sharpshooters aloft on the other ship. Up in the bow, one of Hatch's men toppled backward over the rail.

Both Ted and Henry crouched behind the helm.

"Notice anything queer about that ship, Bold Ted?"

Ted stole another look. "Her gunports are closed!"

"Right, lad. He does not mean to sink us; he means to take us. The gold, Ted. He wants the gold. That means he will fight like a pirate, which we know something about."

Staying down, Henry ran to the open hatch. "Broadside, Ben! Broadside *now!*" The entire right side of the ship erupted with thunder, the smoke still rolling out as Henry called to the helm, "Come about! Hard about! I want him on our port side!"

And now Ted was at the hatch, shouting, "Ben! Heat shot! Solid shot! Hot as you can, and as fast as you can! Don't load until we tell you!"

He rushed back to the helm, musket balls whistling past his ears.

Henry was smiling at him. "What are you thinking?"

Ted smiled back. "We have two powder magazines on this ship. I am thinking . . . I am *hoping* that our construction and theirs is one and the same."

Henry nodded. "I know what you are about, lad. Let us pray that it is so."

FIFTY-ONE

My father was praying. That was what I noticed first. Not the police filling out reports at the nurses' station. Not the people with ice packs, Ace wraps, or ashen faces, sitting in the hard plastic chairs, waiting to be called.

I saw Phil Rackham, standing with Betty, Panhead Mikey, alone and looking worried, and my father, who was off to the side of them and on his knees.

I went to a door marked *To Surgery*, gave it a push. Nothing. It was locked.

"Greg?" My father had looked up and was coming my way. "Greg, I'm glad you're—"

"What happened? What did you do?"

"Greg, just sit a second so I can—"

I shoved him and he staggered back. To my right, I saw one of the cops setting down his clipboard and turning toward me.

"What did you *do*?" I repeated.

"Greg, she's back there." He pointed at the door leading to surgery. "Now, if you'll just . . ."

My mother. Her unborn child. Sheila. All of them, I saw them in my mind's eye, being stolen from me. My father was reaching out for me.

I cocked my fist. The cop began to trot toward us.

Then my arm was gripped in what felt like a vise, and before I could throw the punch, I was being turned.

FIFTY-TWO

The two ships turned about each other, tight pirouettes that cut white wake behind them. The other ship had closed within a hundred feet, and the musket fire was so thick that Ted and Henry had fallen to their bellies and lay next to the deck rail.

Ted lifted his head enough to clear the rail. *Valeroso* had no men in her rigging; there had been no time to send shooters aloft, and now the fire was too murderous to risk it. The other ship's commander, fine plumed hat upon his head, was at the rail, directing the fire. Ted pulled his pistol, aimed, lifted a bit to allow for the drop of the ball, and pulled the trigger.

The sound of the small gun was a mere *pop* compared to the musket fire coming from the other ship, but the opposing commander staggered, put a hand to his shoulder, and when he brought it away, it was red. He shouted, pointed at Ted, and the young man dropped behind the rail again as a dozen musket balls thudded into its far side.

"I think," Henry shouted, "that you have made him angry." The older man was laughing.

Henry crawled to the hatch, staying low. "The shot! Is it hot? Does it glow?"

A shout from below confirmed that it did.

The captain looked at Ted. "Where away, lad?"

"Aft of the mainmast," Ted shouted back. "And low! As close to the waterline as possible! Concentrate every gun there."

Thatch repeated the instructions. The deck below resounded with the shouts of gun crews wedging their barrels to lower them.

Up in the opposition's rigging, men were whirling grappling hooks.

"Fire!" Henry shouted.

Valeroso thundered. For a moment, nothing seemed to have changed. Then the ship heeled over sharply as the other vessel exploded in red and orange, pieces flying skyward as her powder magazine blew.

Ted looked at Henry. Henry looked back and nodded.

Then the rains overtook them again, and Ted staggered back to his feet.

FIFTY-THREE

I almost lost my footing.

"We're cool, Jerry," I heard Phil say. It was his hand pinioning my arm.

"You sure, Phil?" The cop didn't look convinced.

"Sure thing. Bad day. Right?" Phil's other hand clapped me on my shoulder, and I nodded. The cop backed off.

Betty came up to me and started rubbing my neck, and that worked. I began to calm.

"What happened?" I asked. "How is she?"

"It's . . ." Phil began. Then he looked up. "Wait. Here he is."

The doors to the surgical wing opened and a man in green scrubs came out. The first thing I noticed was that the mask dangling from his neck was red . . . with blood.

"Are you Greg?" The doctor asked.

I nodded.

"She had one lucent moment. Just barely. She said that I should talk to you. Is this your father?" I nodded again.

"Well, you can thank him," the doctor said. "He saved your girl's life."

I looked at the doctor, at my father, at the doctor again. "What? How?"

"I'm Commander Larsen, flight surgeon in the Naval Reserve," the doctor said, "temporarily at NAS Key West, doing physicals. Lucky for you, in my civilian life, I'm a neurosurgeon at Johns Hopkins. From what I understand, your father and your girl were waiting to go into the Little White House when . . . Sheila—that her name?"

I nodded.

"When Sheila got a severe headache, vision blurring, nausea. And your father—" Dr. Larsen looked at him. "Are you a doctor, sir?"

My dad shook his head. "EMT. Used to be."

Dr. Larsen nodded. "Well, most doctors wouldn't know to check her for nuchal rigidity—pain with moving the neck—but the security guard on the scene told 9-1-1 that you did. That's how you knew the vessel hadn't ruptured, isn't it?"

Dad nodded.

"Your father's a wise man," the surgeon told me. "He recognized the signs of a cerebral aneurysm about to burst. Blood vessel ballooning at the base of the brain, like an old bicycle inner tube. He didn't wait for 9-1-1. He put her in a taxi outside and had him beat feet for the medical center and—here's the important part—called us on his cell phone and said we needed to have a neurosurgeon prepped when they arrived.

"You see, an aneurysm is very time sensitive. You get to it before it ruptures, and all the person might have later is an interesting scar under her hairdo, and we closed her very carefully so she might not have even that. But let it rupture, and there's usually nothing we can do. Massive stroke and intracranial hemorrhage. Blood pressure drops to nothing, and most people die in the ER lobby. Sheila didn't. And we checked her carefully. There was just the one vessel. Probably congenital; she had it all her life and it didn't get symptomatic until now. She's going to be fine. Pop here saved her life."

I nodded, looked at my dad. The world began to feel as if it were turning about me.

FIFTY-FOUR

In the blackness of the storm-swept night, the ship spun and bucked, like an unbroken colt trying to lose the unfamiliar presence of a rider. Ted, Captain Thatch, Ben the first mate, and Jack the gunner all clung to the stern rail, soaked to the skin, wind whipping them as though to flay them alive. It had taken them half an hour to tie the ropes off on the stern rail, yet the hardest part of the job was still facing them: Saturated with water, the large roll of canvas at their feet weighed hundreds of pounds.

Sewn over the course of an hour, a maddening task in a ship that dipped and rocked so as to threaten its capsizing, the roll of canvas was to serve as an anchor, in effect a big bucket, one big enough to hold ten men. It was secured to the stern rail with two hundred feet of line and, if deployed correctly, would drag against the ship, orienting the vessel perpendicular to the wind.

Thatch had called for it, Ben and Jack had sewn it, and while the thirty men below had all helped to get the rolled anchor and its line up to the quarterdeck, none but the four of them were brave enough to take on the task of dropping it into the angry sea.

"We need more men!" the gunner screamed at the top of his lungs, but his voice was a poor match for the howling wind.

"No others volunteered," Hatch reminded him, shouting into his ear. "I'll not order a man to come to our aid, and I doubt any would obey. We must do it alone."

The mate nodded and they bent to one end of the rolled canvas.

As they lifted, Ted was glad for the weight of the load. It made him less fearful that he would be blown clear of the deck, swept off into the heaving, mountainous sea. He could only make out bits of white at the wave tops, although they were much higher than the quarterdeck. He was glad for this as well. He felt certain that, had he been able to see their situation clearly, the enormity of it would have frozen him in fear.

All four men moved to one end of the canvas.

"Heave!" Thatch grunted and they lifted.

"Heave!" They got the end of the roll even with the rail.

"Heave!" The end cleared the rail.

"Heave!" The roll was now draped over it.

"Now, the rest of it with care, lads!" Thatch ordered.

The four men worked their load bit by bit, Ted straining until he could feel his eyes bulging. The wind had found the canvas, and the sodden load thrashed as if a living thing. When a loose flap hit Ted in the head, he saw stars.

"Heave!"

The canvas was balanced now, lifting and thrashing still, but balanced. It was clear that the next bit would put it over.

"Heave!"

Finally the roll slid off toward the sea, but then it caught on a lantern standard a foot below the rail. Even above the screaming wind, Ted could hear it beginning to tear.

"Over!" Thatch shouted the command, and the four men clambered over the pitching rail. It was all Ted could do to cling to the outside of the ship, his bare toes on the slim purchase of the carved lintels above the stern castle windows. The men grabbed the flapping canvas, lifted it free.

"Away!" Thatch's voice was barely audible to Ted, who was closest to the captain.

Ted let the canvas go, vaguely saw movement, and heard someone let out a shriek. The men clambered back over the rail. Ted squinted against the pelting rain. Now there were only three of them.

"Where's Ben?" Ted's hand gripped the captain's shirt as he asked it, steadying him while seawater crashed over them.

"Canvas took him," Thatch shouted. "He's gone."

Ted peered into the night.

The rope at their feet whistled as it paid out. Then it went taut, the stern rail creaking in protest as it took the load. But it held. The ship swung—a weight at the end of a line—until it was perpendicular to the waves, still rising and falling with them but no longer in danger of rolling over.

Without another word, the men crawled to the ladder and headed belowdecks.

Only one lantern burned on the crew deck, and even though it was hung with stout chain, a deckhand had been assigned to stay near it with a bucket of sand, ready to douse it if the lantern fell and started a fire.

Jack staggered off to find a hammock. Ted and Thatch slumped against a bulkhead. For several minutes they remained silent, the water running from their clothing in small rivers. Around them, the ship groaned and screamed like a tortured animal under the whip.

"Near as I can tell, the heart of the storm is still over us," Thatch said. "We are blowing north."

Ted's tired eyes widened. "You said there was a reef to our north."

Thatch nodded. "And that reef would be a welcome sight, truth be told. If we can ground on it, and hold there, that is better than sinking in the deep. But either we have found a gap in the reef and the Keys, or we have been blown all the way past Cayo Hueso."

"What is north of Cayo Hueso?"

Thatch shrugged. "Shallow water, if God loves us."

For an hour they rode the storm, neither man speaking. In the dim light of the lantern, Ted shook his head.

"Peace, lad," Thatch told him. "Your wife is safe and on her way to Boston, and you are not drowned yet."

Ted shook his head again. "I killed him."

"You are wrong. The storm killed him."

"Not Ben. Mr. Bascombe. The vicar. Had he not gone after me, he never would have come to Tortola. And had he not come to Tortola, he would not have had to flee with us. And had he not fled, he would not have tried to save my Sally."

The ship dropped into a trough, then quickly rose again.

"The man who killed him is in hell right now," Thatch said. "But revenge is not as sweet as it sounds—is it, lad?"

Ted looked down at his feet. "He died thinking I hated him."

"He died loving you. As for your forgiveness, you'll see him again someday, and then you can tell him the truth."

The timbers of the ship creaked loudly.

"But, lad . . ." In the lantern light Ted could see the captain smiling as he spoke. "Let us hope that day is not today!"

Ted woke with a start. The deck beneath him was lifting, the night filled with the sound of crashing wood.

The lantern still burned, and he could see Thatch smiling.

"Henry? Are we dying?"

The captain shook his head. "No. We are aground."

The ship stuck fast, and the winds howled on for another hour. At last they began to lessen. Then, as though someone had closed a shutter, they were gone.

The thirty-three men in the hold looked at one another, crossed the sloping deck, and went up the ladder. When the first man opened the hatch, sunlight streamed in, and the company cheered.

Ted climbed with Thatch to the slanting quarterdeck. The clouds were receding to the east of them, the sky above clear and blue. Just to their west was a low, flat island. On the deck below, men were throwing spare yardarms—anything loose and made of wood—into the water.

"Here, Jack," Thatch called down. "What are you about?"

"The men want to swim to yon island, Cap'n."

"Keep them here," Thatch said. "I've been in these storms before. This calm will not last. The storm will regain us ere they can reach the island."

"Aye, Cap'n, I've told them that. But they wish to try, and I am going with them."

Thatch shook his head. "You cannot make it, Jack."

"Cap'n, I'd rather die with air above my head than be trapped in a coffin of a hold."

"Climb a mast with us. Tie to the top. If we blow off and we sink in water that is shallow enough, perhaps we will be saved."

"Perhaps," Jack nodded. "But I'd rather take my chances with the swim."

"Then Godspeed, my friend."

"You too, Henry."

Thatch turned to Ted. "What of you, lad? Do you go with them, or do you climb?"

Ted gazed up at the tall mast. "Up there? In a storm as long as the last?"

"You take rope with you and you lash yourself on. This ship will float no longer. If we blow off these shallows and into deeper waters, we will surely sink. But God has loved us once and grounded us. Perhaps He will love us once again and sink us in the shallows."

The crew was already in the water, clinging to bits of wood and kicking for the shore, half a mile distant. Already Ted could see cloud mounting the western horizon.

"Let me fetch one thing," he said, "and then I will climb."

Ted hurried to the stern cabin and found what he was looking for, the wood smooth beneath his fingertips.

FIFTY-FIVE

The maple fretboard felt like hard satin beneath my fingers. I nodded to the music, picking the melody. From the kitchen chair across from me, my father played the harmony, smiling as his fingers danced. We ended and the resonators rang.

"That was great," he told me. "You picked that up quick. You've got to sit in with me on Sunday."

"Maybe."

"I know what you're thinking, Greg, but they don't risk infection around somebody who's had that sort of surgery. It'll be a good two weeks before you can see her."

"They only let us talk on the phone the one time."

"They don't want her moving around a lot. She needs to heal."

"She kept telling me that she was sorry. I told her it was not her fault, but she kept saying it, so I said, 'Fine. Promise me you'll never have an aneurysm again and I'll forgive you.' And she started laughing so hard, they made her hang up."

"There you go." My dad put his banjo aside, opened the refrigerator door, and got out a pitcher of iced tea. He poured two glasses and handed me one.

"Thanks," I said. And then, "I'm sorry."

My father shook his head. "That's my line. Not yours."

"But I didn't want to go see you."

"I don't blame you."

"If we hadn't, if you hadn't been there, she'd be dead right now."

My father set his glass of tea on the counter and smiled. "There was a guy I met in rehab, the last time, Greg. College professor from a Baptist university. Pretty smart dude. And one morning we were eating breakfast, and he looked over at me and he said, 'You know what, Teddy? All the devil's stories start with the same word: *if.*' I remembered that, man. I remember it every day. That, and prayer and faith and hope. That's what gets me through the day."

I reached out. Took his hand. My eyes were so teared up I could barely see him. "Dad . . . I am so sorry."

He wiped his eyes with the back of his hand. "Me too, son. Me too."

And that was it. Nobody said *I forgive you.* Nobody had to. We just held each other's hands and we squeezed.

FIFTY-SIX

Ted awoke to the feel of bonds, a tightness about his chest and abdomen. He opened his eyes and saw water, calm water, not four feet below his face. Yet he was dry.

"Lad!" The voice was familiar. "Do you live?"

"Yes," Ted responded weakly. "I think I do." He looked back, behind him. The mast sloped into the water, the form of the ship barely visible many yards beneath the water's surface.

Ted reached to his leg, found the knife strapped there and, working carefully, cut himself free. As he worked around so that he was atop the mast, he felt a weight within his shirt. A wooden box.

He was free enough now to take in their situation. Henry had cut his bonds as well and was above water but by only a few feet. He had climbed the mizzenmast, insisting Ted take the taller mainmast. As it turned out, both masts proved tall enough to carry their occupants through the storm.

Ted opened the box.

"What have you there?" Henry called.

"The navigator's kit," Ted answered. He took out the instruments and, with his back to the sun, shot the shadow. "How long are we from sunrise?"

The captain peered toward the sun, thought for a moment.

"One hour," Henry called over to him. "It feels like one hour precisely."

Local sunrise, early July. Ted did the calculations in his head, factoring in the semidiameter of the sun, recalling the grids of figures in his log. "We are at twenty-four degrees, thirty-nine minutes north, sir, give or take, for what that is worth."

"And those"—Henry pointed to a group of low islands on the horizon—"are the Dry Tortugas, due south of us. For what it is worth."

"So that is where we are." Ted dropped the instruments into the sea.

"Do you think you have strength to swim it, lad?"

Ted squinted at the distant land. "I'm sorry, sir. I doubt I could. The storm has sapped me."

"As it has me."

"Then we wait?" Ted asked.

"Aye, lad. We wait."

They remained on their mast tops all that day and all through the night. And then the next morning, a sail appeared: a Bermuda-built sloop, rigged for fishing. The marooned men were hatless, so they waved their hands in order to get the attention of those on the sloop.

"What ship are you?" called a man in a tricorner hat, who was hailing them from the deck.

"The *Tulip*," Henry called back. "From Great Inagua."

The vessel pulled nearer to Henry and Ted and dropped ropes. But they were useless, the two men being exhausted, so deckhands were sent to carry them up.

"God must love someone," the sloop's captain said as he poured them each some grog. "The *Tulip*, eh? Was she carrying anything valuable?"

Thatch shook his head, said nothing.

Ted thought of the gold bars in the forward magazine, and of the sacks of jewels under the decking. "Nothing," he told the man. "We were ferrying her to Jamaica for a refit, and she was carrying nothing at all."

FIFTY-SEVEN

The earrings, the ruby and the emerald, lay on the table next to Sheila's hospital bed. They didn't look valuable to me anymore. They just looked like stones. I looked in her eyes and I kissed her cheek, and I said, "Hey, you."

"Hey, you too." She spoke in the sleepy voice of someone on pain medication. She touched her head, the bandages. "I'm glad all you can see is the bandages. They shaved me."

"Your hair was short anyhow. It'll grow back in no time."

"You met my mum, my dad?"

"I did. And your mom's a hoot—for somebody who's *nutters*." Sheila began to laugh and I shushed her. "They'll kick me out."

Her face grew serious. "They said I can't dive again."

"Won't need to, post-Revelation. But I'll love you even if you're not a water baby."

She grimaced. "Well, I'm going to get a second opinion, and a third, and a tenth, until I find a doctor who says I can dive. A bit, at least."

"I just want you to have a long life." I squeezed her hand. "Because I certainly plan on having one. And I need you."

She smiled, squeezed back.

The door opened, and the room began to crowd: Phil, Betty, Malibu, Mikey, Robin. And in the back, my dad.

"Got to make this quick," Phil said. "I gave the ward nurse a Spanish reale, but that only buys us ten minutes. Guess the rules say only two visitors at a time, so long as she's in intensive care."

"Stuff the rules," Sheila said.

"That's the spirit."

Then everyone was talking at once, and Betty was patting Sheila's hand, and Phil ended up by me.

"Thanks, boss," I said. "I feel guilty, being here while you work the site."

"We're just cleaning up the grids," he said. "Found a few more jewels, but not much. Couple months we'll move up to where you and Hans found those big magnetometer hits, see if they're cannon."

I smiled. "You know, it's a good thing we write this stuff down. I woke up this morning, and my log's back on the boat, and I was trying to remember the coordinates, and all I can recall is the latitude: twenty-four degrees, thirty-nine minutes north."

He shrugged. "I don't remember either. Eighty-two, fifty-four, or eighty-two fifty-five. It's something like that. I know it's just north of the Dry Tortugas, though."

"Well, I want to be first to dive it."

"Me too," Sheila piped up from the bed.

"You'll be first in the water," Phil told me. He looked at Sheila. "And you—we'll talk about it, okay? But I promised not to work the site until you're on the boat. Fair enough?"

"Brilliant!"

And Sheila smiled.

TOM MORRISEY—the author of six previous novels including *Wind River* and *In High Places*, as well as numerous short stories—is a world-renowned adventure-travel writer, whose work has appeared in *Outside*, *Sport Diver*, and other leading magazines. He holds an M.A. in English Language and Literature from the University of Toledo, and an M.F.A. in Creative Writing from Bowling Green State University. Tom lives with his family in Orlando, Florida. To learn more about the author and his books, visit *www.tommorrisey.com*.

More From Tom Morrisey

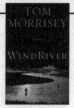

When a backcountry fly fishing trip turns into a race for survival, both Soren Andeman and Ty Sawyer must own up to their pasts or risk being consumed.

Wind River by Tom Morrisey

If You Enjoyed *Pirate Hunter*, You May Also Like:

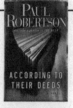

Rare books dealer Charles Beale discovers more than he bid on in a prized volume: hidden documents incriminating a host of major political figures. Knowing this blackmail may have led to murder, he must untangle a complicated knot of dangerous secrets before he becomes the next victim.

According to Their Deeds by Paul Robertson

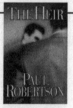

When given the throne to his father's corrupt business empire, Jason Boyer only wants to walk away. Yet despite his efforts, the power intoxicates him, and he soon finds himself battling for his soul...and his life.

The Heir by Paul Robertson

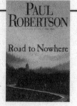

When a controversial road project tears a peaceful town in two, everyone starts looking to their own interests. But things take a deadly turn when somebody is willing to commit murder to make sure things go their way.

Road to Nowhere by Paul Robertson

Stay Up-to-Date on Your Favorite Books and Authors!

Be the first to know about new releases, meet your favorite authors, read book excerpts and more with our free e-newsletters.

Go to www.bethanyhouse.com to sign up today!

Calling All Book Groups!

Read exclusive author interviews, get the inside scoop on books, sign up for the free e-newsletter—and more— at www.bethanyhouse.com/AnOpenBook.

An Open Book: A Book Club Resources Exchange